PAWN TO KING

The notion of a supertelepathic superlevitator was patently absurd—but the opposition would swallow the absurdity when it came along in the guise of a self-evident fact. There would be considerable boosting of blood pressure in the hidden Venusian hierarchy when they learned that the first act of Earth's new chess piece was to abolish a natural law.

The thought gratified him. To date he had achieved nothing spectacular by the standards of the day and age. That was good because it was highly undesirable to be too spectacular. But at least he'd created considerable uneasiness in the ranks of the formerly overconfident enemy. Indeed, if they had bolted this multitalent mutant notion and speculated on the dire possibility of still more formidable types yet to come, they would have every reason to feel afraid.

It was a pity they could not be told the truth.

SENTINELS FROM SPACE

Eric Frank Russell

A Del Rey Book

BALLANTINE BOOKS • NEW YORK

A Del Rey Book
Published by Ballantine Books

ISBN 0-345-32758-6

Manufactured in the United States of America

First Ballantine Books Edition: June 1986

Cover Art by Barclay Shaw

Introduction

by Jack L. Chalker*

Eric Frank Russell (1905–1978) entertained generations of science fiction readers over his career, and influ-
enced a large number of contemporary SF writers.

A number of common themes run through the bulk of
Russell's work, including contempt for authority in any
form and a totally cynical attitude toward humanity's in-
stitutions. A number of his stories from the forties and
fifties, most notably "And Then There Were None...,"
have become the philosophical building blocks of modern-
day libertarianism. Yet, in most writers, this consistent
attitude would produce gloomy and negative tales, either
very downbeat or very idealogical, or both. Russell, on
the other hand, somehow managed to be consistently op-
timistic about humanity's future. Although absolutely
convinced we'd be tied up in bureaucratic knots and do
all the wrong things for all the wrong reasons, he also
recognized that this was as true of the past as the future

---

*Jack L. Chalker is a popular science fiction and fantasy author who has
been a long-time admirer of the works of Eric Frank Russell and who feels
that Russell was a strong influence on his own writing. Most of the facts used
in this introduction came from letters written by Russell over the years to
Chalker and mutual friends. Chalker's enthusiasm was instrumental in bringing
about Del Rey's revival of Russell's work.

and that, as we always had, we would muddle through.

The other major theme that runs through all Russell's work is Forteanism—the study of real events that can not be explained by conventional science and the belief that intellectual dogmatism and bureaucracy prevented us from finding the true explanations. He had a lifelong obsession with the idea that we might be the property, or the playthings, of superior beings.

Nowhere does every theme in Russell's work blend more completely with his incredible storytelling abilities than in *Sentinels From Space*, although it is one of his least-known novels. A synthesis of all his previous work, it's also the only one in which our invisible masters are not only the central characters but, in fact, the good guys, and never have more cosmic themes been played out according to the strict rules of science fiction. This is the scientific rationalist's view of the supernatural, and it is a stunning concept.

Yet this theme is played out against an equally exotic and highly unusual science fiction suspense plot. The future Earth that Russell creates, with its hierarchies of paranormals with terrifying abilities, is at once totally exotic and yet very recognizable to us. The intrigue to be revealed is rooted both in the theme of anti-imperialism and in the very real and very understandable fears of a brilliant and powerful—but *normal*—man who sees the rest of the increasingly paranormal race as an enemy. The villain here has the intellect of a Mao and the ruthlessness of a Hitler, yet he is totally comprehensible to us. We, who are not telepaths or hypnos or any of the other rather ordinary folk born with extraordinary powers, can readily put ourselves in his shoes.

Sentinels, then, is two totally different books, one a serious look at how one man's paranoia can create revolutions and manipulate even his most powerful enemies; the other the more cosmic and mystic. That the two blend well shows Russell's total command of plotting, pacing, and characters. Russell's stories always had what most of his contemporary SF writers lacked—strong, believable characterization, around which you can build the most exotic of plots and worlds. The general theme of his best books, that of one man being able to shake or revolutionize or even defeat whole movements or whole worlds, makes this fun as well.

Like almost all of Eric Frank Russell's work, *Sentinels From Space* is also a whale of a good story, expertly plotted and paced and told. And, like almost all Russell, it's not only a good read, but a good re-read, over and over again. Perhaps the time for this book has finally come.

Chapter 1

The World Council sat solemn and grave as he walked toward them. They numbered twelve, all sharp-eyed, gray or white of hair, their faces lined with many years and much experience. Silently with thin lips, firmed mouths, they studied his oncoming. The thick carpet kept saying *hush-hush* as his feet swept through it. The expectant quietness, the intent gaze, the whispering of the carpet and the laden weight of deep, unvoiced anxieties showed that this was a moment distinct from other minutes that are not moments.

Reaching the great horseshoe table at which the council members were seated, he halted, looked them over, starting with the untidy man on the extreme left and going slowly, deliberately around to the plump one on the far right. It was a peculiarly penetrating examination that enhanced their uneasiness. One or two fidgeted like men who feel some of their own sureness beginning to evaporate. Each showed relief when the soul-seeking stare passed on to his neighbor.

In the end his attention went back to the leonine-maned Oswald Heraty, who presided at the table's center. As he looked at Heraty the pupils of his eyes shone and the irises were flecked with silver and he spoke in slow, measured tones.

He said, "Captain David Raven at your service, sir."

Leaning back in his chair, Heraty sighed, fixed his attention upon the immense crystal chandelier dangling from the ceiling. It was difficult to tell whether he was marshaling his thoughts, or carefully avoiding the other's gaze, or finding it necessary to do the latter in order to achieve the former.

Other members of the council now had their heads turned toward Heraty, partly to give full attention to what he was about to say, partly because to look at Heraty was a handy pretext not to look at Raven. They had all watched the newcomer's entrance but none wanted to examine him close up, none wanted to be examined by him.

Still frowning at the chandelier, Heraty spoke in the manner of one shouldering an unwanted but immovable burden: "We are at war."

The table waited. There was only silence.

Heraty went on, "I address you vocally because I have no alternative. Kindly respond in the same manner."

"Yes, sir," was Raven's inadequate return.

"We are at war," Heraty repeated with a slight touch of irritation. "Does that not surprise you?"

"No, sir."

"It ought to," put in another Council member, somewhat aggrieved by the other's refusal to emote. "We have been at war for about eighteen months and have only just discovered the fact."

"Leave this to me," suggested Heraty, waving aside the interruption. For an instant—only an instant—he met Raven's eyes as he asked, "Have you known or suspected that we are actually at war?"

Smiling to himself, Raven said, "That we would be involved sooner or later has been obvious from the start."

"From what start?" inquired the fat man on the right.

"From the moment we crossed interplanetary space and settled upon another world." Raven was disconcertingly imperturable about it. "War then became inherent to the newly created circumstances."

"Meaning we blundered in some way or other?"

"Not at all. Progress demands payment. Sooner or later the bill is presented."

It did not satisfy them. His line of reasoning ran too swiftly from premise to conclusion and they were unable to follow the logic of it.

Heraty took over again. "Never mind the past. We, as present day individuals, had no control over that. It's our task to cope with immediate problems and those of the near future." He rubbed his bluish jowls, added, "Problem number one is this war. Venus and Mars are attacking us and officially we can't do a thing about it. Reason: it's a war that isn't a war."

"A difference of opinion?" asked Raven.

"It began with that. Now it has gone a whole lot further. They have turned from words to deeds. Without any formal declaration of war—indeed, with every outward appearance of friendship and blood-brotherhood—they are implementing their policies in a military manner. If you can call it military. I don't know how else to describe it." His voice sounded more ireful. "They've been at it for something like eighteen months and we've only just discovered that we are being hit, often and hard. That sort of thing can go on too long."

"All wars go on too long," Raven observed.

They viewed this as a profound thought. There was a murmur of agreement, much nodding of heads. Two of them went so far as to glance straight at him, though as briefly as possible.

"The worst of it is," continued Heraty, morbidly, "that they have got us cunningly fixed in a tangle of our own devising and—officially at any rate—there's no way out. What's the answer to that?" Without waiting for suggestions he provided one himself. "We must take action that is unofficial."

"Me being the goat?" put in Raven, shrewdly.

3

"You being the goat," Heraty confirmed.

For a moment the silence returned while Raven waited politely and the Council occupied itself with various thoughts. There was good cause to ponder. There had been wars before in the far past, the very far past; some slow and tortuous, some swift and bloody. But they had all been Earth wars.

A conflict between worlds was something new, something different. It posed unique problems to which bygone lessons could not apply. Moreover, a new style war, conducted with novel weapons, employing previously unheard of techniques posed fresh problems not solvable on the basis of past experiences. There was nothing to go by other than the hard, grim facts of today.

After a while, Heraty said moodily, "Venus and Mars have long been settled by *homo sapiens*, our own kind, our very flesh and blood. They are our children but no longer see it that way. They think they are now grown up and plenty old enough to go where they like, do what they like, come home any time they want. They've been agitating for self-government the last couple of centuries. They've been demanding the key of the house while they're still damp from their christening. We've consistently refused them their desire. We've told them to wait, be patient." He sighed again, long and deeply. "See where it puts us!"

"Where?" invited Raven, smiling again.

"Squarely on the horns of a dilemma—and both of them uncomfortably sharp." He shifted in his seat as if his southern aspect were peculiarly susceptible to suggestion. "Without self-government the Martians and Venusians remain Terrestrials, officially and legally, sharing this world with us, enjoying all our rights as equal citizens."

"And so?"

"That means they can come here as often and for as long as they please, in any numbers." Bending forward, Heraty slapped the table to emphasize his annoyance.

"They can walk straight in through the ever-open door while crammed to the top hairs with arson, sabotage and every other imaginable form of malicious intent. And we can't keep them out. We can't refuse entry except by making them precisely what they want to be, namely, aliens. We won't make aliens of them."

"Too bad," sympathized Raven. "I take it you have good reasons?"

"Of course. Dozens of them. We don't put the brakes on somebody else's progress out of sheer perversity. There are times when we must temporarily sacrifice that which is desirable in order to deal with that which is desperately necessary."

"It would be clearer if it were plainer," suggested Raven.

Hesitating a second or two, Heraty went on, "One major reason is known only to a select few. But I'll tell you: we are on the verge of getting to the Outer Planets. That is a jump, a heck of a big jump. To back it up to the limit, get properly established and settle ourselves in strength we'll need all the combined resources of three worlds unhampered by any short view quibbling between them."

"I can well imagine that," agreed Raven, thinking of Mars' strategic position and of the immensely rich fuel deposits on Venus.

"And that's not all, not by a long shot." Heraty lowered his tone to lend significance to his words. "In due time there will be another jump. It will take us to Alpha Centauri or perhaps farther. There is some unpublished but rather convincing evidence that ultimately we may come head on against another highly intelligent life-form. If that should occur we'll have to hang together lest otherwise we hang separately. There will be no room for Martians, Venusians, Terrestrials, Jovians or any other planetary tribes. We'll all be Solarians, sink or swim. That's how it's got to be and that's how it's going to be whether nationalist-minded specimens like it or not."

"So you're impaled on yet another dilemma," re-

5

marked Raven. "Peace might be assured by publishing the warning facts behind your policy—and thereby creating general alarm plus considerable opposition to further expansion."

"Precisely. You've put it in a nutshell. There's a conflict of interests which is being carried too far."

"H'm! A pretty set-up. As sweet a mutual animosity as could be contrived. I like it—it smacks of an enticing chess problem."

"That's exactly how Carson sees it," Heraty informed. "He calls it super-chess for reasons you've yet to learn. He says it's time we put a new piece on the board. You'd better go see him right away. Carson's the man who raked the world for someone like you."

"Me?" David Raven registered mild surprise. "What does he think is so special about me?"

"That I wouldn't know." Heraty showed himself far from anxious to discuss the subject. "Such matters are left entirely to Carson and he has his own secrets. You must see him at once."

"Very well, sir. Is there anything else?"

"Only this: you were not brought here merely to satisfy our curiosity but also to let you see for yourself that the World Council is behind you, though unofficially. Your job is to find some way of ending this war. You'll have no badge, no documents, no authority, nothing to show that your personal status is different from that of any other individual. You'll have to get along by benefit of your own abilities and our moral support. No more!"

"You consider that should be sufficient?"

"I don't know," admitted Heraty worriedly. "I'm in poor position to judge. Carson's more capable in that respect." He leaned forward, added with emphasis, "For what little it is worth my own opinion is that very soon your life won't be worth a moment's purchase—and I sincerely hope I'm wrong."

"Me, too," said Raven, blank-faced.

They fidgeted again, suspecting him of secret amusement at their expense. The deep silence came back and their formerly evasive eyes were on him as he bowed and walked away with the same slow, deliberate, confident gait as when he'd entered. Only the carpet whispered and when he went out the big door closed quietly, without a click.

"War," remarked Heraty, "is a two-way game."

Carson masqueraded as a mortician so far as personal appearance went. He was tall, lean, sad-faced, had the perpetual air of one who regrets the necessity and expense of floral offerings. All this was a mask behind which lurked an agile mind. A mind that could speak without benefit of lips. In other words, he was a Type One Mutant, a true telepath. There's a distinction here: true telepaths differ from sub-telepaths in being able to close their minds at will.

Glancing with glum approval at Raven's equally tall but broader, heavier frame, and noting the lean, muscular features, the dark gray eyes, the black hair, Carson's mind made contact without an instant's hesitation. Invariably a Type One recognizes another Type One at first sense, just as an ordinary man perceives another simply because he is not blind.

His mind inquired, "Did Heraty give forth?"

"He did—dramatically and uninformatively." Seating himself, Raven eyed the metal plate angled on the other's desk. It bore an inscription reading: *Mr. Carson. Director—Terran Security Bureau.* He pointed to it. "Is that to remind you who you are whenever you become too muddled to remember?"

"In a way, yes. The plate is loaded on the neural band and radiates what it says. The technical boys claim that it's antihypnotic." A sour grin came and went. "To date there's been no occasion to try it out. I'm in no great hurry to test it either. A hypno who gets this far isn't going to be put off by a mere gadget."

"Still, the fact that someone thinks you could do with

7

it is a bit ominous," Raven commented. "Has everyone got the heebies around here? Even Heraty insinuated that I've already got one foot in the grave."

"An exaggeration, but not without basis. Heraty shares something with me, namely, the dark suspicion that we've at least one fifth columnist on the Council itself. It's no more than a dark thought but if there's anything to it you're a marked man from now on."

"That's pleasant. You dig me up in order to bury me."

"Your appearance before the Council was unavoidable," Carson told him. "They insisted on having a look at you whether I approved or not. I didn't approve and Heraty knows it. He countered my objection by turning my own arguments against me."

"How?" Raven invited.

"Said that if you were only one-tenth as good as I claimed you ought to be, there was no need for anxiety. The enemy could do all the worrying instead."

"H'm! So I'm expected to live up to an imaginary reputation you've concocted for me in advance. Don't you think I've enough grief?"

"Plunging you into plenty of grief is my idea," declared Carson, displaying unexpected toughness. "We're in a jam. Nothing for it but to flog the willing horse."

"Half an hour ago I was a goat. Now it's a horse—or maybe part of a horse. Any other animal imitations you'd like? How about a few bird calls?"

"You'll have to call some mighty queer birds to keep pace with the opposition, much less get ahead of it." Sliding open a drawer, Carson took out a paper, surveyed it unhappily. "This is as far as we've got with a top secret list of extra-Terrestrial varieties. Nominally and according to law they're all samples of *homo sapiens*. In deadly fact they're *homo-something-else*." He glanced at his listener. "To date, Venus and Mars have produced at least twelve separate and distinct types of mutants. Type Six, for instance, are Malleables."

Stiffening in his seat, Raven exclaimed. *"What?"*

"Malleables," repeated Carson, smacking his lips as if viewing an especially appetizing corpse. "They are not one hundred percenters. No radical alteration of the general physique. They can do nothing really startling from a surgeon's viewpoint. But they've been born with faces backed with cartilage in lieu of bones, are incredibly rubber-featured and to that extent are good, really good. You would kiss one thinking he was your own mother if it struck his fancy to look like your mother."

"Speak for yourself," Raven said.

"You know what I mean," Carson persisted. "As facial mimics they have to be seen to be believed."

Indicating the highly polished surface of his desk, Carson continued, "Imagine this is a gigantic checkerboard with numberless squares per side. We're using midget chessmen and playing white. There are two thousand five hundred millions of us against thirty-two millions of Venusians and eighteen million Martians. On the face of it that's a huge preponderance. We've got them hopelessly outnumbered." He made a disparaging gesture. "Outnumbered in what? *In pawns!*"

"Obviously," agreed Raven.

"You can see the way our opponents view the situation: what they lose in numbers they more than make up for in superior pieces. Knights, bishops, rooks, queens and—what is so much the worse for us—new style pieces endowed with eccentric powers peculiar to themselves. They reckon they can produce them until we're dizzy: mutants by the dozens, each one of them worth more than a regiment of pawns."

Raven said meditatively, "Acceleration of evolutionary factors as a direct result of space conquest was so inevitable that I don't know how it got overlooked in the first place. A child should have seen the logical consequence."

"In those days the old-timers were obsessed by atomic power," responded Carson. "To their way of thinking it needed a world-wide holocaust created by radio-active materials to produce mutations on a large scale. It just

9

didn't occur to them that hordes of Venus-bound settlers could not spend five solid, searing months in space, under intense cosmic ray bombardment, their genes being kicked around every hour and every minute, without there being normal working of cause and effect."

"It's occurring to them now."

"Yes, but in bygone days they couldn't see wood for trees. Heck, they went so far as to build double-shelled ships containing ray absorbing blankets of compressed ozone, cutting down intensity to some eighty times that at Earth level—yet failed to realize that eighty times still remains eighty times. The vagaries of chance even themselves up over a long period of time so that we can now say that Venus trips have created about eighty mutants for every one that would have just come naturally."

"Mars is worse," Raven pointed out.

"You bet it is," agreed Carson. "Despite its smaller population Mars has roughly the same number and variety of mutants as Venus. Reason: it takes eleven months to get there. Every Mars settler has to endure hard radiations about twice as long as any Venus settler—and he goes on enduring them because of Mars' thinner atmosphere. Human genes have a pretty wide tolerance of massive particles like cosmic rays. They can be walloped again and again and again—but there are limits." He paused, his fingers tapping the desk while he reflected briefly. "Inasmuch as a mutant has military value, Mars' war potential fully equals that of Venus. In theory—and it's faulty theory, as we must show them—Mars and Venus together can put enough into the field to give us a run for our money. That is precisely what they are trying to do. Up to the present they've got away with it. We've now reached the point where it has ceased to be funny."

"Seems to me," observed Raven, thoughtfully, "that they're making a mistake similar to that made by the original pioneers: in sheer excess of enthusiasm they're overlooking the obvious."

"Meaning that this planet mans the space fleets and therefore can find some mutants of her own?"

"Yes."

"They'll learn in the same way that we've had to learn. And you're going to show them—I hope."

"Hope springs eternal. In what way do you suggest that I show them?"

"That's up to you," said Carson, dexterously passing the buck. Searching through the papers on his desk, he extracted a couple, looked them over. "I'll tell you of one case that illustrates the squabble in which we're involved and the methods by which it's being fought. It was this particular incident that told us for the first time that there is a war on. We'd got suspicious of a long series of apparently disconnected events, laid several camera-traps. Most were put out of action. A few failed for no known reason. But one registered."

"Ah!" Raven bent forward, eyes keen, attentive.

"The camera showed how three men destroyed some extremely important spaceship data that can't be replaced in less than a year. The first of this trio, a Type One Mutant, a true telepath, kept mental watch for interrupters. The second, a Type Two, a floater—"

"Meaning a levitator?" Raven chipped in.

"Yes, a levitator. He got them over two twenty-foot walls with the help of a rope ladder and then took the ladder up to a high window. The third one, a Type Seven Mutant, a hypno, took care of three guards who intervened at different times, stiffened them into immobility, erased the incident from their minds and substituted false memories covering the cogent minutes. The guards knew nothing of the camera-traps and therefore were not able to give them away to the telepath unwittingly. But for a camera we wouldn't know a darned thing except that in some mysterious manner the data had gone up in smoke."

"Humph!" Raven seemed more amused than aghast.

"There have been several big fires of such strategic importance that we're inclined to blame them on pyrotics—though we can't prove it." Carson shook his head mournfully. "What a war! They make their own rules as they go along. Their antics play hob with military logistics and if there were any brass hats these days they'd be ripe for mental treatment."

"Time has marched on," Raven contributed.

"I know, I know. We're living in modern days." He shoved a sheet of paper at his listener. "There's a copy of my list of known Mars-Venus mutations numbered according to type and lettered for military value, if you can call it that." He sniffed as if there were some doubts about calling it that. "*D* means dangerous, *D-plus* more so, while *I* means innocuous—perhaps. And that list may not be complete. It's as far as we've got to date."

Raven glanced rapidly down the list, asked, "So far as you know all these remain true to type? That is to say, the floaters can levitate only themselves and anything they are able to carry at the time but cannot cause levitation of independent objects? The teleports have the reverse aptitude of levitating objects but cannot lift themselves? The telepaths aren't hypnotic and the hypnos aren't telepathic?"

"That is correct. One man, one supernormal ability."

Raven began to study it carefully. It read:

1. True Telepaths.	D+.
2. Levitators.	D.
3. Pyrotics.	D+.
4. Chameleons.	I.
5. Nocturnals.	I.
6. Malleables.	D.
7. Hypnos.	D+.
8. Supersonics.	I.
9. Mini-engineers.	D+.
10. Radiosensitives.	D.
11. Insectivocals.	D+.
12. Teleports.	D+.

"So!" Smiling to himself, Raven stuffed the list into a pocket, got up, went to the door. "And they're all under the delusion that Old Mother Earth ain't what she used to be?"

"You said it," Carson endorsed. "They say she's aged, decrepit, dimwitted and hopelessly out of touch with the facts of life. She's got nothing left but her last dying kick. You go administer said kick—and where it'll best be felt."

"I'll do just that," Raven promised, "provided I can stay in one piece long enough to take aim." He went out, carefully closing the door behind him.

He was on his own.

Chapter 2

The fun started right outside on the street. It could hardly have been more prompt though, naturally, it lacked the finesse that might have been evident had the organizers enjoyed longer warning and greater time for preparation. A little more elbow room and they'd have been in at the kill. As it was, the spur-of-the-moment tactic gained in swiftness what it lost in thoroughness.

Raven walked boldly through the front entrance of the Security Bureau Building, gave the come-hither sign to an aerial taxi prowling overhead. The machine did a falling turn into the lower northbound level of traffic, dropped out of that and into the sitting level, hit the street with a rubbery bounce.

The taxi was a transparent ball mounted on a ring of smaller balls designed to absorb the landing shock. There were no wings, jets or vanes. It was a latest model antigrav-cab worth about twelve thousand credits but its driver hadn't bothered taking depilatory treatment costing two fish.

Opening the door, the driver suffused his beefy features with professional hospitality, noted that the customer did not respond and made no attempt to enter. Welcome gradually faded from the mat. He scowled, scratched his blue-stubbled chin with a cracked fingernail and spoke with a cracked voice.

"See here, Mac, unless I'm imagining things you gave me the—"

"Shut up until I'm ready for you," said Raven, still on the sidewalk and some ten feet from the cab. His eyes were watching nothing in particular; his air was that of one whose mind is elsewhere—listening, perhaps, to far-away fairy bells—and resents a disturbance.

The cabbie intensified his scowl, gave the stubble another rake in the sonic imitation of a space-mechanic sand-papering the venturis. His right arm was still extended, holding the door open. Something wafted the sleeve of the arm, depressing it slightly as if an unseen breath had blown upon it. He failed to notice it.

Raven returned his attention to the cab, approached it but did not get inside. "Have you got a melter?"

"Sure! Where'd I be without one if a bounce-arm snapped?" The cabbie extracted one from the instrument board pocket. It resembled a tiny hand gun. "What d'you want it for?"

"I'm going to burn your seat," Raven informed, taking it from him.

"Are you now? That's quite an idea, ain't it?" The other's small, sunken eyes went still smaller, more sunken. A smirk broke across his leathery face, revealed two gaps in his molars. "It's your unlucky day, Daffy." His hand dived again into the pocket, came out holding another melter. "I happen to carry them in pairs. So you fix my pants and I'll fix yours. That's fair, ain't it?"

"A pants-fixing performance would interest several scientists more than mightily," assured Raven, "when done with instruments effective only upon metals." He smiled at the other's sudden look of uncertainty, added, "I was referring to the back seat of the cab."

With that he stuck the nozzle of the midget autowelder into the seat's upholstery, squeezed the handle.

Nothing visible came from the melter though the hand holding it gave a slight jolt. A thin spurt of strong-smelling fumes shot out of the plasticoid upholstery as something concealed within it fused at high heat. Calmly Raven climbed into the cab, closed the door.

"All right, on your way, Shaveless." Bending forward, he put the melter back into its pocket.

The cabbie moped confusedly at his controls while the anti-grav machine soared to five thousand feet and drifted southward. His heavy brows waggled from time to time with the effort of striving to think it out. His eyes continually shifted from the observation window to the rearview mirror, keeping surreptitious watch on this passenger who might be capable of anything up to and including setting the world on fire.

Taking no notice of the other's attitude, Raven shoved an investigatory hand into the still warm gap in the upholstery, felt hot metal, brought up a badly warped instrument no longer than a cigarette and not as thick. It was gold colored, had stubby wings curled and distorted by heat. Its pointed front end bore a shining lens half the size of a seed pearl. Its flattened rear was pierced with seven needle-fine holes that served as miscroscopic jets.

He did not have to pull this tiny contraption to pieces to discern what was inside. It was all there and he *knew* it was there: the lilliputian engine, the guiding scanner, the miniscule radio circuit that could yell *pip-pip-pip* for hours, the match-head-sized self-destroying charge—all in a weight of something under three ounces. Yet but for its destruction it could have loaded the cab with an electronic drag-scent that the hounds would follow for endless miles and in three dimensions.

Turning, he had a look through the rear window. So many cabs, tourers, sportsters and official machines were floating around on various levels that it was quite impossible to decide whether he was still being followed visually. No matter. A mess of traffic effectively hiding the hunters could equally well conceal the hunted.

Tossing the winged cylinder into the pocket occupied by the melters, he said to the driver, "You can have that thingumbob all for your very own. It contains items worth some fifty credits—*if* you can find someone capable of picking it apart without wrecking it entirely."

"There's ten owing for that hole in the seat."

"I'll pay you when I get out."

"All right." The other perked up, took the winged cylinder out of the pocket, fingered it curiously, put it back. "Say, how did you know this thing was there?"

"Somebody had it in his mind."

"Huh?"

"People who shoot gadgets through cab doors should not think of what they're doing even if they are a quarter of a mile away in no detectable direction. Thoughts can be overheard sometimes. They can be as effective as a bellowed warning." He eyed the back of the cabbie's neck. "Have you ever been able to do anything without thinking about it at all?"

"Only once." Holding up his left hand he showed the stump of a thumb. "It cost me this."

"Which goes to show," said Raven, and added mostly to himself, "Pity that mini-engineers aren't also true telepaths."

In silence they covered another forty miles still at the same altitude. Sky traffic was thinning out as they got well beyond the city limits.

"Forgot to bring my mittens," hinted the cabbie. "Shouldn't ought to forget my mittens. I'll need them at the South Pole."

"In that case we'll call it a day partway there. I'll let you know when." Raven had another look behind. "Meanwhile you can put in some practice at shaking off any followers we may have. Not that I can tell whether there are any, but it's possible."

"Dropping the procession will cost you fifty." The cabbie studied him via the rear view mirror, speculating as to whether he'd priced the service too high or too low.

"And that includes a shut mouth, guaranteed unopenable."

"You're rash with your guarantees—you'll open for them because you won't be able to help it," Raven informed darkly. "They have techniques involving compulsion and no cash." He emitted a sigh of resignation. "Oh, well, by the time you talk it will be too late to matter. The fifty is yours just for delaying things a while." He grabbed the seat-grips as the cab swayed, darted sidewise, shot into a cloud. The world became hidden by thick fog which whirled around and slid past in streaks of yellow and clumps of dirty white. "You'll have to do better than this. You're not radarproof."

"Give me time. I ain't properly started yet."

Two hours later they thumped upon the lawn behind a long, low house. Nothing was visible in the sky except a high flying police patrol heading north. The patrol bulleted steadily onward in complete disregard of the sphere upon the lawn and whined out of sight.

The woman within the house was a little too big, a little too generously proportioned and moved with the deliberation of those weighty above the average. Her eyes were very big, widely spaced and blackly brilliant. Her mouth was large, her ears likewise, and her hair a huge, coal-black mop. Full-busted and heavy-hipped, there was too much of her to suit the tastes of most men. Nevertheless, although physically no sylph, at one time or another twenty suitors had pursued her and had treated her rejections with despair. The reason: what burned within her shone visibly through those great eyes and made her surpassingly beautiful.

Giving Raven a warm, big-fingered hand, she exclaimed, "David! Whatever brings you here?"

"You would already know had I not thought it expedient to keep my mind closed."

"Of course." She switched from vocal to telepathic means of communication solely because it came easier. "What is it?"

He responded in the same manner, mentally, "Two birds." He smiled into the orbs that made her lovely. "The two I hope to kill with one stone."

"Kill? Why do you have to use that dreadful thought *kill*?" A touch of anxiety came into her face. "You have been talked into something. I know it. I can feel it despite your keeping it hidden from me within your mind. You have been persuaded to interfere." Seating herself on a pneumatic lounge, she gazed morbidly at the wall. "It is the unwritten law that we must never be tempted to interfere except with the prime motive of thwarting the Denebs. We might give ourselves away just sufficiently to frighten humankind, and frightened people tend to strike blindly at the source of their fear. Besides, noninterference lulls all suspicions, encourages them to think we are not capable of it."

"That is excellent logic providing your premise is correct and unfortunately it isn't. Circumstances have changed." He took a seat opposite, studied her gravely. "Leina, we've slipped a little in one respect, namely, that they're shrewder than we expected."

"In what way?"

"Entangled in their own contradictions they became desperate enough to search the world on the million-to-one chance of finding someone able to unravel the strings. And they traced me!"

"Traced you?" Her alarm heightened. "How did they manage to do that?"

"In the only possible way, genetically, through the records. They must have classified, dissected and analyzed some ten, fifteen or twenty successive generations, wading through data on endless births, marriages and deaths, knowing nothing of what they might eventually find but hoping for the best. My determinedly conventional pseudoancestors legalized all their alliances and left a long series of documentary pointers leading straight to me. So ultimately the line became reeled in and I was the fish gasping at the end."

"If they can do that with you they can do it with others," she commented without happiness.

"On this particular planet," he reminded, "there are no others. Only we two. And you are exempt."

"Am I? How can you be sure?"

"The sorting out process has already been completed. I've been grabbed, but not you—maybe because you're a female. Or perhaps you are concealed by benefit of ancestors allergic to official documents, such as one or two healthy but immoral pirates."

"Thank you," she said, slightly miffed.

"The pleasure's mine," he assured, grinning.

Her eyes keened into his. "David, what do they want you to do? Tell me!"

In full detail he informed her of what had happened, ending, "So far the Mars-Venus combine has been satisfied merely to try crippling us by degrees—the technique of long maintained and gradually increasing pressure—knowing that unless we can think up some really effective counter-action we're going to crack sooner or later. To put it another way, they are taking a pint of our blood every chance they get. Someday we'll be too feeble to stand, much less make defensive gestures."

"It's no business of ours," she decided. "Let argumentative worlds fight it out between themselves."

"That's exactly how I was tempted to view the situation," he admitted, "until I remembered how history shows that one darned thing leads to another. Look, Leina, it is only a matter of a short time before Earth decides it's had more than enough and must hit back. If Earth can't strike with finesse it will strike without finesse, roughly and toughly. Mars and Venus promptly become more riled than ever, get really hard. Tempers rise, each side's boosted by the other's. Restraints are thrown away one by one, then in bunches. Scruples are poured down the drain until some badly frightened crackpot on one side or the other plants a hydride bomb to show who's boss. Your own imagination can take it from there."

"It can," she agreed without relish.

"Much as I dislike poking a finger into human affairs," he went on, "I have an even stronger distaste for the notion of hiding under a mountain while the atmosphere flames and the world shudders all around and multimillion humans walk clean off the stage of life. Carson over-optimistically thinks I can do something about it, single-handed. All the same, I'm willing to have a shot at it providing the opposition lets me live long enough. Nothing ventured, nothing gained."

"Oh, dear!" Her fingers toyed together. "Why must these creatures be so stubborn and idiotic?" Without waiting for an answer, she asked, "What do you wish me to do, David?"

"Keep yourself from becoming involved," he said. "I've come back to destroy a few papers, that's all. There's a chance they'll catch up with me before I leave. In that event, you can perform one small service."

"And that is—?"

"Look after my best suit for a little while." He tapped his chest with much significance. "It fits me perfectly and it's the only one I've got. I like it and don't want to lose it."

"David!" Her mental impulse was sharp and immeasurably shocked. "Not that! You can't do *that*! Not without permission. It is a fundamental violation. It isn't ethical."

"Neither is war. Neither is mass-suicide."

"But—"

"Hush!" He raised a warning finger. "They are coming already. It didn't take them long." He glanced at the wall clock. "Not quite three hours since I left the Bureau. That's what I call efficiency." His gaze came back to her. "Do you sense their approach?"

She nodded and sat waiting in silence while Raven hurried away and dealt with his papers. He came back. Presently the door gongs chimed softly. Standing up, Leina hesitated a moment, glanced at the other. Raven responded with a careless shrug. She went to the door, opened it. Her manner was that of one deprived of initiative.

Five men were grouped by a bullet-shaped sportship four hundred yards from the house. Two more waited on her doorstep. All wore the black and silver uniform of security police.

The pair at the door were burly, leather-face specimens alike enough to be brothers. It was no more than type-similarity because inwardly they were different. The mind of one probed at Leina's while the other's did not. One was a telepath; the other something else. The sudden and fierce thrust of the first one's mind temporarily prevented her examining the second one's and thus identifying his peculiar talent, for perforce she countered the telepath by snapping her own mind shut. The other mentality immediately sensed the closure and recoiled.

"Another Tele," he told his companion. "Just as well we came along in a bunch, isn't it?" Not waiting for comment, he spoke to Leina vocally, "You can talk to me of your own free will." He paused to enjoy a harsh chuckle, went on, "Or you can talk to my friend involuntarily, whichever you please. As you can see, we are police."

Tartly she gave back, "You are nothing of the kind. A police officer would refer to another as his fellow officer and not as his friend. Neither would he utter implied threats before so much as stating his business."

The second man, who had remained silent up to that point, now chipped in. "Rather talk to me, eh?" His eyes gained a strange, eerie light, growing like little moons. A hypno.

Ignoring him, she said to the first man, "What do you want?"

"Raven."

"So?"

"He's here," he insisted, trying to peer over her shoulder. "We know he's here."

"So?"

"We're going to take him along for questioning."

Raven's voice sounded from the room at back. "It is most kind and thoughtful of you, Leina, to try to detain the gentlemen. But it is futile. Please show them in."

She shivered slightly. Her face was a mirror of emotions as she stood aside and let them brush past her. They went in eagerly like steers galloping into the slaughterhouse. She knew what was coming. The doorknob in her hand grew colder and colder.

Chapter 3

The invaders slowed up as they entered the room. Their expressions became wary, they had small bluesteel guns in their hands, and they kept well apart as if suspecting their quarry of the ability to lay both of them at one swipe.

Not bothering to come to his feet, and obviously amused by their alertness, David Raven said as he picked their identities out of their minds, "Ah, Mr. Grayson and Mr. Steen. A telepath and a hypno—with a gang of other skewboys waiting outside. I am greatly honored."

Grayson, the telepath, snapped at his companion, "Listen who's calling us skewboys." Making an impatient motion at Raven, he added, "All right, Brain-picker, on your feet and start walking."

"To where?"

"You find out when you arrive."

"So it seems," agreed Raven drily. "The ultimate destination is not recorded in your mind, from which I conclude that you do not enjoy the confidence of your superiors."

"Neither do you," Grayson retorted. "Take the weight off your tail. We can't stand here all day."

"Oh, well." Coming erect, Raven stretched himself,

yawned. His gaze rested on Steen, the hypno, as he inquired, "What's eating you, Squinty? Never found anyone so fascinating before?"

Maintaining the openly curious stare with which he had fixed Raven from the very start, Steen responded, "When there's any fascinating to be done *I'll* do it!" He carried on with, "I'm wondering what all the excitement is about. You haven't got four arms and two heads. What's supposed to make you so marvelous?"

"He isn't so marvelous," Grayson interrupted with impatience. "Seems to me that headquarters has been stirred up by an exaggerated rumor. I know what he's got and it isn't so much."

"You do?" asked Raven, looking at him.

"Yes, you're merely a new breed of telepath. You can still probe other minds even when your own is closed. Unlike the rest of us, you don't have to open your own before you can snoop into others. It's a nice trick and a useful one." He sniffed his disdain. "But as an interesting variation it's not big enough to worry two planets."

"Then what *are* you worrying about?" Raven pressed. "Having learned the worst you've learned the lot. Now leave me to ponder with pleasure over the sins of my youth."

"We've been ordered to bring you in for questioning. That is to say, in one piece. So we're bringing you." Grayson's contempt grew more evident. "We're dragging back the tiger even though it smells to me of kitten."

"And by whom will I be questioned, the Big Chief or some no-account underling?"

"That's no affair of mine," said Grayson. "All you've got to do is come along and provide the answers."

"Leina, please fetch me my hat and bag." Raven threw an open and meaningful wink to where she stood silently in the doorway.

"No you don't," Grayson rasped at her, naturally not liking the wind. "You stay put." He turned to Raven. "Go fetch them yourself." Then to Steen. "You go with him.

I'll keep an eye on the large lady. Do your stuff on him if he so much as clicks his teeth."

The pair walked stolidly into the adjoining room, Raven leading and Steen close behind. Steen's eyes already were glowing with power that was better than bullets. Squatting on one arm of a pneumaseat, Grayson rested his gun-hand on a knee, eyed Leina speculatively.

"Another mental oyster, aren't you?" Grayson said. "Anyway, if you're hoping he'll manage to pull a fast one on Steen you can save your brain the strain of thought. He'll never do it between now and Christmas."

Offering no comment, she continued to gaze expressionlessly at the wall, showing no hint of apprehension.

"Any telepath can outwit and outmaneuver any hypno at a distance because he can read intentions and has space in which to get out from under." Grayson gave it with the authority of personal experience. "But close up he hasn't the chance of a celluloid cat. The hypno is the winnah every time. I know! Many's the lousy hypno trick I've had played on me, especially after a session with a few quarts of Venusian mountain dew."

She did not respond. Her generous features were blank, impassive as she strove to listen through and beyond his chatter. Grayson made a swift and vicious thrust at her mind, hoping to catch it unaware, and struck nothing but an impenetrable shield. She had resisted him without effort and continued listening, listening. A faint almost unhearable scuffle sounded in the other and was followed by the merest whisper of a gasp.

Grayson swiveled round on one heel, looking like one who suspects himself of failing to hear something he should have heard. "Besides, there's me here with this gun and there's a tough bunch waiting outside." He glanced at the other room's door, became restless. "All the same, they're slow in there."

"Not a chance," she murmured, barely loud enough for him to catch. "Close up there's not a chance."

Something about her face, her eyes, or the tone of her

voice aroused his suppressed suspicions, created vague alarm. His lips thinned and he motioned to her with his gun.

"Move, Buxom. Walk in there slowly two paces ahead of me. We'll see what's keeping them."

Leina got up, bracing herself a moment on the arm of the pneumaseat. Reluctantly she turned to face the door, her eyes lowered as if to delay the vision of what lay behind the door or at any second might come through it.

Steen came through it, rubbing his chin and grinning with self-satisfaction. He was alone.

"He tried to be funny," announced Steen, addressing Grayson and pointedly ignoring Leina. "I had a notion he was going to do just that. Result: he's stiffer than a tombstone. We'll need a long board to carry him away."

"Hah!" Grayson relaxed, let the gun droop as the other continued toward him. Triumphantly he said to Leina, "What did I tell you? He was a dope to try it close up. Some people will never learn!"

"Yes," agreed Steen, coming nearer, nearer. "He was a dope." He stopped face to face with Grayson, looking straight at him, gaze level with gaze. "Not a chance, close up!" His eyes were brilliant and very large.

Grayson's fingers twitched, loosened. The gun dropped from them, thumped upon the carpet. His mouth opened and shut. Faint words came out, uttered with difficulty.

"Steen . . . what the heck . . . are . . . *doing*?"

The eyes swelled enormously, become monstrous, irresistibly compelling. Their blaze seemed to fill the cosmos and sear the onlooker's brain. A deep, droning voice came with the blaze, at first faintly, but racing nearer over immense distances at immense velocity and building up to a masterful roar.

"Raven's not here."

"Raven's not here," mumbled Grayson in dreamy tones, his mind overwhelmed.

"We have seen nothing of him. We were too late."

Grayson repeated it like an automaton.

27

"Too late by forty minutes," the mentally paralyzing voice of Steen insisted.

"Too late by forty minutes," endorsed Grayson.

"He took off in a gold colored, twenty-tube racing craft number XB109, the property of the World Council."

Grayson echoed it word for word. He had the rigid pose and inane expression of a waxy one gathering dust in a tailor's window.

"Destination unknown."

That, too, was parroted.

"There is nobody in this villa but a fat woman, a telepath of no consequence."

"There is nobody," mumbled Grayson, glassy-eyed, half blind, half dead and mentally enslaved. "There is nobody...nobody...but a fat woman of no conse-quence."

Steen said, "Pick up your gun. Let's go back and tell Haller."

He pushed past the fat woman of no consequence, Grayson following sheeplike. Neither favored Leina with so much as a glance. Her own attention was on Steen, studying his face, reaching for what lay behind the mask, silently talking at him, reproving him, but he took no notice. His disregard was obvious, deliberate and deter-mined.

She closed the door behind them, sighed and wrung her hands in the manner of women since the beginning of time. There were stumbling sounds behind her. Turning she faced the figure of David Raven swaying uncertainly two yards away.

The figure bent forward, hands over its face, rubbing its features as though not sure on which side of its head they were placed. It was feeling the alien, the unfamiliar, and horrified by its own sense of touch. The hands came away, revealed a tormented countenance and eyes full of fundamental shock.

"Mine," he said in a voice that was neither Raven's nor Steen's but combined some of the characteristic qualities of both. "He snatched away that which is mine and mine alone! He deprived me of myself!"

He paused staring at her in manner not quite sane while his face continued to picture the psychic struggle within him. Then he edged forward, arms outstretched, fingers crooked.

"You knew about this. By the blackest clots in space, you knew about it and helped. You big ungainly schemer, I could kill you for it!" His fingers trembled with sheer emotion as he reached for her neck while she stood unmoving, impassive, an indescribable something shining through her great orbs. The hands touched her neck, closed around. She made no move to resist.

For several seconds he held her like that, hands cupped around her throat, gripping lightly and not contracting, while his features underwent a peculiar series of contortions. Finally he let go, backed away hurriedly with shock added to shock. He found his voice again.

"Heavens above, you *too*!"

"What one can do another can do and that was the bond between us." She watched him sit down and feel the face he did not know. "There is a law as strong and basic as that of physical survival. It says, 'I am Me—I cannot be Not-Me.'"

He remained silent but rocked to and fro and nursed the face.

"So always you will hunger for that which is rightfully yours. You will hunger as one in imminent danger of death yearns tremendously for life. Always you will crave yourself badly, madly, and never know peace, rest, tranquility, never know *completeness*, unless—"

"Unless?" His hands came away fast as he looked up startled.

"Unless you play it our way," she informed. "If you do, then what has been done can be undone."

"What do you want of me?" He was upright now, a gleam of hope showing.

"Implicit obedience."

"You shall have it," he promised fervently.

Briefly and inanely she felt relieved of the problem of Raven's suit and the owner-who-wasn't-the-owner.

The boss of the waiting gang was a thin-boned individual named Heller, six feet tall, Martian born and a Type Three Mutant, a pyrotic. Leaning against the tail of his ship, he fiddled with a silver button on the jacket of his phoney police uniform and registered disappointment as Steen and Grayson came up.

"Well?"

"No luck," said Steen. "Gone."

"How long has he been gone?"

"Forty minutes," informed Steen.

"He had three hours' start," Haller said, picking at his teeth, "so that means we're catching up. Where's he making for?"

"That," said Steen casually, "is something he omitted to divulge to the generous helping of femme he left in the house. All she knows is that he came in an antigrav cab, snatched some stuff he had planted here and shot off in XB109."

"A female in the house." Haller stared at him. "What's her place in his life?"

"Ha!" said Steen, smirking.

"I see," declared Haller, not seeing at all. His gaze transferred to the silent, dummylike Grayson, lingered there a while. Eventually a frown corrugated his forehead as he asked, "What the devil is afflicting *you*?"

"Eh?" Grayson blinked uncertainly. "Me?"

"You're a telepath and supposed to be able to read my mind although I can't read yours. I've just asked you ten times mentally whether you've got a bellyache or something, and you've reacted as if thought is a strange phenomenon confined to some outlandish place the other side of Jupiter. What's the matter with you? To look at you one would imagine you were suffering from an overdose of hypno."

30

"An overdose of his own medicine," Steen put in, quickly smothering Haller's awakening suspicions. "He tangled with the lady who happened to be one of his own kind. How'd you like to be nagged to death telepathically as well as vocally?"

"Heaven forbid!" said Haller soothed. Dismissing the question of Grayson's peculiar lack of zip he added, "Let's take steps. This Raven isn't giving us any time to waste."

He climbed into the ship, the others following. While the lock closed and the propulsion tubes warmed, he dug out his interplanetary register, thumbed its pages, found the item for which he was seeking.

"Here it is, XB109, a berilligilt-coated single seater with twenty tubes. Earth-mass three hundred tons. Maximum range half a million miles. Described as a World Council courier boat bearing police and customs exemption. H'm! That makes it awkward to intercept openly with any official witnesses around."

"Assuming that we ever find it," Steen qualified. "One world is a big place."

"We'll get our cross hairs dead on it," asserted Haller, with complete confidence. "That half million range is a comfort. It ties him down to Earth or Moon. We know he can't have sneaked away direct to Mars or Venus."

He consulted a coded list of radio channels correlated with times. Three-thirty: channel nine. Pressing the appropriate stub, he spoke into a hand-microphone. What he said went out in pulses, scrambled, and was much too brief to permit detection and unsorting by any eavesdropper. "Combine call: Haller to Dean. Find XB109."

Turning the pilot's seat sidewise, Haller sat in it, lit a black Venusian cheroot fifteen inches long, puffed luxuriously. He put his feet up on the edge of the instrument board, watched the loudspeaker.

It said, "XB109. Not listed in today's departures. Not shown on any of today's police observation reports. Stand by."

"Service!" boasted Haller, sending an appreciative glance along the cheroot and toward Steen.

Five minutes, then, "XB109. Not in Council parks one to twenty-eight. Stand by."

"Queer," remarked Haller, taking a long suck and blowing a lopsided smoke ring. "If it's not on the floor it must be off the floor. But he couldn't lift it today without getting it marked airborne."

"Maybe he took it yesterday or the day before and stashed it here," Steen suggested. Carefully he closed the door of the pilot's cabin, made sure that it was firmly shut. Sitting on the edge of the instrument board alongside Haller's feet, he waited for the next message. It came after ten minutes.

"Dean to Haller. XB109 in charge of Courier Joseph McArd at Dome City, Luna, refueling for return. Closing channel nine."

"Impossible!" Haller ejaculated. "*Im*-possible!" He stood up, bit an inch off his cheroot, spat it on the floor. "Somebody's lying!" His ireful eyes came level with Steen's and promptly he added, "You?"

"Me?" With a pained expression Steen also stood up. He was almost chest to chest with the other.

"Either that or the dame gave you a cockeyed registration number and Grayson was too dopey to detect the deception in her mind." Haller waved the cheroot. "Maybe it was the dame. She pointed down a blind alley and laughed herself silly when you two went yipping into it. If so, Grayson's to blame for that. He was the mind-probe of you two. Send him in to me—I've got to get to the bottom of this."

"How could Grayson penetrate a mind as flat and blank as a mortuary slab?" asked Steen.

"He could have told you he was stymied and let you put her under the influence. After you'd made her play statues he could have dug out her taste in paper sunshades, couldn't he? Where's the point of you going around in pairs if you're too dumb to co-operate?"

"Not dumb," denied Steen, unoffended.

"Somebody's nursing a month-old mackerel," Haller insisted. "I can smell it. Maybe that darned woman stuffed it up Grayson's vest. He's got the stupefied air of someone whose best friends have just told him. That's not like Grayson. You go fetch him—I want to give him a going over."

"I don't think we'll need him," said Steen, very softly. "This is just between us two."

"Is it?" Haller's self-command and lack of surprise revealed him as a hard character. There was a gun on his desk but he made no attempt to grab it as he gently placed his cheroot beside it and turned to face the other. "I'd a notion it was you who lied. I don't know what's come over you but you'd better not let it go too far."

"No?"

"No! You're a hypno but what of it? I can burn away your insides some three or four seconds before you can paralyze mine, and moreover paralysis wears off after a few hours, whereas charring does not. It's decidedly permanent."

"I know, I know. That is power, pyrotic power." Steen gestured and his hand touched Haller's casually, almost accidentally.

The hand stuck. Haller tried to pull his own away, found he couldn't. The two hands adhered at point of contact like flesh united to flesh—and something outrageous was happening at the junction, through the junction.

"This, too, is power," said Steen.

Far beneath the innocuous pile of warehouses nominally belonging to the Transpatial Trading Company there existed a miniature city that to all intents and purposes was not part of Earth though sited upon it. Unknown to and unsuspected by most surface dwellers it had been taken over long since.

Here was the field headquarters of the Mars-Venus underground movement, its very heart. A thousand came and went along its cool, lengthy passages and through a series of great cellars, a hand-picked thousand none of whom were men as others are men.

In one cellar worked a dozen slim-fingered oldsters who moved around slowly, fumblingly, in the manner of those seven-eighths blind. Their eyes were not eyes but something else, something too short-focused to photograph clearly anything more than three or four inches from the tip of the nose. Yet they were quasi-visual organs that within those brief limits could count the angels dancing on the point of a pin.

The oldsters worked as if continually smelling the objects of their tasks, fingers almost to nose, their not-eyes directed at abnormal angles and functioning with supernormal vividness. These were Type Nine Mutants, generally called mini-engineers. They thought nothing of building a seven-year radium chronometer so incredibly minute that it could serve as the center jewel in a diamond ring.

And in an adjacent cellar were beings similar but not the same. Pranksters continually testing their eerie powers on one another.

The two men sat opposite each other. A swift change of facial features, altering them out of all resemblance. "There you are—I'm Peters."

An equally swift and precisely similar facial change on the part of the other. "That's funny—so am I!"

Two hollow laughs. As alike as twins they sit down and play cards, each surreptitiously watching the other for the first moment when a rubber face would forgetfully relax and betray its owner's true identity.

Two more enter with the motive of turning the card game into a foursome. One registers a moment of intense mental strain, floats clean over the table and into a chair on the opposite side. The second glares at a nearer chair which trembles, hesitates, then places itself under him as if shifted by invisible hands. The twins accept these phenomena as normal, everyday occurrences and proceed to redivide the cards.

The second entrant, the chair-mover, makes his share leap straight into his ready fingers, grunts as he studies them, says with much boredom, "If you two dummies feel that you just *have* to be Peters let's have different smells so we'll know who from which." Another grunt. "I pass."

Someone going along the outer passage pauses to have a look through the door then goes on his way grinning. Ten seconds later the first Peters makes to suck his cigarette and discovers that it is now lit at both ends. With a hearty curse he leaves his chair and shuts the door, taking his cards with him lest during his absence they turn over twice of their own accord.

Grayson came into this subterranean menagerie with his mind closed against all possible intrusions, his eyes alert, suspicious, his manner jumpy. He was in a hurry and had the air of one with every reason to fear his own shadow.

At the end of a long passage where it terminated in a heavy steel door, Grayson came face to face with a hypno guard who said, "No further, chum. This is where the boss lives."

"Yes, I know. I want to see Kayder at once." Grayson stared back along the passage, made an impatient gesture. "Tell him he'd better hear me before all this blows up under us."

The guard eyed him calculatingly, then he opened the mike-trap in the door and spoke to it. Seconds later the door opened.

Grayson went through, tramped across the long room to where its sole occupant was seated at a small bureau.

A squat, broad-shouldered man with heavily underslung jaw, Kayder was of Venusian birth and probably the only Type Eleven Mutant located on Earth. He could converse in low, almost unhearable chirrups with nine species of Venusian bugs, seven of them highly poisonous and willing to perform deadly services for friends. Kayder, therefore, enjoyed all the appalling power of one with a nerveless, inhuman army too vast in numbers to destroy.

"What is it this time?" he snapped, removing his attention from a wad of documents. "Make it quick and to the point. I feel low this morning. This world doesn't suit me."

"Me, too," Grayson endorsed. He went on with, "You dug up something on this David Raven and ordered that he be brought in."

"I did. I don't know what he's got but it's alleged to be good. Where have you put him?"

"Nowhere. He got away."

"Not for long," assured Kayder with confidence. "I know that he is hell-bent for a hideout someplace. It will take a little while to pry him out." He waved a hand in dismissal. "Keep on the trail. We'll get him in due time."

"But," said Grayson, "we did get him. He was flat on his belly with his tongue hanging out and his sides heaving. A fox right at the last lap. And he got away."

Kayder rocked back on the hind legs of his chair. "Mean to say you actually had him? You let him slip? How was that?"

"I don't know." Grayson was badly worried, made no effort to conceal the fact. "I just don't know. I can't make it out. It has got me baffled. That's why I've come to see you."

"Be more specific. What happened?"

"We broke into his hiding place. A woman was with him—true telepaths, both of them. Steen was with me, as good a hypno as any we've got. Raven made a monkey of him."

"Go on, man! Don't stand there enjoying dramatic pauses!"

"Steen gave *me* the treatment," continued Grayson, hurriedly and morbidly. "He caught me on one leg and made me marble-minded. He compelled me to return to the ship and tell Haller that we'd seen nothing of Raven. Then he went into Haller's cabin."

A small, spidery thing scuttled many-legged up one side of Kayder's pants. Lowering a casual hand, he caught it, helped it onto the bureau. It was thin and bright green with eight crimson pinheads for optics.

Distastefully watching this creature, Grayson said, "A few hours later my wits drifted back. By then Haller was crazy and Steen had disappeared."

"You say Haller was crazy?"

"Yes, he was babbling. Seemed as if his brain had been twisted right round and sort of got itself back to front. Kept talking to himself about the infantile futility of Mars-Venus, Terra squabbles, the supreme wondrousness of the universe, the glory of death and so forth. Acted as if for two pins he'd jump straight into the afterlife but needed time to work up the guts."

"Haller's a pyrotic," Kayder observed. "You are a telepath. Did you overlook those simple facts? Or were you too stupefied by events to remember them?"

"I was not. I had a look inside his skull."

"And what did you find?"

"It was mussed up something awful. His think-stuff was like freshly stirred porridge. He was nursing long chains of pseudologic and working through them like prayer beads. One said, 'Steen is me is Raven is you is the others is everyone.' Another said, 'Life is not-life is soon-life is wonder-life but not other-life.'" He screwed a finger above his right ear. "A complete imbecile."

"Bad overdose of hypno," diagnosed Kayder, undisturbed. "Haller must have had hypno-allergy. There's no way of detecting it until a victim goes off the beaten track. Probably it's permanent, too."

"Maybe it was accidental. Steen wouldn't know that Haller was susceptible. I like to think so."

"That's because you hate to believe that a pal of yours could or would turn on his friends and make them squint down their own spines. Whether by accident or not, Steen put paid to Haller, one of his own crowd and his immediate superior to boot. We have a nasty name for that kind of game. It's treachery!"

"I don't think so," insisted Grayson, doggedly. "Raven's got something to do with this. Steen wouldn't do us dirt without good reason."

"Of course he wouldn't," agreed Kayder, his beefy face sardonic. He threw several tiny chirrups at the green spiderthing. It performed a bizarre little dance that might have meant something.

Kayer continued, "Everyone has a reason, good, bad or indifferent. Take me, for instance. Reason why I'm an honest, loyal and absolutely trustworthy citizen of Venus is because nobody's ever offered me enough inducement to be otherwise. My price is too high." He tossed a knowing glance at the other. "I can make a shrewd guess at what's wrong with Steen. He's a low-priced man and Raven found it out."

"Even if he's the sort to be bought over, which I doubt, how could he be? He made no contacts."

"He was alone with Raven, wasn't he?"

"Yes," admitted Grayson. "For less than a couple of minutes and in the adjoining room with me still listening in. Raven's mind remained blank. Steen's mind told that Raven turned to face him as if about to say something. Raven touched him—and Steen promptly went blank too. A hypno can't do that. A hypno can't shut off like a telepath—but he did!"

"Ah!" said Kayder, watching him.

"That hit me immediately. It was mighty queer. I got up to see what had happened. Then Steen reappeared. I was so relieved that I failed to notice he was still blank. Before I could catch on to that fact he had me where he wanted me." Apologetically Grayson finished, "I was naturally wary of Raven but completely off guard with Steen. You don't expect an ally suddenly to knock you down."

"Of course not." Kayder chirped again at the spider which obediently moved aside while he reached for his desk-mike. "We'll make it a double hunt. Just as easy to look for two as for one. We'll soon have Steen dragged in for examination."

"You're forgetting something," Grayson offered. "*I'm* here." He paused to let it sink in. "Steen knows of this place, too."

"Meaning you think he might rat on us and we're due for a raid?"

"Yes."

"I doubt it." Calmly Kayder pondered the point. "If Terran counter-forces had learned of this center and decided to put it out of business they'd have moved fast. We'd have had our raid hours ago while there was still an element of surprise."

"What's to stop them being craftier and tougher than that? What's to stop them biding their time while they make suitable preparations and then blowing the entire place sky-high?"

"You're jumpy," scoffed Kayder. "We've got too much talent around here—and besides failure could drive us into hiding. Better the devil you know than the devil you don't."

"I suppose so." Grayson was moody, uncertain.

"Anyhow, they've no publicly satisfactory excuse for taking such drastic measures. They can't take active and open part in a war while pretending it doesn't exist. Until they admit what they don't want to admit we've got them where we want them. The initiative is ours and remains ours."

"I hope you're right."

"You bet I'm right." Kayder sniffed his contempt of any other outlook. He switched his mike, activating it. "D727 Hypno Steen has gone bad on us. Get him at all costs and with minimum of delay!"

Muffled by the heavy door an outside loudspeaker repeated, "D727 Hypno Steen." Then another, farther away along the labyrinth of corridors. "D727 Hypno Steen . . . get him . . . with a minimum of delay!"

At the other end of the underground maze and nearer

the secret entrance a nose-close worker threw an irritable nod at a loudspeaker he could not see, then delicately inserted into its miniscule holder a triode-hexode radio tube the size of a match-head. Next door, an unshaven pyrotic slapped his jack of clubs on a floater's five of hearts.

"Socko! You owe me fifty." He leaned back, rubbed his chin bristles. "Gone bad on us, eh? Never heard of such a thing."

"He'll be sorry," prophesied a kibitzer.

"Nuts!" said the first. "Nobody's sorry after they're dead!"

Chapter 4

Leina sensed him returning, glanced through the window, saw him entering the path. A hint of disapproval showed in her fine eyes. She drew away from the curtains.

"He's back. Something has gone wrong." She opened the door to the adjoining room. "I refuse to stay here to watch your meeting. Wrong is wrong and right is right. I cannot see it any other way even as a matter of expediency."

"Don't leave me alone with him. Don't, I tell you! I won't be able to control myself. I'll try to kill him though he may kill me. I'll—"

"You will do nothing of the sort," she reproved. "Would you foolishly slaughter your own, your very own self?" She paused, hearing a mental voice call, "Leina!" but not answering it. "Remember your promise: absolute obedience. Do as he tells you; it's your only chance."

She went through, closing the door and leaving him to deal with his fate as ordered. Finding a chair, she seated herself primly. Her air was that of a schoolmarm determined not to be involved in a piece of inexcusable vulgarity.

Someone came into the other room, his mind reaching

through the wall and nudging her gently. "It's all right, Leina, you can come out in a minute." Then vocally to the other, "You ready to get back?"

Silence.

"Surely you *want* to get back, don't you?"

A whisper, "You damn vampire, you know I do!"

"Here then!"

Leina closed her eyes though there was nothing to see. A few swift, subdued gasps and one small sob came from the next room. They were followed by a deep and thankful breathing. She stood up, taut-faced, and went to the door. She looked at Steen who sat limp and pale on the pneumatic settee, noted the frightened introspection in orbs that at other times could burn with fierce, hypnotic intensity.

Raven said to Steen, "I took possession of your body. Even though you are an enemy I apologize for that. It is not proper to usurp the persons of the living without their willing permission."

"The *living*?" Steen went two shades paler as he put emphasis on that last word. Is it therefore proper to usurp the persons of the *dead*? His mind was in a turmoil. "You mean—?"

"Jump to no wild conclusions," advised Raven, seeing the other's thoughts as clearly as if they were a page of print. "You might be right. You might be hopelessly wrong. Either way it won't help you one iota."

"David," put in Leina, eyeing the window, "what if they soon come back in greater strength and better prepared?"

"They'll come," he assured, unworried. "But not just yet. I'm gambling on them thinking it would be nonsensical for the prey to return to the trap. It will occur to them sometime and they'll come along to check up, by which time they'll be too late." He resumed with Steen. "They are scouring the planet for me, attributing to me an importance out of all proportion. Somebody must have given them information to make them so excited. Somebody high up in Terran affairs must have betrayed his trust. Do you know who it is?"

"No."

He accepted the denial without hesitation, for it was written indelibly on the other's mind.

"They're hunting for you as well."

"Me?" Still shaken, Steen tried to pull himself together.

"Yes. I made a bitter mistake. I blundered badly by trying to take over the commander of your vessel. He proved to be something more than a standard pyrotic. He had intuitive perceptiveness, a well developed form of extra-sensory vision. It enabled him to see or sense or estimate things that he is not entitled to know."

He glanced sideways as Leina drew in a quick breath and put a hand to her throat.

"I did not expect that. There was no evidence of it and it caught me by surprise," Raven went on. "There's the beginning of a Type Thirteen, a pyrotic with e.s.p. He doesn't realize it himself, doesn't know he's slightly out of the ordinary even for a mutant." Studying the floor, he doodled with the toe of one shoe on the nap of the carpet. "The instant that we made contact he knew me as you will never know me—and he found it too much to bear. He made a frantic snatch at what he conceived to be the only form of self-preservation immediately available. He was wrong, of course, but people don't think logically in a crisis. So he made himself useless to me."

"Meaning?" inquired Steen, looking ghastly.

"He's whirly," said Raven. "They blame *you* for that."

"Blame me?" echoed Steen. "My body?" He stood up, felt himself around the chest and face, studied himself in a mirror. He was like a child ensuring the faultlessness of new clothes. "My body," he repeated. Then with heated protest, "But it wasn't *me*!"

"Try convincing them of that."

"They'll put a telepath to work on me. He'll read the truth. I can't feed them a lot of lies—it's impossible."

"Nothing is impossible. The word ought to be expunged from the dictionary. You could tell outrageous lies all the way from here to Aldebaran if you'd first been conditioned by a hypno more powerful than yourself."

"They wouldn't kill me for that," mused Steen, greatly troubled. "But they'd plant me someplace safe and for keeps. That's a worse fate, being put away. I couldn't endure it. I'd rather be dead!"

Raven chuckled. "You may not know it but you've got something there."

"You're in a sweet position to consider it funny," Steen snapped back, missing the point because it was too far out of reach for him to capture. "Who could put *you* in cold storage when within five minutes you could confiscate the person of a guard and walk out on his legs? Why, you could carry on from there, go grab the right official and sign an order for your own release. You could ... you could—" His voice trailed off as his thoughts roared along in a mighty flood and tried to carry endless possibilities to an utterly fantastic limit.

Tracking his mind, Raven registered a faint smile as he said, "You certainly can extend it fast and far. But even if in the end I did swap places with the secret lord of the Mars-Venus combine I doubt whether I'd seal the peace I'd imposed by marrying Terra's leading beauty. Tsk-tsk! You've been reading too many of those cheap and lurid Martian romances, or watching them on the spectroscreen."

"That may be," conceded Steen, long accustomed to having his inward notions dragged out and criticized. "All the same it looks like someone will have to blow you apart to stop you." His attention shifted to Leina, came back. "Even that wouldn't do much good if there are any more of your type around, ready to fill your place."

"Beginning to think of us as on the winning side, eh?" Raven smiled again, said to Leina, "Seems it's just as well I did take him over."

"I say it's wrong," she responded, firmly. "Always has been, always will be."

44

"I agree with you in principle," Raven answered. He returned to Steen. "Look, I've not come back here solely for the fun of it. I've a reason and it concerns you."

"In what way?"

"First of all, are you now willing to play on our side or do you insist on sticking to your own?"

"After this experience," explained Steen, fidgeting, "I feel that changing sides should be the safest. But I can't do it." He shook a positive head. "I'm not made that way. The fellow who'll renege on his own kind is a louse."

"So you remain anti-Terran?"

"No!" He shuffled his feet around, avoided the other's steady gaze. "I won't be a traitor. At the same time I feel that all this anti-Terran business is crazy—gaining nothing." His voice drifted off as morbidly he considered the situation. "All I really want is to get home, sit tight and be neutral."

That was true. It showed in his troubled mind. Steen had been shaken to his psychic roots, was fed up and lacked all original enthusiasm. It is a great shock to lose a limb; greater to be deprived of a body.

"Back home you're likely to have a rough time trying to sit on the fence," Raven suggested. "When parochial hysterics look around for easy marks on whom to vent their spite they usually choose a neutral."

"I'll take my chance on that."

"Have it your own way." Raven nodded toward the door. "There's your road to freedom; the price is one item of information."

"What do you want to know?"

"As I've told you, some high up Terran ratted on me. Someone on our side is a stinker. You've already said you don't know who it is. Who's likely to know?"

"Kayder," said Steen, mostly because he was in no position to refuse the information. The name popped into his mind automatically, could be read by the other as if inscribed in neon lights.

"Who is he? Where does he live?"

That was easier, not too dangerous. Where does he *live*? It enabled him to picture Kayder and his private residence while managing to suppress all thought of the underground center. Nor need his conscience bother him. Outside of the secret center Kayder cynically exercised his Terran rights to the full, even ran a small but genuine Venusian import agency. Kayder was fully capable of looking after himself.

"What's his special talent, if any?" Raven asked, having read the answers.

"I'm not certain of that. I've heard it said he's a bug-talker."

"That will do me." He jerked an indicative thumb toward the door. "Out you go. As a neutral you may be lucky."

"I'll need to be," Steen admitted. Pausing on the outer step, he added fervently, "And I hope I never see either of you again." With that he glanced skyward, rapidly walked away.

"Notice that?" Leina became a little edgy. "He looked upward, kept his expression under control, but his mind revealed what his eyes were seeing. A helicopter coming down!" She had a quick and wary look herself. "Yes, it's falling fast. David, you talked too much and stayed here too long. What are you going to do now?"

He eyed her serenely. "It seems a woman remains a woman."

"What do you mean?"

"When you become jumpy you slide right off humanity's neutral band. You think so hard that you forget to listen. Not everyone is an enemy."

Mastering her anxiety, she did listen. Now that her full attention had returned she could detect the overhead jumble of thoughts radiating from the helicopter. There were four personalities in the descending machine, their mental impulses growing stronger every second and making no attempt to blank out. Pawn-minds, all of them.

"House looks quiet. Who's that turning out of the path and into the road?"

"Dunno, but it isn't him. Too short and lumpy." Pause. "Anyway, Carson said there'd be a voluptuous Amazon here. We can talk to her if we can't find Raven."

"Hear that?" invited Raven. "You've got an unsuspected admirer in the shape of Carson."

"Never met him. You must have been telling him things." She watched the window and continued to listen. The eerie mind-voices were now over the roof.

"They ought to have given us a telepath. I've heard that the best of them can pick a mind right out to the horizon."

Another mind commented, "There will never be a brain-picker in the squad this side of the last trump. The public won't stand for it. Ever since that hullabaloo about thought-police two centuries ago the rule has been that no telepath can become a cop."

A third, with open scorn, "The public! They make me sick!"

Urgently this time, "Hey! Zip those vanes another hundred. That garden is made of dirt, not sponge rubber. Can't you talk without closing your eyes?"

"Who's juggling this gadget, you or me? I was landing 'em on a spread handkerchief when you were biting the bars of your playpen." Pause. "Hold tight, here we touch!"

Dangling from twin circles of light the thing lowered past the window, pressed its balloon tires into a bed of marigolds. Four men emerged, one propping himself boredly against the stubby fuselage while the other three headed toward the house. All were in plain clothes.

Meeting them at the door, Raven asked, "What's this? Is it something urgent?"

"I wouldn't know about that." The leader eyed him up and down. "Yes, you're Raven all right. Carson wants to talk to you." He signed toward the waiting machine. "We came in this drifter because it carries a security beam. You can speak to him direct from here."

"All right."

Climbing into the machine, Raven settled in its cubbyhole, allowed the other to switch the beam for him.

Presently the screen livened, glowed, and Carson's features showed themselves in it.

"That was quick," he approved. "I've got ten patrols out for you and thought it might take them a week to locate you." Adjusting a control at his end, he made his image sharper. "What has happened, if anything?"

"Not much," Raven informed. "The opposition has made two fast passes at me. I've made two at them. Nobody has won a battle. At the moment we're sitting in our corners, sucking lemons, waiting for the bell and throwing ugly looks at each other."

Carson frowned. "That's your end of the poker. Ours is less comfortable. In fact right now it's white hot."

"How come?"

"The Baxter United plant went sky-high this A.M. The news is being kept off the spectroscreens for as long as we can."

His hands involuntarily tightening, Raven said, "Baxter's is a pretty big place, isn't it?"

"Big?" Carson's face quirked. "The overnight shift, which is their smallest, was just ending. That cut down the casualties to approximately four thousand."

"Great heavens!"

"It has the superficial appearance of an industrial disaster born of some accident," Carson went on, his tones harsh, "which means a heck of a lot because every such incident is an accident so far as we know. We can't tell otherwise unless a few traps are sprung."

"Were there any in this case?"

"Plenty. Dozens of them. The place has immense strategic value and was guarded accordingly. We're leery, see?"

"So—?"

"Ninety-five percent of our traps were blown to kingdom come. The few remaining were too damaged to function or recorded nothing of an incriminating nature. A score of patrols composed partly of telepaths and hypnos soared with the rubbish."

"No survivors?" Raven inquired.

"Not exactly. There were some eyewitnesses. You could hardly call them survivors since the nearest of them was a mile from the plant. They say there was a sharp tremor in the ground, a tremendous whump and the entire outfit rained around. There was plenty of force behind the blast. A two-hundred-ton shunting locomotive was tossed a thousand yards."

Raven said, "According to what you first told me, the enemy's technique has been one of crafty but effective sabotage carried out without spectacular loss of life, in fact with minimum bloodshed. After all, there are ties of common blood." He studied the screen, went on, "But if in grim fact this is another of their jobs it means a considerable change of sentiment. They've now decided to rush us along by sheer ruthlessness."

"That is precisely what we fear," endorsed Carson. "Drunk on his own successes, some Venusian or Martian fanatic may have decided to run ahead of public opinion in his own world and force the issue by any means to hand. We can't stand for that!"

Nodding agreement, Raven glanced out of his cubbyhole. The helicopter's crew were hanging around well out of earshot, talking, smoking, watching the sky. Far to the east something curved high above the horizon and vanished into the blue, leaving a thin vapor trail behind it. A space liner, outward bound.

"Why call me? Is there something special you want me to do?"

"No," said Carson. "Not any more than indirectly. What you do is mostly up to you. I've given you the information, let you see what it may mean." He emitted a sigh, rubbed his forehead wearily. "The Mars-Venus idea is to arrange natural looking misfortunes that gradually sap our power to the point where we've got to give in. But *real* misfortunes do occur from time to time even in the best regulated communities. Without evidence of some convincing sort we've no way of telling a real disaster from a manufactured one."

"Of course not."

"It's a strong temptation to blame the opposition for a major accident at which they may be as aghast as ourselves. On the other hand, if we *knew* they were responsible, and which individuals had done it, we'd hang them in dangling rows. Terran citizenship wouldn't save them. Murder remains murder any place in the cosmos."

"Would you prefer me to drop everything while I look into this?"

Carson's features sharpened. "Not by any means. Ending this senseless dispute somehow—if it can be ended—is more important than coping one at a time with its incidents. I'd rather you went straight ahead with whatever you've planned. But I also want you to make full use of any opportunity to dig up data on this blast. If you find anything, throw it to me as fast as you can." His jaw lumped, his eyes narrowed. "I'll then take action."

"All right. I'll keep my eyes open and my ears perked. You will get anything I happen to find." Regarding the other curiously, Raven asked, "Just what was this Baxter plant doing, anyway?"

"You would ask me that?"

"Something I shouldn't be told?"

"Well . . . well—" He hesitated, went on, "I know of no satisfactory reason why you shouldn't. If Heraty disapproves he'll have to get on with it. I don't see why operatives should wander around only half informed." He stared hard at the screen as if trying to view his listener's background. "Anyone close up or within hearing distance?"

"No."

"Then keep this strictly to yourself. Baxter's was within two months of completing a battery of one dozen new type engines employing an equally new and revolutionary

50

fuel. A small pilot model ship fitted with such an engine, and under auto-control, did a return trip to the Asteroid Belt end of last year. Nothing has been said to the general public—yet."

"Meaning you're getting set for the Big Jump?" inquired Raven, strangely imperturbable about it.

"We *were*." Carson displayed a touch of bitterness as he employed the past tense. "Four triple-engined jobs were going to be aimed at the Jovian system. Moreover, that was to be a tryout, a mere jaunt, only the beginning. If they made it without trouble—" He let the sentence hang unfinished.

"The farther planets? On to Pluto?"

"A jaunt," he repeated.

"Alpha Centauri?"

"Maybe farther still than there. It's much too early to estimate the limit, but it should be far away, very far." His attention concentrated more on the other. "You don't look particularly excited about it."

Offering no reason for this unnatural phlegmaticism, Raven asked, "This new fuel is highly explosive?"

"Definitely! That is what has got us all tangled up. It could be an accident despite every imaginable precaution."

"H'm!" He let it stew a moment, then said, "There's a skewboy around here, a Venusian named Kayder. He operates the Morning Star Trading Company. I'm going to chase him up."

"Got anything on him?"

"Only that he is reliably said to be on Terra for purposes other than trade. My informant seems to think he is Mister Big in this part of the battlefield."

"Kayder," repeated Carson, making notes on a pad not in view. "I'll check with Intelligence. Even though he's legally Terran they will have him on file as a native-born Venusian." He finished scribbling and looked up. "Okay. Make use of that copter if you need it. Is there anything else you want?"

"One fertile asteroid for my very own."

"When we've taken over a few hundreds of them I will reserve one for you," promised Carson, without smiling. "At the rate we're going it will be ready for occupation a hundred years after you're dead." His hand reached forward, made a twisting motion. The screen went blank.

For a short time Raven sat gazing at it absent-mindedly. Faint amusement lay over his lean, muscular features. A hundred years after you're dead, Carson had said. It was a date completely without meaning. A point in time that did not exist. There are those for whom the dark angel cannot come. There are those impervious to destruction at human hands.

"*Human* hands, David," broke in Leina's thought-stream coming from the house. "Remember that! Always remember that!"

"It is impossible to forget," he gave back.

"Perhaps—but don't temporarily ignore the memory, either."

"Why not? There are two of us here: one to remember while the other is excusably preoccupied."

She did not respond. There was no weighty answer she could give. She shared with him a mutual function, willingly accepted, willingly faced. It must always be remembered, never mentioned.

Leina feared neither man nor beast, light or dark, life or death. Her anxieties stemmed from only one source: she was afraid of loneliness, the terrible, searing loneliness of one with an entire world to herself.

Struggling out of his cramped space, Raven stamped his feet around to ease his muscles, put Leina out of his mind. One does not attempt to soothe with sympathy a superior intelligence as powerful as one's own. He spoke to the pilot as the waiting four came up.

"Take me to this address. I'd like to get there soon after sundown."

Chapter 5

Kayder came home as twilight surrendered to darkness, dumped his sportster on the rear plot, watched two men stow it in its little hangar. They fastened the sliding door, joined him in walking to the back door of the house.

"Late again," he griped. "The cops are jumpy tonight. They're swarming all over the sky. I was stopped three times. Can I see your license, please? Can I see your pilot ticket? Can I see your certificate of air-worthiness?" He sniffed his contempt. "Wonder they didn't demand a look at my birthmarks."

"Something must have happened," ventured one. "There's been nothing out of the ordinary on the spectroscreen, though."

"Seldom is," remarked the second. "Three weeks have gone by and still they've not admitted that raid on—"

"Sh-h-h!" Kayder jogged him with a heavy elbow. "How many times do I have to tell you to keep it buttoned?"

He paused on the step, key in hand, searched the rim of the sky in vain hope of glimpsing a white brilliance he rarely saw. It was an aimless habit for he knew it would not appear before early morning. On the opposite side, halfway to the zenith, a pink light shone. He ignored that one. An ally it might be but that was all. Kayder thought of Mars as an opportunist sphere which had had the sense to ride the Venusian bandwagon.

Unlocking the door, he went inside, warmed his hands at a thermic panel. "What's for dinner?"

"Venus duck with roasted tree almonds and—"

The door gongs clanged sonorously. Kayder shot a sharp look at the taller of the two.

"Who's that?"

The other's mind reached toward the front, came back. He said, "Fellow named David Raven."

Kayder sat down. "You sure of that?"

"It's what his mind says."

"What else does it say?"

"Nothing. Only that his name is David Raven. The rest is blank."

"Delay him a while then show him in."

Going to his huge desk, Kayder hurriedly pulled out a drawer, took from it a small ornamented box of Venusian bogwood. He flipped its lid upward. Beneath lay a thick pad of purplish leaves mixed with dry spike-shaped blossoms. Scattered lightly over the center of this pad was what appeared to be the merest pinch of common salt. He chirruped at the box. Promptly the tiny glistening grains moved, swirled around.

"He knows you're keeping him waiting and why," the tall man pointed out. With ill-concealed uneasiness he kept watch on the box. "He knows exactly what you're doing and what you have in mind to do. He can snatch all your thoughts straight out of your head."

"Let him. What can he do about it?" Kayder poked the box across the desk and nearer the facing chair. A few shining specks soared out of it, danced around the room. "You worry too much, Santil. You telepaths are all alike: obsessed by the fancied danger of open thoughts." He chirped again, giving his lips a peculiarly dexterous twist and somehow creating a ripple of well inaudible sounds between his front teeth. More living motes ascended, spun into invisibility. "Show him in."

Santil was glad to get out, his companion likewise. So far as they were concerned, when Kayder started playing around with his boxes the best place was elsewhere. All thoughts of Venus duck and roast tree almonds could be abandoned for the time being.

Their attitude gratified Kayder. It enhanced his sense of personal power. Superiority over pawns is a thing worth having, but to rise above those with redoubtable talents of their own is greatness indeed. His self-satisfied gaze swung slowly round the room, traveling from box to case to exotic vase to lacquered casket, some open, some closed, and he did not care who was reading his mind. A little green spider-thing stirred in its sleep in his right-hand pocket. He was the only man on Earth who had a nerveless, courageous, almost invincible army within sweep of his hand.

The professional smile of a trader welcoming big business suffused his heavy features as Raven came in. He pointed to a chair, was silent as he weighed up the black, glossy hair, the wide shoulders, narrow hips. Collar-ad model, he decided, except for those silver-flecked eyes. He did not like the latter feature, not one little bit. There was something about those eyes. They sort of looked too far, penetrated too deeply.

"They do," said Raven, without expression. "Very much so."

In no way disconcerted, Kayder gave back, "I'm not nervous, see? I've had too many mind-pickers around me too long. Sometimes I can't think up a smart crack without six of them snickering all over the place before I've had time to voice it." He favored the other with another swift, calculating once-over. "I've been looking for you."

"So nice of me to come. What's the motive?"

"I wanted to know what you've got." Kayder would much rather have stalled over that and offered something deceptive. But as he'd remarked he was accustomed to telepaths. When your mind is as wide open as a spectroscreen's Sunday colorstrips the only thing you can do is admit what is on it. "I'm led to believe you're extraspecial."

Leaning forward, hands on knees, Raven asked, "Who led you?"

Kayder gave a grating laugh. "You want to know that when you can read it in my mind?"

"It isn't in your mind. Perhaps a hypno dutifully eliminates it for you every now and again as a safety measure. If so, something can be done about it. A stamp can be erased but not the impression underneath."

"For somebody extra-special you lag behind in the matter of wits," Kayder opined. He was always pleased to reduce the status of a telepath. "What a hypno can do, another and better hypno can undo. When I want to keep something right out of my skull I can find better and more effective ways."

"Such as?"

"Such as not taking it into my mind in the first place."

"Meaning you get your information from an unknown source?"

"Of course. I asked that it be kept from me. What I don't know I can't tell and nobody can lug it out of me against my will. The best mind-picker this side of Creation can't extract what isn't there."

"An excellent precaution," approved Raven, peculiarly pleased with it. He swiped at something in mid-air, swiped again.

"Don't do that!" Kayder ordered, registering a deep scowl.

"Why not?"

"Those marsh midges belong to me."

"That doesn't entitle them to whine around my ears, does it?" He smacked hands together, wiped out a couple of the near-visible specks. The rest sheered away like a tiny dust cloud. "Besides, there are plenty more where these came from."

Kayder stood up, his face dark.

In harsh, threatening tones he said, "Those midges can do mighty unpleasant things to a man. They can make his legs swell until each one is thicker than his torso. The swelling creeps up. He becomes one immense elephantine bloat utterly incapable of locomotion."

Obviously deriving sadistic satisfaction from the power of his private army, he continued, "The swelling reaches the heart, at which point the victim expires somewhat noisily. But death does not halt the process. It goes on, makes the neck twice as wide as the head. Finally it blows up the head to a ghastly balloon with hair scattered singly across its overstretched scalp. By that time the button eyes are sunk four to six inches deep." He stopped while he relished his own descriptive ability, then ended, "A midge victim is by far the most repulsive cadaver between here and Sirius."

"Interesting if melodramatic," commented Raven, cool and undisturbed. "How unpleasant to know I'm unlikely to be the subject of their attentions."

"What makes you think that?" Kayder beetled black brows at him.

"Several items. For example, what information are you going to get out of me when I'm bloated and buried?"

"None. But I won't need it when you're dead."

"An excusable error on your part, my friend. You would be surprised by how much vital information you lack but are going to acquire someday."

"What do you mean?"

"Never mind." Raven motioned it aside. "Sit down and compose yourself. Think of the consequences of bloating me. Nobody but a Venusian insectivocal could arrange such an end. So far as we know you're the only one on this planet."

"I am," admitted Kayder with some pride.

"That narrows the suspects, doesn't it? Terran Intelligence takes one look at the corpse and plants a finger straight on you. They call it murder. They've a penalty for that."

Observing the dust cloud, Kayder said meaningly, "*If* there is a body for Intelligence to brood over. What if there is not?"

"There won't be a body. I'll arrange for it to be disintegrated and thus tidy things up a bit."

"You will arrange it? We're talking about your corpse, not mine."

"We are talking about what is neither yours nor mine."

"You're way out in the blue," declared Kayder, feeling a horrible coldness on the back of his neck. "You're along where the Moon shines." Bending forward, he pressed a button on his desk, meanwhile eyeing the other as one would watch a suspected lunatic.

Santil opened the door, edged partway through. His entry was reluctant and represented the minimum necessary to answer the summons.

"Have you heard anything?" Kayder demanded.

"No."

"Have you been trying?"

"It was no use. I can overhear only your mind. He can talk and think and feel around while his own mind pretends it's a vacuum. That's more than I can do, more than any telepath I ever met could do."

"All right. You may go." Kayder waited until the door closed. "So you're a new kind of mind-probe, a sort of armor-plated telepath. One who can pick without being picked. That confirms what Grayson told me."

"Grayson?" echoed Raven. He shrugged. "He who is only half informed is ill informed."

"That goes for you too!"

"Of course it does. I've plenty to learn." Idly he swung a foot to and fro, studying it with a bored air, then said with casual unexpectedness. "I'd like to learn who organized the Baxter blowup."

"Huh?"

"They suffered a big blast this morning. It was bad, really bad."

"Well, what's that to me?"

"Nothing." Raven admitted, deeply disappointed.

There was good cause for his discontent. A rush of thoughts had poured through Kayder's mind in four seconds flat, and he had perceived every one of them.

A big blowup at Baxter's? Where do I come in? What is he getting at? Putting that huge dump out of action would be rather a masterstroke but we haven't got round to it yet. I wonder whether higher-ups back home have started arranging special jobs without reference to me. No, they wouldn't do that. Besides, there's no point in duplicating organizations and keeping one hidden from the other.

But he suspects me of knowing something about this. Why? Has some false clue led him this way? Or could it be that those itchy Martians have begun to pull fast ones of their own in such a way that we get saddled with the blame? I wouldn't put it beyond them. I don't trust the Martians overmuch.

Raven ended his train of thought by opining, "I doubt whether you trust anyone or anything except, perhaps, these bugs of yours." His attention went to the still swirling cloud. He seemed to have no trouble in distinguishing and identifying every microscopic creature within it. The unflinching gaze roamed on, examining boxes, cases, vases, caskets, estimating the relative powers of their contents, sitting in judgment upon each. "And someday even those will let you down if only because bugs must always be bugs."

"When you talk about insects you're talking to an authority," growled Kayder. He glowered straight ahead. "You've read all my thoughts. I can't blank them out like a telepath and therefore they've been wide open to you. So you know that this Baxter affair is no business of mine. I had nothing whatever to do with it."

"I concede it willingly. No hypno wiped it off your

mental slate else you wouldn't have been so confused and frankly speculative about it." He pulled thoughtfully at one ear. "An hour ago I'd have betted heavily that you were the guilty party. I'd have lost. Thanks for saving my money."

"You must need it. How much did you pay Steen?"

"Nothing. Not a button."

"Do you expect me to believe that?"

"Like everyone else, Steen can stand only so much," Raven informed. "Time comes when a man is called upon to put up with more than he can stomach. Either he runs out while the going is good or he stands fast until he cracks. You'd better write Steen off as a case of battle fatigue."

"He'll be dealt with in due course," promised Kayder, lending it menace. "What did you do to Haller?"

"Not so much. Trouble with him is that he's overeager and trying to summon up some gumption. He'll be dead pretty soon."

"I'm told his brain is—" Kayder's voice drifted away, came back on a higher note. "Did you say *dead*?"

"Yes." Raven studied him with cold amusement. "What's wrong with that? We all die eventually. You'll be dead someday. Furthermore, it's only a couple of minutes since you yourself were openly gloating over what I'd look like after your bugs had been to work on me. You enjoyed death then!"

"I can enjoy it right now," Kayder retorted, his blood-pressure shooting upward. His thin, mobile lips took on a queer twist.

The telephone yelped on his desk as if in protest of what was in his mind. For a moment he gaped at the instrument in the manner of one who had forgotten its existence. Then he grabbed it.

"Well?"

It chattered metallically against his ear while a series of expressions chased across his features. Finally he racked it, leaned back in his seat, wiped his forehead.

"Haller has done it."

Raven shrugged with a callousness that appalled the other.

"They say," continued Kayder, "that he babbled a lot of crazy stuff about bright-eyed moths flying through the dark. Then he put himself down for keeps."

"Was he married?"

"No."

"Then it's of little consequence." Raven dismissed it like a minor incident unworthy of a moment's regret. "It was to be expected. He was overeager, like I told you."

"What do you mean by that?"

"Never mind. It's too early. You're not yet old enough to be told." Standing up he seemed to tower over the other. His right hand contemptuously brushed the dust cloud away. "All I will tell you is this: in the same circumstances you would sit in front of me and joyfully cut your own throat from ear to ear, laughing as you did it."

"Like heck I would!"

"Yes, like heck you *would*!"

Kayder pointed an authoritative finger. "See here, we've met each other. We kidded ourselves we were going to take each other and we've found it's not worth the bother. You've got nothing out of me, nothing. I've got all I want out of you, which is that as something super-super you bear a strong resemblance to a flat tire. There's the way out."

"Think as you please." Raven's smile was irritating. "What I hoped to get out of you was the identity of a traitor and perhaps, something on this Baxter case. Intelligence can deal with anything else."

"Bah!" Laying a hand palm upward on his desk, Kayder emitted inviting chirrups. Whirling motes descended and settled over his fingers. "Terran Intelligence has mooched behind me for months. I'm so used to their company I'd feel lost without them. They'll have to produce a better hypno than any we have got before they can arrange some effective unblanking." Tipping his hand over the box he watched the midges pour down like powder. "Just to show you how little I care I don't mind telling you they've every reason to try to nail me down. So what? I'm a Terran engaged in legitimate business and nothing can be proved against me."

"Not yet," qualified Raven, going to the door. "But remember those bright-eyed moths that Haller mentioned. They should have an especial interest for you as an insectivocal—even though the laugh is on you!" He went out, glanced through the open door and finished by way of afterthought, "Thanks for all that stuff on your underground base."

"*What?*" Kayder dropped the box, midges and all.

"Don't reproach yourself or the hypno who expunges it from your mind every time you leave the base. He made a good, thorough job of it. There wasn't a trace." The door swung to, the click of its lock sounding right on top of his concluding remark, "But it made a beautifully detailed picture in friend Santil's mind."

Diving a hand under his desk, Kayder pulled out a mike, switched it on. His hand trembled and his voice was hoarse. Veins of fury stood out on his forehead.

"Get on the jump and shoot this around: an Intelligence raid is due shortly. Number one cover-up plan to operate at once. Number two plan to be prepared in readiness." His angry glare was directed toward the door as he went on, knowing full well that the escapee must still be near enough to pick up every word. "David Raven is now on the run from this address. Trip him up on sight. Put him out of business any way you can. That's top priority— get Raven!"

The door opened and Santil came in saying, "Look, he caught me napping in a way I—"

"Idiot!" interjected Kayder, bristling at the sight of him: "You telepaths kid yourselves you're superior examples of Nature's handiwork. Pfah! Thank the fates I'm not one myself. Of all the mentally gabby dopes you represent the lowest limit!"

"He was blank, see?" protested Santil, flushing. "When you're born and bred a telepath you can't help being conditioned by it. I forgot this fellow could still feel around while mentally deader than a dead dog and accidentally let slip a thought. He snatched it so quickly I didn't realize he had it until he spoke just now."

"You forgot," jibed Kayder. "It's top of the list of famous last words, 'I forgot.'" His irate features became darker. His gaze shifted to a large, mesh-covered box standing in one corner. "If those jungle hornets were able to recognize individuals I'd send them after him. No matter how far he's gone they'd reach him and strip him down to his skeleton before he could utter a squeak."

Keeping his attention away from the box, Santil said nothing.

"You've got a mind or what passes for one," Kayder went on, acid-toned, slightly vicious. "Come on, use it! Tell me where he is now."

"I can't. He's blank like I said."

"So are you—blanker than a stone wall." He picked up the telephone, dialed, waited a while. "You, Dean? Put those emergency pips on the air. Yes, I want to speak to the-man-we-don't-know. If he phones back tell him Raven's likely to put the finger on local base. I want him to use his influence either to postpone or minimize a raid." Racking the instrument, he pondered irefully, meanwhile plucking at his bottom lip and releasing it with little plopping sounds.

"He's got good range. Ten to one he overheard you," Santil pointed out.

"That is taken for granted. Lot of good may it do him when we don't know ourselves whom we're talking to."

The phone shrilled again.

"This is Murray," announced a voice at the other end. "You sent me to dig up stuff on this Raven."

"What have you got?"

"Not so much. I'd say the Terrans are becoming desperate, scouring the planet and making wild guesses."

"Take care not to make a few of your own," Kayder snapped. "Heraty, Carson and the others are no fools even if they have got a ball and chain shackled to each leg. Give me what you've got and leave the guessing to be done at this end of the line."

"His father was a pilot on the Mars run, an exceptionally efficient telepath coming from four telepathic generations. There was no mixing of talents maritally speaking until Raven's parents met."

"Go on."

"The mother was a radiosensitive with an ancestry of radiosensitives plus one supersonic. According to Professor Hartman, the product of such a union would most likely inherit only the dominant talent. It's remotely possible that the offspring—meaning Raven—might be telepathically receptive across an abnormally wide band."

"He's wrong there. This skewboy can pull others in even while he's holding them off."

"I wouldn't know about that," Murray evaded. "I'm no professional geneticist. I'm only telling you what Hartman says."

"Never mind. Let's have the rest."

"Raven followed in his father's footsteps to a limited extent. He got his Mars-pilot certificate and thus holds the space rank of captain. That's as far as he went. Though fully qualified he hasn't worked at it. He's never taken a ship Marsward. Having acquired his rank he appears to have done little more than mooch aimlessly around this plant until Carson hauled him in."

"H'm! That's strange!" Kayder's brows became corrugated with thought. "Any reason that you could discover?"

"Maybe he feels that his health won't stand for any Mars trips," hazarded Murray. "Not since he was killed."

"Eh?" His back hairs stiffening, Kayder urged, "Say that again."

"He was at the spaceport ten years ago when the old

64

Rimfire exploded like a bomb. It wrecked the control tower and did some slaughter. Remember?"

"Yes, I saw it on the spectroscreen."

"Raven was picked up with the other bodies. Definitely he was one of the dear departed. Some young doc played with the corpse just on whim. He lifted splintered ribs, injected adrenalin, shoved the head into an oxygen auto-breather and massaged the heart. He brought him back from wherever he'd gone. It was one of those rare returned-from-the-grave cases." Murray paused, added, "Since then I reckon he's lost his nerve."

"Nothing more?"

"Is all."

Racking the phone, Kayder lay back, stared at Santil. "Lost his nerve. Bunkum! From what I saw of him he never had any to lose in the first place."

"Who says he lost it?" Santil inquired.

"Shut up and let me think." The spider-thing crept out of his pocket, blinked around. Putting it on the desk, he let it play with his finger-tip while he mused aloud.

"Raven had a weirdly inhuman attitude toward death. He guessed Haller would do the dutch about ten minutes before it happened. That's because it takes one nut to recognize another."

"Maybe you're right."

"It suggests that his own extremely narrow escape has left him queer in the head. He regards death as something to be despised rather than feared because he has defied it once and argues that he can do it again and again." His attention transferred from the spider to Santil. "Raven's death data is so unusual that he makes loony computations upon it. You see what it means?"

"What?" asked Santil, uneasily.

"Unlimited, foolhardy, crackpot courage. He's a better-than-average telepath with the mental attitude of a religious fanatic. One taste of death has killed his fear of it. He's likely to try anything that strikes his fancy at any given moment. That makes him totally unpredictable.

Doubtless Carson is counting on precisely those factors: a high-grade adept who thinks nothing of rushing in where angels fear to tread—as he did right here."

"I expected he'd be a lot more than that," Santil ventured.

"So did I. Goes to show that the farther a rumor is passed along the more it becomes exaggerated. I have the measure of him now. Give him enough rope and he'll hang himself."

"Meaning—?"

"Meaning it's always the onrushing, headstrong animals that fall into the pit." He tickled the spider-thing under its crinkled belly. "He is the kind that runs out of one trap straight into another. All we need do is bide our time and wait for him to drop down a hole."

Something went *pip-pip-pip* under the floor. Pulling open a drawer he took from it another and smaller telephone.

"Kayder."

"Ardern here. The raid is on."

"How's it going?"

"Hah! It would give you a big laugh. The hypnos are weighing and bagging tree almonds; the mini-engineers are assembling ladies watches; the teleports are printing news-from-Venus sheets and everyone's acting like they're being good at school. The entire place is happy, peaceful, innocent."

"Got the blanking done in time?"

"Most of it. Six weren't treated when Intelligence burst in. We smuggled them out through the chute. They got away all right."

"Good," said Kayder, with satisfaction.

"That's not all. You've put out an urgent call for a smoothie named David Raven? Well, we've pinned him down."

Kayder sucked in his breath with a low hiss that made the spider jump. He soothed it with a finger.

"How did you manage to find him?"

"No trouble at all. Metaphorically speaking, he walked into the cage, locked the door on himself, hung his identity card on the bars and yelled for us to come look at him." His chuckle sounded hearty over the wires. "He has stitched himself up in a sack and consigned himself to us."

"I'm too leery of him to see it that way. There's something funny going on. I'm going to check on it myself. Expect me around in ten minutes."

Hiding the phone and closing its drawer, he ignored Santil and the spider-thing while he stared introspectively at the desk. For some reason he could not identify he felt apprehensive. And for some other reason equally dodgy his mind kept returning to the notion of bright-eyed moths that glide through the dark.

Brilliant, glowing, soaring through the endless dark.

Chapter 6

Kayder made it in seven minutes. The unpretentious house to which he went was the terminal of the secret chute from underground base. This was where the half dozen unblanked escapees from the Intelligence raid had emerged, taken to the streets and gone their several innocent ways.

The man waiting for him was small, thin and had features permanently yellowed by past spells of Venusian valley fever. He was a Type Two Mutant, a floater with a bad limp acquired in his youth when once he overdid the altitude and exhausted his mental power while coming down.

"Well?" demanded Kayder, staring expectantly round the room.

"Raven's aboard the *Fantôme*," informed Ardern.

Kayder's ire started to rise with characteristic ease. "What d'you mean by giving me that stuff about having him caged with his card on the bars?"

"So he is," insisted Ardern, unabashed. "As you well know, the *Fantôme* is a homeward boat about to blow for Venus."

"With a Terran crew. All spaceship crews are Terrans."

68

"What of it? Neither he nor they can get up to any tricks in mid-space. They've got to land. This Raven will then be on our own planet, among our own millions, and subject to our own local authority. What more could you want?"

"I wanted him to deal with myself." Going to the window, Kayder mooned through the dark at a string of green lights marking the distant spaceport where the *Fantôme* rested.

Ardern limped across, joined him. "I was by the gangway when this fellow came from the copter as if he'd only ten seconds to spare. He gave the checker his name as David Raven and claimed a cabin. I thought to myself, 'That's the guy Kayder's screaming for,' whereupon he turned, grinned at me like an alligator grinning at a naked swimmer and said, "'You're dead right, my boy!'" He shrugged, finished, "So, of course, I made a dash for the nearest phone and told you."

"He's got enough bare-faced impudence to serve a dozen," Kayder growled. "Does he think he's invincible or something?" He paced rapidly to and fro, afflicted with indecision. "I could dump a box of bugs on that boat but what's the use? My little soldiers don't know one individual from another unless one can talk to them."

"And you don't have much chance to get aboard, anyway," Ardern pointed out. "The *Fantôme* is due to lift in the next five minutes."

"Who's on her that we know?"

"It's too late to get a complete passenger list. She carries some three hundred, not counting the crew. Part of them will be Terrans, the rest plain, ordinary Venusians and Martians incapable of doing or thinking anything not connected with trade." Ardern mused it a moment. "Pity we can't search the lot and pick out the few skewboys. The only ones I know are twelve of our own men returning for fourth-year leave."

"What types are they?"

"Ten mini-engineers and two teleports."

"An ideal combination of talent to send a pinhead explorer through his keyhole and smear him across his bed," said Kayder with much sarcasm. "Bah! He'd read their every intention the moment it jelled and be twenty jumps ahead of them all the way."

"He has to sleep," Ardern ventured.

"How do we know that? Nocturnals never sleep and maybe he doesn't either."

"Tell you what, there's still radio contact so let's get those twelve to search the ship for a homeward-bound telepath. They could then enlist his help."

"No good," scoffed Kayder, waving it aside. "Raven can make his mind feel like a lump of marble. If a telepath made a pass at him through the cabin door and got a complete blank, how could he tell whether Raven was awake or asleep? And how could he tell whether or not his own bumps were being felt?"

"I reckon he couldn't," Ardern admitted, frowning.

"Some mutational aptitudes give me the gripes." Kayder returned his attention to the far-off lights. "Now and again I get fed up with our so-called array of superior talent. Bugs are best. Nobody can pick a bug's mind. Nobody can hypnotize a bug. But bugs obey those they love and that's that. Let me tell you it's plenty!"

"I once saw a pyrotic burn a thousand of them."

"Did you now? And what happened afterward?"

"Ten thousand came and ate him."

"There you are," said Kayder, feeding his own ego. "Bugs—you can't beat them!"

He meandered to and fro, pausing now and again to scowl at the lights, then said, "Nothing for it but to pass the buck."

"How d'you mean?" asked Ardern.

"We'll let them handle him at the other end. If an entire world can't cope with one not-so-hot skewboy we might as well give in right now."

"That's what I told you in the first place. He's caged himself."

70

"Maybe he has and maybe he hasn't. I'm sitting on *his* world and I'm not caged, am I?"

The faraway lights were suddenly outshone by a vivid shaft of intense white fire that crawled upward from ground level and increased speed until eventually it was spearing into the heavens. Soon after came a deep roaring that made the windows rattle. Darkness swamped back and the green lights reappeared, by contrast seeming dimmer than before.

Ardern screwed up his yellowish face, looked bothered. "I had to leave the gangway to go to the phone—"

"And so—?"

"How do we know he's actually on that boat? He's had all the time in the world to walk off it again. That cabin booking could have been an act to send us snuffling along the wrong trail."

"Could be." Kayder didn't like it. "He's artful enough to try something like that. But we can check up. Are those snoops out of the base yet?"

"I'll see." Ardern flipped a tiny wall switch, spoke into the aperture above it. "Those Intelligence characters still messing around?"

"They've just gone."

"Swell, Philby. I'm coming along with Kayder to—"

"Don't know what's so fine about it," interrupted Philby. "They took eight of our men with them."

"Eight? What the devil for?"

"Further questioning."

"Were those eight thoroughly blanked?" Kayder chipped in.

"You bet they were!"

"Then why worry? We're coming to use the short-wave transmitter so get it warmed up."

Reversing the wall switch, Ardern said, "First time they've dragged people away for questioning. I don't like it. Do you suppose they've found a way to break mental blocks?"

"Then why didn't they seize the entire bunch and come

71

after you and me as well?" Kayder made a gesture of disdain. "It's a gag designed to show they're earning their keep. Come on, let's deal with a thing at a time and get in touch with the *Fantôme*."

The receiver's big screen cleared, showed the features of a swarthy individual with a chest-mike hanging from his neck. The *Fantôme*'s operator.

"Quick, Ardern, give me that list of names of our men." Kayder took it, licked his lips in readiness to begin.

"Name, please?" requested the operator, looking at him.

"Arthur Kayder. I want to talk to—"

"Kayder?" put in the operator. His face grew momentarily fuzzy as the screen clouded with static. Long streaks whirled diagonally across the fluorescent surface and were followed by other erratic patterns. Then it cleared once more. "We have a passenger waiting to speak to you. He was expecting your call."

"Hah!" commented Ardern, nudging Kayder. "One of our men has got him marked."

Before Kayder could reply, the operator bent forward, adjusted something not in view. His face flashed off the screen and another one replaced it. The newcomer was Raven.

"Could you learn to love me, Louse-ridden?" he inquired.

"You!" Kayder glowered at him.

"Me in person. I guessed you'd check up when the boat lifted but you were slow, very slow. Tsk-tsk!" He shook his head in solemn reproof. "I've been waiting your call. As you can see for yourself I am really and truly on board."

"You'll be sorry," Kayder promised.

"Meaning when I reach the other end? I know that your next move will be to tell them I'm coming. You'll get on the interplanetary beam and warn a world. I can't help but find it most flattering."

"The word will prove to be *flattening*," said Kayder, with unconcealed menace.

"That remains to be seen. I'd rather live in hope than die in despair."

"The one will be followed by the other whether you like it or not."

"I doubt it, Bugsy, because—"

"Don't call me Bugsy!" Kayder shouted, his broad features dark red.

"Temper, temper!" Raven chided. "If your looks could kill I'd drop dead right now."

"You're going to do it anyway," Kayder bawled, now completely beside himself. "And as soon as it can be arranged. *I'll* see to that!"

"Sweet of you to say so. Public confession is so good for the soul." Raven eyed him calculatingly and added, "Better put your affairs in order as quickly as you can. You may be away quite a spell."

He switched off, giving the furious Kayder no opportunity for further retort. His features vanished from the screen. The operator came back.

"Do you want someone else, Mr. Kayder?"

"No—it doesn't matter now." Immobilizing the transmitter with a savage flip of the thumb, he turned to Ardern. "What did he mean about me being away quite a spell? I don't get it."

"Me neither."

For some time they stood stewing the problem, feeling inwardly bothered, until Philby came along and said, "There's a call waiting from you-don't-know-who."

Kayder took the phone, listened.

The familiar but unknown voice rasped, "I've more than enough on my plate without taking unnecessary risks to cover up loud-mouthed blabs."

"Eh?" Kayder blinked at the instrument.

"It's like getting down on one's knees and begging for a kick in the rear to utter homicidal threats over an open transmission system with half the Intelligence listening in," continued the voice, acid-toned. "Under Terran law the penalty is five to seven years in the jug. They can pin it on you beyond my power to unpin."

"But—"

"You're a choleric character and he knew it. You let him bait you into shouting illegal intentions all over the ether. You brainless cretin!" A pause, then, "I can't cover you without giving myself away. There's nothing you can do but get out fast. Take the boxes and burn them, contents and all. Then bury yourself until somehow we can smuggle you home."

"How am I going to manage that?" asked Kayder, feeling futile.

"It's your worry. Get out of that base—you mustn't be found there. And be careful about visiting your house for those boxes. They may have a guard on the place already. If you can't collect your stuff in the next hour you'll have to abandon it."

"But my army is there. With them I could—"

"You could do nothing," contradicted the voice, sharply. "Because you won't be given the chance. Don't stand there arguing with me. Get out of sight and lie low. We'll try to put you on a boat after the hue and cry has died down."

"I can fight the charge," Kayder pleaded. "I can say it was no more than meaningless abuse."

"Look," came back the voice wearily, "the Intelligence Service *wants* to tie you down. They've been seeking a pretext for months. Nothing can save you now except Raven's own evidence that he knew you were ribbing—and you won't get *that*. Now shut up and make yourself hard to find."

The other went off the line. Lugubriously Kayder cradled the phone, felt lost for suitable comment.

"What's the matter?" asked Ardern, watching him.

"They're going to try to lug me in for five to seven years."

"Why? What for?"

"Threatening murder."

"Holy smoke!" Ardern backed away, limping as he went. "They can do it too if they set their minds to it." His face became strained with mental effort, his body appeared to lengthen itself slightly, then his feet left the ground and he soared slowly toward a ceiling shaft. "I'm going while there's time. I don't know you. You're a complete stranger to me." He drifted up the shaft.

Kayder went out, surveyed his house from a vantage point, found it already covered. He walked the streets and back alleys until two in the morning, thought bitterly of those potent boxes lying in the back room of his home. Without them he was no better than any ordinary pawn. How could he reach them undetected? From how far beyond a ring of guards can one throw a stream of unhearable chirrups?

He was slinking cautiously along the darkest side of a square when four men came out of a black archway, barred his path.

One of them, a telepath, spoke with authoritative assurance. "You're Arthur Kayder. We want you!"

It was useless to dispute a mind-probe, useless to battle against odds of four. He went with them surlily but quietly, still thinking of his precious boxes, still convinced that bugs are best.

Chapter 7

The great crawling mists of Venus lay thick and yellow over the forepeak ports when Raven went into the main cabin for a look at the radar screen. A glistening serration across the fluorescent rectangle marked the huge range of the Sawtooth Mountains. Beyond these lay the rain forests that covered shelf after shelf down to the wide, lush plains on which mankind had established its strongest footholds.

A constant shuddering went through the entire length of the *Fantôme* as its great power plants strove to cope with their most difficult task: the relatively slow maneuvering of a giant designed for superfast motion. It was not easy. It was never easy.

Far below, hidden deep in the greenery of the rain forests, lay four crushed cylinders that once had been ships. At this moment the sole purpose of the *Fantôme*'s crew was to ensure that the number did not become five.

All passengers likewise recognized that this was the critical stage of their journey. The inveterate card players became tense and still. The chatterers were silent. The *tambar* drinkers sobered up. All eyes were on the radar screen, watching jaws of rock widen and grow larger as all too sluggishly the ship lowered past them.

In a flat, unemotional voice an officer in the pointed forepeak was reciting over the loudspeaker system, "One forty thousand, one thirty-five, one thirty thousand."

Not sharing the general anxiety, Raven studied the screen and bided his time. The mountains passed center, moved toward the screen's base, slid completely off it. Somebody sighed with relief.

Presently the oval edge of the great plain revealed itself, became clearer, more detailed, streaked with broad rivers. Vibration was now violent as the ship fought to hold its tonnage in near-balance with the planet's gravitational field.

"Twenty thousand. Nineteen five hundred."

Raven arose from his seat and left the cabin, several startled glances following his unusual action. Walking rapidly along a metal corridor he reached the forestarboard airlock. This, he decided, was as good a time as any. The crew had their hands full, their minds completely occupied. The passengers were concerned with the safety of their own skins.

Although long accustomed to humanity's absorbed interest in self-preservation he still found the tendency amusing. So far as they were concerned, it was a case of ignorance being woe. Now if only they were better informed...

He was smiling to himself as he operated the automatic door, stepped into the lock, closed it behind him. That action would light a crimson telltale in the control room, set an alarm ringing, and someone would hotfoot along to see who was fooling with the exit facilities at this touchy stage. No matter. Any irate official would be at least half a minute too late.

The lock's own little speaker was muttering in sympathy with its fellows scattered throughout the ship. "Fourteen thousand, thirteen five hundred, thirteen twelve five hundred."

Swiftly he released the seals of the outer door, unwound it, opened it wide. None of the vessel's air poured out but some higher pressure Venusian atmosphere pushed in, bringing with it a warmth, dampness and strong odors of mass vegetation.

Somebody started hammering and kicking upon the airlock's inner door, doing it with the outraged vigor of authority successfully defied. At the same time the loudspeaker clicked, changed voices and bawled with much vehemence.

"You in Airlock Four, close that outer door and open the inner. You are warned that operation of the locks by any unauthorized person is a serious offense punishable by—"

Waving a sardonic goodby to the loudspeaker, Raven leaped out. He plunged headlong into thick, moist air, fell with many twists and turns. At one instant the *Fantôme* was a long, black cylinder flaming high above him; at the next there was a whirling world of trees and rivers rushing up to meet him.

If anyone on the ship were quick enough with binoculars, he would derive much food for thought from the figure's sprawling, tumbling, apparently uncontrolled descent. Conventionally, only two kinds of people jumped out of spaceships: suicides and fugitive floaters. The latter invariably used their supernormal power to drift down at safe and easy pace. Only the suicides fell like stones. Only two kinds of people jump out of spaceships—and it was inconceivable that there could be any who were not exactly people!

The drop took longer than it would have on Earth. One falls with regular acceleration only until effectively braked by mounting air-pressure, and here the cloying atmosphere soon piled up before a moving object.

By the time he was four hundred feet above the treetops the *Fantôme* had reduced to a foreshortened, pencil-sized vessel about to land just over the horizon. It was impossible for anyone aboard to witness his fate. At that point Raven slowed in mid-air.

This braking was a curious phenomenon having nothing in common with the taut-faced, mind-straining deceleration of an accomplished levitator. The sudden reduction of his rate of fall occurred casually, naturally, much in the manner of a dropping spider that changes its mind and pays out its line less rapidly.

At treetop height, still three hundred and fifty feet above ground, he was descending as if dangling from an invisible parachute. Between enormous top branches as thick as the trunks of adult Earth-trees he went down like a drifting leaf, hit ground with enough force to leave heel marks in the coarse turf.

This point was little more than a mile from the rim of the great plain. The gigantic trees were thinned out here, growing widely apart with quiet, cathedral-like glades between them. Fifty or sixty miles westward the real Venusian jungle began, and with it the multitudinous bad-dream forms of ferocity that only lately had learned to keep their distance from the even deadlier form called Man.

He was not at all worried about the possible appearance of a stray member of this planet's thousand and one killers. Neither had he any apprehension about more efficient huntsmen of his own biped shape despite their being after him in full cry soon.

The news of his jump would gall whatever deputation might be waiting for him at the spaceport. But it would not fool them for a moment. Kayder's message—assuming that they had received it—would tag him as a telepathic oddity to whom Terran characters like Heraty and Carson attached greater importance than apparently deserved. From that they'd deduce that whatever warranted this importance had been missed by Kayder and had yet to be discovered.

Now they'd face the fact that he had left the ship in the manner of a levitator but had not gone down like a levitator. Without hesitation they'd now accept the existence of some new and previously unsuspected quasi-levitatory talent and, adding that to what they'd already got, classify him as the first example of a creature often postulated and mightily feared: the multi-talented offspring of mixed mutants.

Sitting on a lump of emerald bark three feet thick, he smiled to himself as if at a secret joke. A multi-talented sample of mutational posterity. No such individual had ever been discovered though humanity kept constant watch on three worlds for such a one. Genetically there was excellent reason to believe that no such a person ever would be found or could exist as a viable strain.

For reasons peculiarly her own, Nature had long ordained that the children of mixed mutant unions inherited only the dominant talent if any at all. The subordinate aptitude invariably disappeared. Often the dominant one would skip a generation, in which case the skipped generation consisted of mere pawns.

The notion of a super-telepathic super-levitator was patently absurd—but the opposition would swallow the absurdity when it came along in the guise of a self-evident fact. There would be considerable boosting of blood pressure in the hidden Venusian hierarchy when they learned that the first act of Earth's new chess piece was to abolish a natural law. They would want him badly and quickly, before he started playing hob with other man-made laws esteemed for making cash profits or personal power.

The thought of this gratified him. To date he had achieved nothing spectacular by the standards of the day and age. That was good because it was highly undesirable to be too spectacular. Such was the gist of Leina's case against interfering, the basis of her disapproval of the part he'd chosen to play: that at all times one should be unobtrusive, unnoticed and not be tempted to interfere.

But at least he'd created considerable uneasiness in the ranks of the formerly over-confident enemy. Indeed, if they had bolted this multi-talent mutant notion and speculated on the dire possibility of still more formidable types yet to come, they would have every reason to feel afraid. And their fears would divert them from the truth, the truth they must never know lest others pick it out of their minds.

It was a pity they could not be told the truth—but there are facts of life not told to the immature.

No natural laws had been or could be abolished.

A supernatural phenomenon is one that accords with laws not yet known or identified.

There were no multi-talented humans.

There were only bright-eyed moths that swoop and soar through endless reaches of the eternal dark.

He sent out a powerful, light-beamed mind-call far above the normal telepathic band. "Charles!"

"Yes, David?" It came back promptly, showing that the other had been expecting the summons. The incoming mental impulses impinged on twin receiving centers and proved slightly out of phase.

Raven turned to face the sender's direction as instinctively as one pawn would turn to look at another.

"I dived out of the ship. Doubt whether it was necessary but thought I'd play safe."

"Yes, I know," gave back the distant mind. "Mavis got a call from Leina. As usual they gabbled an hour about personal matters before Leina remembered she'd come through to tell us you were in the *Fantôme*. It seems she'd sooner you had kept to your proper job."

"Females remain females throughout the whole of eternity," Raven offered.

"So I went to the spaceport," continued Charles, "and I'm outside it right now. Can't get in because it's barred to the public and heavily guarded. Frustrated pawns who've come to meet the passengers are hanging around in clusters, biting their nails and swapping baseless rumors. The ship is down and a lot of bellicose officials are behaving as if someone's just swiped their pay checks."

"'Fraid I'm to blame for that."

"Why come on a ship, anyway?" asked Charles. "If

for some mysterious reason you had to do it the slow way couldn't you have inflated a small balloon and drifted here?"

"Occasionally there are considerations more important than speed," answered Raven, seeing nothing nonsensical in the question. "For instance, I'm wearing a body."

"It's precisely your body they'll be hunting. It's a give-away."

"Perhaps so, but it's what I want them to seek. Hunting for a nice human-looking body will stop them getting other ideas."

"You know best," Charles conceded. "You're coming to our place I take it?"

"Of course. I called to make sure you'd be there."

"We will. See you shortly, eh?"

"I'm starting right now."

Forthwith he set off through the shadowy glades toward the plain, striding swiftly along and keeping watch more with his mind than with his eyes. It was always possible to hear things lurking unseen. They could not spy on him without radiating even their rudimentary thoughts. Such as that pair of screech owls glowering in a dark hole two hundred feet up a tremendous tree trunk.

"Man-thing below! *Aaaargsh!*"

At the fringe of the trees came first evidence of the hunt. He stood in the darkness close by a mighty bole while a copter floated over the green umbrella of top branches. It was a big machine held up by four multi-bladed rotors and bearing a crew of ten. Their minds could be counted as they tried to probe the maze beneath.

There were half a dozen telepaths listening, listening, eager to catch any stray mental impulse he might be care-less enough to let go loose. Also one insectivocal cuddling a cage of flying tiger-ants to be tipped over any likely spot indicated by a telepath.

The relief pilot was a nocturnal content to do nothing but wait his turn should the search continue after dark. The remaining pair consisted of a hypno steadily cursing

Raven for taking him away from a profitable game of jimbo-jimbo, and a flap-eared supersonic straining to catch the thin whistle of the radium chronometer which the quarry was wrongly assumed to possess.

The menagerie of mutants passed right above and zig-zagged onward unaware of his existence immediately under them. A similarly composed outfit was scouring a wide path on a roughly parallel course two miles to the south, and yet another two miles northward.

He let them get well behind him before he stepped into the open, followed the outskirts of the trees until he struck a broad dirt road. Once upon the highway he behaved less warily.

These flying search parties might be made of exceptionally gifted humans far above pawn standard, but they still tended to fall into pawn errors. They took it for granted that anyone boldly strolling in plain sight, along a road, could have nothing to hide. In any event, if one of them did see fit to display excess of zeal and swoop over him for a pry into his cranium, he'd give them a boring selection of dunderhead pawn thoughts. What's for dinner? If I'm given fried slimefish again I'll go crazy!

There remained the risk, albeit a slight one, that a clear pictorial record of his features might be in circulation and a hunter might drop low enough to identify him visually.

But nobody showed above-average curiosity until he came within a short distance of Plain City. At that point a copter drifted overhead and he felt four minds spiking simultaneously into his own. For their pains he rewarded them with pictures of a sordid domestic wrangle in a squalid home. He could almost hear them snort with contempt as they withdrew their mental probes, whirled their rotors faster, and sped toward the rain forest.

At the city's edge he stepped off the road and made way for a ponderous tractor dragging a steel-barred trailer. Two hypnos and one teleport were in charge of this belated addition to the chase, chief feature of which consisted of a score of drooling tree-cats in the trailer. These could follow a spoor one week old and literally sprint up the trunk of any forest giant not smothered in spikes.

As became a pawn he chewed a piece of purplish grass and stared with dull-eyed curiosity as this lot creaked and rumbled past. The minds of the whole bunch were like open books. One of the hypnos was nursing a *tambar* hangover, the other missing a night's sleep and frequently pinching himself to keep alert.

Strangely enough, the teleport was worried lest they catch their prey and he be saddled with the blame should Terran authority get to hear of it. In the days of his youth he had been well and truly kicked in the pants for obeying orders and he was determined to resent it to his dying day.

Even the tree-cats broadcast their own feline desires and schemings. Ten glared longingly at Raven from behind their bars, dripped saliva, and promised that one fine day they would sample the flesh of the master race. Six more were weighing their chances of escaping into the forests and remaining beyond reach of mankind for keeps. The other four had decided exactly what they would do should glorious fate ordain that the hunted man's trail be crossed by that of a female tree-cat. Evidently this quarter's notion of private enterprise was to mix business with pleasure.

On they clanked and rattled down the road, a futile cavalcade made doubly absurd by the mock-dopey watch of its very quarry. Probably by fall of dark they would catch and tear to bloody shreds a rare jungle hobo or an illicit *tambar* distiller and return flushed with success.

Continuing into the city, Raven found his way to a small granite house with brilliant orchids behind its window-panes. He had no trouble in the finding although this was his first visit to Plain City. He made his way straight to his destination as if it were clearly visible from the beginning, or as one heads through encompassing darkness toward a distant light. And when he reached the door he did not have to knock. Those waiting within had measured his every step and *knew* the moment of arrival.

Chapter 8

Mavis, petite, blonde and blue-eyed, curled herself in a deep chair and observed him with the same deep penetration that his own eyes often showed to the considerable discomfort of others. It was as if she had to look right into him to see his real self behind a concealing mask of flesh.

The other one, Charles, was a plump and rather pompous little man blessed with the lacklustre optics of a low-grade pawn. Any talented human would take one look at Charles and unhesitatingly classify him as a fat nitwit. A veneer of matching nitwittery lay over his brain and served to confirm the first impressions of any outer mind that might choose to probe. More by good luck than good management Charles was an entity exceptionally well concealed and therefore much to be envied.

"Naturally we're pleased to see you," said Mavis, speaking vocally for the pleasure of feeling her tongue wag. "But what has happened to the rule that one stays on one's appointed ball of dirt?"

"Circumstances alter cases," Raven said. "Anyway, Leina is still there. She can handle anything."

"Except being alone, entirely alone," retorted Mavis, taking Leina's part. "No person can handle that!"

"You're right, of course. But nobody remains isolated for ever. In the end there's always a reunion." He chuckled with queer humor, added, "If only in the sweet by-and-by."

"Your theology is showing," commented Charles. He took a pneumaseat beside Mavis, squatting comfortably with his pudgy legs stretched out, his paunch supported in linked hands. "According to Leina, you are busily sticking your fingers into other peoples' affairs. Is that right?"

"About half right. You've not had the full story. Someone on this planet—aided by unknown co-operators on Mars—is having a good time pulling Terra's hair. They are like mischievous children playing with a gun, neither knowing nor caring that it might be loaded. They are out to gain complete independence by a form of coercion amounting to new style war."

"War?" Charles was doubtful.

"That's what I said. The trouble is that wars have a habit of getting hopelessly out of hand. Those who start one usually find themselves quite unable to stop it. If it can be done, this one must be prevented from starting in real earnest, by which I mean becoming bloodier."

"Ugh!" Charles rubbed a pair of smooth chins. "We know there's a strong nationalist movement on this planet but we've ignored it as being of no especial interest from our viewpoint. Even if they go so far as to swap bombs and bullets with Terra, and murder each other wholesale, what does it matter to us? It's all to the merry, isn't it? Their loss is our gain."

"In one way but not in another."

"Why?"

"The Terrans are badly in need of unity because they are heading toward the Denebs."

"They're heading—?" Charles' voice trailed off. For a moment his dull eyes shone with formerly hidden fires.

"Are you telling me that Terran authorities actually *know* about the Denebs? How the deuce *can* they know?"

"Because," Raven told him, "they are now at development stage four. A lot is going on that the general public doesn't suspect, much less those here or on Mars. The Terrans have built a better drive and already tried it out. They're about to test it farther and are unable to forecast its limits. For matterbound folk they're doing pretty well."

"Evidently," endorsed Charles.

"I've not yet been able to discover exactly how far they have gone or what data has been brought back by test pilots, but I know they've found enough to arouse suspicions that sooner or later they may collide with some other unnamed, undescribed life-form. You and I know that can only be the Denebs." He wagged an emphatic finger. "We also know that the Denebs have long been milling around like a pack of hounds with five hundred trails to follow. They don't know which way to go for the best, but their general trend is in this direction."

"That is true," put in Mavis. "But the last prognosis gave them a minimum of two centuries in which to discover this solar system."

"A reasonable conclusion based on the data then available," answered Raven. "Now we have a new and weighty item to include in our computations, namely, that Homer Saps will soon be rushing out to meet them. The flag is being hoisted, the smoke fires lit and everything is being done to attract attention to this neck of the cosmos. That kind of caper is going to cut down the time before the Denebs are in a hurry to look over what is here."

"Have you reported this?" demanded Charles, fidgeting.

"Most certainly."

"And what was the response?"

"Thanks for the information."

"Nothing more than that?" He lifted an eyebrow.

"Nothing," assured Raven. "What else do you expect?"

"Something more emotional and less coldly phleg-matic," Mavis interjected. "You males are all the same, just so many brass buddhas. Why can't you stand on a table and scream?"

"Would it do any good?" asked Charles.

"Don't you get logical with me," she snapped. "It would take some pressure off the glands. I possess a few glands, in case you don't know it."

"That is a subject about which I am passably in-formed," said Charles, pointedly. "Moreover, I have glands myself. One of them makes me fat and inclined to laziness, but I appear to lack the one that is bothering you at the moment." He pointed a plump digit. "There's the table. Climb up and let go a few shrill bellows. We won't mind."

"I am not in the habit of bellowing," said Mavis.

"There you are!" He threw a glance at Raven and gave a careless shrug. "Women for you. Cold and calculating. Can't take the steam off their zip-bits."

Mavis promised, "Someday I'll trim your wings, Porky."

"Fancy me with wings." Charles laughed until his paunch trembled. "Diving and soaring like an obese angel. Or fluttering like a fat moth." He wiped his eyes, laughed again. "What an imagination!"

Producing a tiny, lace-edged handkerchief, Mavis wept into it very softly and quietly.

Charles stared at her aghast. "Well, what have I said wrong now?"

"You voiced a stimulator." Going over to Mavis, Raven patted her shoulder. "There, there! It isn't right to remain here if memories are growing too strong for you. It isn't right to stay if you want out. We can find another pair who—"

She whipped down the handkerchief and spoke fiercely. "I don't want out. I'll go when it's time and not before. What sort of person do you think I am? Can't a girl have a good cry if she wants to?"

"Sure she can, but—"

"Forget it." She stuffed the handkerchief into a pocket,

blinked a couple of times, smiled at him. "I'm all right now."

"Does Leina ever do that?" asked Charles, looking at Raven.

"Not while I'm around."

"Leina was older when . . . when—" Mavis let the sentence go unfinished.

They knew exactly what she meant.

Nobody else could have guessed it, not even the Denebs, but these few knew.

They were silent quite a while, each busy with entirely personal thoughts that remained hidden behind mental shields. Charles was the first one to cease ruminating and become vocal.

"Let's get down to business, David. What are your plans and where do we come in?"

"The plans are elementary enough. I want to find, identify and effectively deal with the opposition's key man on Venus, the one who decides ways and means, settles all disputes, generally rules the nationalistic roost and is indisputably the big boss. Take away the locking-stone and the whole arch falls down."

"Sometimes," qualified Charles.

"Yes, sometimes," Raven agreed. "If their organization is half as good as it ought to be they'll have a deputy leader held ready to replace him if necessary. Maybe more. Then our task will be more complex."

"And after all that there will still be the Martians," Charles suggested.

"Not for certain. It all depends on how they react to whatever happens here. Mars-Venus liaison is to a great extent boosted along by mutual encouragement. Each keeps giving the other the loud hurrah. Take away the applause and the act doesn't seem so good to the remaining partner. I'm hoping they'll pipe down when Venus drops out."

"One thing I don't understand." Charles was thoughtful. "What's to stop Terra paying back the insurgents in their own coin? Sabotage and all that stuff is a game at which two can play."

Raven told him.

"Ah!" He had another rub at his chins. "The local boys can make a mess of what they regard as other people's property while the Terrans can louse up only what they consider their own."

"It's no business of ours," put in Mavis. "If it were we would have been told as much." Her eyes were shrewd as they examined Raven. "Have you been requested to interfere by anyone other than Terrans?"

"No, lady, and it's not likely I shall be asked."

"Why not?"

"Because large as the issue may loom in this minor corner of the galaxy, it is small and pitifully insignificant by comparison with bigger issues elsewhere. Things look different from far, far away." His expression showed that he knew he was telling her nothing with which she was not already familiar. "And the accepted rule for the likes of us is to use our own initiative with regard to small matters. So I am using mine."

"That is good enough for me," approved Charles, sitting up and easing his stomach. "What d'you want us to do?"

"Not very much. This is your bailiwick and you know more about it than anyone. Give me the name of the man you consider likeliest to be the inspiration behind this separatist tomfoolery. Give me what data you've got on his talent and other resources and tell me where I can find him. Cogent information is what I need most. Please yourself about offering any more help."

"I propose to offer more." Charles glanced sidewise. "How about you, Mavis?"

"Count me out. I intend to follow Leina's example and keep watch. After all, that's what we're here for. Somebody has to do it while you mulish males go gallivanting around."

Raven said, "You're dead right. Keeping watch is all-important. I'm thankful for you fair maidens. Us bull-heads are left free for pernicious interfering."

She pulled a face at him but offered no comment.

"The setup here is amusing," Charles informed. "We have an orthodox Terran governor who utters strictly orthodox sentiments and remains diplomatically unaware that the illegal underground nationalist movement already is doing ninety percent of the bossing. The big boss in this movement, the figure the rank and file look up to, is a large and handsome rabble-rouser named Wollencott."

"What's he got that others haven't?"

"The face, figure, and personality for the part," explained Charles. "He is a native-born Type Six Mutant, that is to say, a malleable, with an imposing mane of white hair and an equally imposing voice. Can make himself the perfect picture of a tribal joss any time he wants. He can also speak like an oracle—providing that he has first learned the words by heart. He's incapable of thinking out the words for himself."

"All that doesn't sound so formidable," Raven offered.

"Wait a bit. I've not finished. Wollencott is so well-suited to portray the dynamic leader of a patriotic cause that he might have been especially chosen for the part. And he was!"

"By whom?"

"By a hard character named Thorstern, the *real* boss, the power behind the throne, the lurker in the shadows, the boy who will still be around long after Wollencott is hung."

"The puppet master, eh? Anything extra-special about him?"

"Yes and no. The most surprising feature is that he is not a mutant. He hasn't one paranormal aptitude." Charles paused, ruminated a moment, went on, "But he is ruthless, ambitious, cunning, a top-grade psychologist and has a high-powered, quick-moving brain good enough to serve a thousand monkeys."

"A pawn with high I.Q."

"Exactly! And that means plenty when redoubtable talent doesn't necessarily have redoubtable brains. Given first-class wits, even a pawn can pull the strings of a dopey telepath; his mind can move just that fraction faster than the telepath can pick it up and react."

"I know. I've listened in to one or two such cases. It's the easiest thing in the world for a mutant to fall into the error of underestimating an opponent merely because he is ordinary. Besides, power is never sufficient unto itself; there must also be the ability to apply it. That's where the Denebs excel. They make full use of what they've got." Becoming restless, Raven moved toward the door. "But we haven't to cope with the Denebs just yet, least-ways, not *here*. The immediate objective is Thorstern."

"I'm coming with you." Heaving himself out of the pneumaseat, Charles hitched his middle, let guileless eyes rest on Mavis. "Hold the fort, Honey. If anyone asks, tell them Papa has gone fishing—but don't say for what."

"See that you come back," she ordered. "In one piece."

"In this strange phase of existence of life in death one can guarantee nothing." He released a wheezy laugh, his belly quivering in sympathy. "But I'll try."

With that parting crumb of comfort he followed Raven out, leaving her to get on with her chosen task of standing guard over things that were on the Earth but not earthly.

And like Leina as she sat alone, watching, watching—listening, listening—her chief consolation was that her solitude was shared by other silent sentinels elsewhere.

Chapter 9

The invariable eventide fog was now creeping into the city, rolling with sluggish purpose along its streets and avenues in thick yellowish swirls that became still denser as the hidden sun went down. By midnight it would be a warm, damp, all-obscuring blanket through which nothing would move with certainty except blind men, restless, sleepless nocturnals and a few whispering supersonics "echo-walking," that is to say, finding their way like bats.

In the rain forests it was different; the trees lay on considerable higher levels while the fog hugged the valleys and the plains. The search in the forests would continue, with copters whirring over the treetops and hunters scouring the glades.

Charles and Raven passed a shop window in which an outsize spectroscreen displayed ballet dancers moving delicately through a scene from *Les Sylphides*. The prima ballerina drifted across the stage with infinite grace, pale and fragile like a blown snowflake.

Yet only a few miles away, deep within the encroaching dark, were monstrous forms and monstrous vegetation marking the frontiers of the half-known and the unknown. It was a contrast of extremes that few noticed, few thought about. When a planet has been settled long enough to have a population mainly native-born, erstwhile dreams become humdrum, the alien becomes the familiar, old-time fantasies are replaced by new and radically different ones.

Stopping outside the window and studying the scene, Charles said, "See the ease and grace with which she pirouettes, the lithe slenderness of her limbs, the calm, impassive, almost ethereal beauty of her face. Note how she pauses, hesitates, flirts and darts away like a rare and wonderful butterfly. She is a good example of a rather unearthly type that has enthralled humanity for centuries: the ballet type. She fascinates because she makes me wonder."

"About what?" Raven inquired.

"Whether her type are paranormals not recognized as such and not suspecting it themselves. It is possible to have a talent far too subtle to be named and classified."

"Make it clearer," Raven suggested.

"I wonder whether people like her have a subconscious form of extra-sensory perception that impels them to strain poetically toward a goal they can neither name nor describe. Such intuitive awareness gives them an intense yearning that they can express in only one way." He pointed to the screen. "Butterfly-like. A butterfly is a day-loving moth."

"You may have something there."

"I'm sure I have, David." He left the window, continued onward at a fast waddle. "As a life-form in their own right human beings have made a good accumulation of knowledge. How immensely greater would it be if they could add to it all the items they've got subconsciously or instinctively but cannot correlate on the conscious level."

Raven said, "Brother Carson, who is no stupe, is with you in that. He showed me a list of known mutants and then warned that it might be far from complete—types hanging around undiscovered by themselves, much less by others. It is difficult to identify oneself as an oddity unless the oddness happens to be self-advertising."

Nodding vigorously, Charles contributed, "Rumor has it that an entirely new type was discovered this week and by pure accident. A young fellow who lost his hand in an argument with a buzz saw is now supposed to be growing another."

"A bio-mechanic," defined Raven. "Can service himself with new parts. Well, it's an innocuous faculty, which is more than can be said for some."

"Yes, sure, but the point is that up to then he didn't know he could do it because he'd never lost a piece of himself before. But for that accident he could have gone through life and to his grave without the vaguest notion that he possessed a supernormal power. So I often wonder how many more folk lack adequate knowledge of themselves."

"Plenty. Look at what *we* know."

"I am looking," assured Charles, quietly. "It is so much that it would shake a thousand worlds if they shared it." His fingers curled around the other's elbow, digging hard. "In fact, it's so much we take it for granted that it's all. David, do you suppose that . . . that—?"

Raven stopped in mid-stride. His silver-flecked eyes were bright as he gazed into other eyes similarly illuminated.

"Finish it, Charles. Finish what you were going to say."

"Do you think maybe *we* don't know half as much as we believe? That what we do know is very far from being the whole story? That there are others who do know more, watching us exactly as we are watching these, sometimes laughing at us, sometimes pitying us?"

"I can't say." He registered a wry grin. "But if there are, we do know one thing—they don't interfere with *us*!"

"Don't they? Can we be sure of it?"

"They don't in any manner that we can recognize."

"We recognize Deneb tactics," Charles retorted. "They

95

do plenty of shoving around that is intended for us but not felt by us. Conversely, others could push us without knowing whom they were pushing, without us knowing we were being pushed."

"Better still, they could adopt our own methods to our own confusion," offered Raven, manifestly skeptical but willing to take it along. "They could appear to you and me pretty much as we appear to these, visibly ordinary." He waved a hand to encompass the local citizenry. "Just like any other Joe. Suppose I told you I'm a Deneb in fleshly disguise—do you dare to call me a liar?"

"I do," said Charles, with no hesitation. "You are an unblushing liar."

"I resent having to admit it." He gave the other a reassuring clap on the shoulder. "See, you *know* what I am. Therefore you must have intuitive awareness. Definitely, you're a paranormal and ought to express yourself by taking up ballet dancing."

"Eh?" Charles gloomed down at his ample front. It stuck out like a Christmas parcel carried under his vest. "That's what I call throwing it back at me."

He went silent as three men in uniform came round the corner ahead and stopped in their path.

The trio were dressed as forest rangers, the only organized body—apart from special squads of police—officially permitted to bear arms on Venus. They grouped close together like friends having a last chat before going home, but their attention was on the pair coming toward them. Their open minds revealed that all three were pyrotics looking for a man named Raven.

The leader kept tab of the oncomers out the corners of his eyes, waited until they drew level, wheeled swiftly on one heel and snapped with sudden authority, "Your name David Raven?"

Stopping and lifting a surprised eyebrow, Raven said, "However did you guess?"

"Don't be funny," advised the questioner, scowling.

Raven turned to Charles. His tones were pained. "He tells me not to be funny. Do you think I am funny?"

"Yes," responded Charles, with prompt disloyalty. "You've been that way since you fell on your head at age three." His bland but stupid looking eyes shifted to the ranger. "Why do you want this person named . . . er—?"

"Raven," prompted Raven, being helpful.

"Oh, yes, Raven. Why do you want him?"

"There's money on his head. Don't you ever use your spectroscreen?"

"Occasionally," Charles admitted. "Most times it bores me to tears, so I let it stay dead."

The ranger sneered to his companions. "Now you know why some people stay poor. Opportunity knocks at every door but some refuse to listen." Taking no notice of Raven, he continued with Charles who was looking suitably crushed.

"They've put it on the spectroscreen that he's wanted badly and at once."

"For what?"

"For imperiling the lives of crew and passengers of the *Fantôme*. For opening an airlock contrary to regulations, interfering with navigation, refusing to obey the lawful orders of a ship's officer, landing in a forbidden area, evading medical examination on arrival, evading customs search on arrival, refusing to pass through the antibacterial sterilization chambers and—" He paused for breath, asked one of the others, "Was there anything else?"

"Spitting in the main cabin," suggested that worthy who had long been tempted by that crime merely because a large-lettered notice warned him that he must not.

"I never spit," asserted Raven, giving him the cold eye.

"Shut up, you!" ordered the first one, making it clear that he was taking no back chat from anybody. He switched to Charles, preferring that person's respectful dumbness.

"If you happen to come across this David Raven, or hear anything about him, ring Westwood 1717 and tell us where he is. He's dangerous!" He slipped a sly wink at the others as he emphasized the last word, then promised, "We'll see that you get your fair share of the reward."

"Thanks." Charles was humbly grateful. He said to Raven, "Come on. We're late already. Keep a look-out and remember he resembles you."

They walked off, conscious that the three were watching them go. The trio's surreptitious comments reached them in the form of mental impulses loud and clear.

"Took us for rangers, anyway."

"Let's hope some ranger captain does too, if we happen to meet one."

"We're wasting our time just because a guy on the spectroscreen mentioned money. We could spend a few hours at better than this. There's a *tambar* joint two blocks down, so what say—"

"Why don't they distribute his picture?"

"A telepath would help, like I said. All we'd need do is wait for him to point. Then we'd make the smoke and flames. After that we could wear down our fingers counting the dough."

"Now you mention it, I think there's something queer about that reward. They didn't bid anything like as high for Squinty Mason when he busted those banks and shot a dozen people."

"Perhaps Wollencott wants him for personal reasons."

"Look, fellows, there's a *tambar* joint—"

"All right, we'll go there for half an hour. If anyone catches us there we've got a good excuse. We heard a rumor that Raven was meeting someone in the dump." The mental stream started to fade very slowly. "If Wollencott wants him—"

They continued talking about Wollencott until they dimmed beyond hearing. They thought up twenty ways in which Wollencott would make an example of the culprit.

It was Wollencott, Wollencott, Wollencott all the time.

Not one mentioned Thorstern or so much as gave that name a passing thought.

Which was quite a tribute to the brains of the owner of that name.

Chapter 10

A great black basalt castle was the home of Emmanuel Thorstern. It dated back to the earliest days of settlement when smooth, high walls six feet thick were sure protection against antagonistic jungle beasts of considerable tonnage. Here the little group of first-comers from Earth had clung stubbornly to their alien plot until more shiploads built them up in numbers and strength of arms. Afterward they'd sallied forth, taken more land and held it.

Seven other similar castles elsewhere on the planet had served the same function for a time, then had been abandoned when their need had passed. These others now stood empty and crumbling like dark monuments to this world's darkest days.

But Thorstern had stepped in and restored this one, strengthening its neglected walls, adding battlemented towers and turrets, spending lavishly as though his calculated obscurity in matters of power had to be counterbalanced by blatancy in another direction. The result was a sable and sinister architectural monstrosity that loomed through the thickening fog like the haunt of some feudal maniac who held a countryside in thrall.

Toying thoughtfully with the lobe of an ear, Raven

stood amid swirls of fog and examined this edifice. Only the base was clearly visible in the curling, thickening vapor, the rest becoming shadowy with the growing darkness and merging into the higher haze. Yet his gaze lifted and shifted from point to point as if somehow he could see in full details those features hidden from normal sight.

"Quite a fortress," he remarked. "What does he call it?—the Imperial Palace or Magnolia Cottage or what?"

"Originally it was known as Base Four," Charles replied. "Thorstern renamed it Blackstone. Locally it's referred to as the castle." He stared upward in the same manner as the other, apparently having the same ability to see the unseeable. "Well, what now? Do we go after him in our own way or do we wait for him to come out?"

"We'll go in. I don't feel like hanging around all through the night until some unpredictable time tomorrow."

"Neither do I." He pointed at a high angle. "Do we exert ourselves and go over the top? Or shall we take it easy and walk in?"

"We'll enter like gentlemen, in decent and civilized manner," Raven decided. "To wit: through the front gate." He had another look at their objective. "You do the talking while I hold your arm and let my tongue hang out. Then we'll *both* look simple."

"Thank you very much," said Charles, in no way offended. Strutting officiously up to the gate, he thumbed a bell button, waited with Raven by his side.

Four blasphemous minds located nearby immediately radiated four different but equally potent oaths. They were pawn minds, all of them. Not a mutant in the bunch.

It was to be expected. As an individual without talent other than that provided by above-average brains, Thorstern would make full use of those blessed with paranormal aptitudes but not yearn for their company. So it was likely that the majority of those around him—that is to say, within the castle—would be mere pawns chosen for various merits of loyalty, dependability, subservience to the boss.

In these respects the lord of the black castle ran as true to type as the lowliest of his servitors. All ordinary human beings, clever or stupid, were leery of paranormals, liked them better the farther away they got. It was a natural psychological reaction based on the concealed inferiority complex of Homo Today in the presence of what uncomfortably resembled Homo Tomorrow. The Terran forces controlled by Carson and Heraty could have exploited such instinctive antagonisms to the great discomfort of the opposition—but that would have meant further accentuating human divisions in the name of human unity.

In addition, to stir up masses of pawns against a powerful minority of mutants would be to incite type-riots which—like the racial upsets of long, long ago—could get hopelessly out of hand and spread farther than desired. Terra had some mutants of her own!

So it was a blue-jowled and commonplace kind of pawn who opened a door in the thickness of the wall, came out and peered through the heavy bars of the gate. He was squat, thick-shouldered, irritable, but sufficiently disciplined to try to conceal his ire.

"Wanting someone?"

"Thorstern," said Charles airily.

"It's *Mister* Thorstern to you," reproved the other. "You got an appointment?"

"No."

"He won't see anyone without an appointment. He's a busy man."

"We are not anyone," put in Raven. "We are someone."

"Makes no difference. He's a busy man."

Charles said, "Being so busy he will wish to see us with the minimum of delay."

The guard frowned. He was around I.Q. 70 and steered mostly by his liver. He did not want to use the phone and consult a higher-up lest the reward be a bawling out. More than anything else he yearned for a reasonable excuse to give these callers the easy brushoff. That interrupted game of jimbo-jimbo had reached its most enthralling stage now that he had won first sniff at the green bottle.

"Well?" insisted Charles, fatly bellicose. "You going to keep us here come Monday week?"

The other registered the baffled distaste of a slow mind being pushed faster than it wants to move. The plausible excuse he was seeking seemed strangely elusive. He glowered at the pair as though they had shoved him where he didn't wish to go.

Maybe he *had* better do something about this. The manifold ramifications of Thorstern's business brought all sorts of people to the gate at all times, though seldom as darkness fell. Some were admitted, some were not, and now and again it happened that dopes and crackpots were allowed in while important looking persons were kept out. Anyway, it was his duty only to hold the fort, not to sit in judgment on every caller.

Licking his lips, he asked hoarsely, "What are your names?"

"They don't matter," said Charles.

"Well, what is your business?"

"That *does* matter."

"Cripes, I can't tell them just that!"

"Try it and see," Charles advised.

Hesitating, the guard stared from one to the other, absorbed mental comfort from each without knowing it, went back into the wall. Those in the tiny room beyond greeted him with a chorus of remarks that caused not a whisper outside the door but did spike through the basalt in neural waves and came clearly to the pair waiting outside the gate.

"Oh, Lord, how much longer are you going to be? You're holding up the game."

"What's eating someone, coming along at this hour? It'll be blacker than the inside of a cat pretty soon."

"Who is it, Jesmond? Somebody important?"

"They won't say," informed the guard, with glumness.

Taking the phone off the wall, he waited for its visiscreen to clear and show who was responding at the other end.

At the end of a minute his neck was beet-red and his tone apologetic.

Racking the phone, he threw the three scowling, impatient faces at the table a pained glance, went into the rapidly gathering gloom. The impulse that had driven him to report with no information was now gone, but he sensed its absence no more than he had sensed its presence. "See here, you two, the—"

He stopped, gaped outward through the gate. Those couple of minutes had hastened the night. Visibility was now down to a mere four or five yards. Within that small radius there was nobody in view, nobody at all.

"Hey!" he called into the wall of fog. No reply. Again, much louder. "Hey!"

Nothing but a dismal drip of water from black walls and a dim, subdued mixture of sounds from the city a couple of miles away.

"Darn!" Giving it up, he returned to the door. A thought struck him just as he reached it, he came back, tried the gate, shaking it, examining its bolts and the main lock. It was securely fastened. He glanced at the top. A quadruple row of spikes three inches from the overhead rock made it completely impassable. "Darn their hides!" he said, inexplicably uneasy, and went indoors.

The green bottle was the chief object of his attention. It did not occur to him that a great gate's strongest point is also its weakest—the lock. Neither did it strike him that the most complicated lock can be turned from either side providing one has a key—or a satisfactory nonmaterial substitute!

Darkness became complete as the last dim fadings of light were swept away much as if a gigantic shutter had been drawn across the concealed Venusian sky. A long, narrow courtyard stood behind the gate. Within this area visibility was down to an arm's length. As usual upon Venus, the fall of night caused the fog to be pervaded by a hundred exotic odors drawn from trees and jungles, with a crushed marigolds perfume predominant.

The two invaders halted their progress through the courtyard. Immediately to their right a large bolt-studded door was set in the wall. Though well hidden in the all-enveloping cloud, they *knew* the door was there without having perceived it visually. They moved closer and inspected it.

Charles murmured, "They fitted that gate with a wonderlock containing fourteen tricky wards. Then they fitted the lock itself with an alarm guaranteed to scream bloody murder the moment anyone tried to tamper with it. Finally, they included a cut-off for the alarm in the attendant's room so that it wouldn't operate while he was dealing with a caller." He gave a loud sniff. "That's what I call ingenuity carried to the point of imbecility."

"Not necessarily," Raven differed. "They designed that layout solely for coping with their own kind, mutant or nonmutant. It is quite adequate for such a limited purpose. Dealing with Denebs—or the likes of you and me—is quite another problem. Thorstern and all his hosts would have a deuce of a time trying to solve it."

"I suppose you're right. That gate comes near to the unbustable according to this world's notions of unbustability." Charles ran deceitfully dull-witted eyes over the big door and the black rock around it. "Do you see what I see?"

"Yes, there's an invisible light beam across the passage just behind the door. Open the door and break the beam and curfew rings tonight."

"Everything to delay us," grumbled Charles, impatient of time-wasting futilities. "You would think they'd done it deliberately." He glanced down at his paunch, feeling that frequent inspection never made it any smaller, added in mournful tones, "This is where we're handicapped by our disguise. Without it we could go straight in."

"The same applied a few minutes ago. We're dealing with men and therefore must do things somewhat like men." He eyed Charles with mild humor. "We *are* men, aren't we?"

"No—some of us are women."

"You know what I mean, Gusty. We are men and women."

"Of course. But sometimes I—" His voice trailed off, his plump face quirked, then he said, "That brings back a thought to me, David. I stew it over from time to time."

"What is it?"

"How many horses really are horses? How many dogs really are dogs?"

"Well, that is something to look into after more urgent and important business has been settled," Raven opined. "It will be an interest to divert us through a few millennia to come." He gestured toward the door. "Right now there's this little trap. The beam has to be switched off whenever anyone answers the door from inside. Following the lines back to the switch is going to take a bit of time if it's deep inside the place."

"You trace the lines while I tend to the door," suggested Charles. "One man, one job."

He got on with his part straightaway. It involved no more than standing with hands in pockets and staring intently at the obstacle.

Meanwhile, Raven gazed with equal concentration at the thick rock to one side. On the face of it there was nothing to see worth seeing, nevertheless his pupils shifted slowly, moving rightward, rising and falling occasionally.

Neither made further remark. Each engrossed in his own special task, they stood side by side, unmoving, and stared to the front as if transfixed by a supernatural apparition, invisible to all but themselves. After a short while, Charles relaxed but was careful not to disturb the other.

Half a minute later Raven likewise eased up, said, "The lines go along a corridor then down a passage to the right and into a small anteroom. The switch made a loud click when it snapped up but luckily the room was empty."

Bracing a hand against the door he gave it a shove. It

swung inward, heavily, soundlessly. The two stepped through, closed it behind them, walked along a narrow corridor illuminated by sunken ceiling lights. Their manner had the casual confidence of people who purchased the castle last week and plan to furnish it tomorrow.

"All this gives some indication of the psychology of Thorstern," Raven remarked. "The bolts and bars and invisible light beams could be detected by any mutant endowed with first-class extra-sensory perception, though he'd be unable to do anything about them. On the other hand, a teleport could manipulate the lot without any trouble whatsoever, if only he could see them. So the place is wide open to a multi-talented mutant such as a teleport with e.s.p. Thorstern proceeds on the assumption that there is no such creature, or anything resembling such a creature. He'll hate to think he's wrong."

"He isn't wrong so far as multi-talented humans are concerned."

"Not yet. Not today. But someday he may be. That fellow Haller was classified as a pyrotic and no more, yet he realized too much the moment I touched him. He'd got a rudimentary form of e.s.p. and didn't know it himself until that moment. He'd got one and one-tenths mutational talents."

"A freak," said Charles.

"Yes, you could call him that. So Brother Thorstern is going to be anything but amiable when confronted by two freakier freaks such as ourselves. Being a pawn, even though a clever one, his attitude toward mutants is determined by suppressed fear rather than open jealousy."

"That's a handicap considering that our purpose is to persuade him to see reason."

"Your finger is right on the sore spot, Charles. It's not going to be easy to knock sense into a powerful and ruthless individual motivated by fear. And it's so much the harder when you dare not show him why his suppositions are wrong and his fears utterly groundless."

"Have you ever imagined which of a thousand possible

107

reactions this world would favor were we free to tell it a few cogent things?" asked Charles.

"Yes, many a time. But what is the use of speculating about it? Someday the Denebs are sure to get this far. The less they learn, the better."

"The odds are at least a million to one against them finding anything worth the discovery." Charles was very sure of himself on this point. "Look at Tashgar and Lumina and the Bootes group. They explored the lot, treated the life-forms thereon with contempt and beat it elsewhere, searching, searching always searching and never getting any place. They'd go clean crazy if they knew that a hundred times over they've found what they're looking for but couldn't recognize it when it was right in their hands." He permitted himself a sardonic chuckle. "The Denebs are geniuses who lack the elementary ability to put two and two together and make it four."

"In given circumstances the addition of two and two can be a really tough mathematical problem," Raven pointed out. "Sometimes I feel sorry for the Denebs. If I were in their shoes I'd become boiling mad at frequent intervals and—"

He let the subject drop as they reached the end of the corridor, turned into the right-hand passage and found several men walking toward them.

Before any one of this small bunch had time to react to his suspicions, Raven said brightly and with disarming confidence, "Pardon me, can you tell me the way to Mr. Thorstern's room?"

He was answered by a burly man in the middle who bore himself with a touch of authority. "First turn on the left, second door on the left."

"Thanks."

They stood aside to let Raven and Charles go past, watched in silence as the pair strolled by them. Their expressions said nothing but their minds were shouting their inmost thoughts.

"Any caller for Thorstern is met at the gate and conducted to his room. How come these two are ambling around on their own?"

"Something out of kilter here," pondered a second one. "Not usual for visitors to be left on the loose; in fact, it never happens."

A third was saying to himself, "I don't like this. Why don't I like it? Is it because I haven't enough worries of my own? I've got plenty!" His thoughts veered away. "To heck with them!"

"Second door on the left, eh?" projected a fourth mind, amused and unworried. "Gargan thought fast when he gave them that one. Trust him to play safe. That's why he never gets anywhere, he always plays safe."

The first one, who was Gargan, resumed by deciding, "The moment they get around that next bend I'll give the boss a warning buzz." He commenced edging toward a wall-stud.

Turning the corner, Raven threw Charles a knowing glance, found the second door to the left, paused before it.

"I can pick up a hopeless tangle of thought-streams but not one that says it's coming from Thorstern." He nodded toward the door. "And there are no active minds behind that. The room is empty. Not a soul inside it." Studying the blank panels for a moment, he added, "Half a dozen chairs, a table and a screen cabinet for inter-communication. The walls are solid rock. The door can be sealed by remote control, opened only by remote control. H'm!"

"The better mouse-trap," defined Charles. His fat face developed creases around the mouth. It gave him the look of a child about to break somebody's window. "Just the sort of place I like to enter to show how little I care."

"Me too." Raven gave the door a push. It opened without trouble. Going inside, he relaxed in a chair, eyed the blank screen.

Charles took a seat beside him, making the chair squeak under his bulk. He also turned his attention to the screen but his mind—like Raven's—probed carefully in all directions and tried to sort out the incoherent babble coming through surrounding stonework.

"I was holding two aces when, durn me . . . a typical Martian joint with cold air and warm beer . . . went up with a bang that shook the entire town. We ran for a copter while Intelligence was still . . . left the Terran patrols spinning like dizzy . . . so this stinking skewboy reads my thoughts and beats me to the dame and . . . yes, a hypno named Steen. They wanted him badly, I don't know . . . I tell you these skewboys aren't to be . . . *what's that*?"

"Here it comes," remarked Raven, licking his lips.

"This Steen, it is said that he . . . *Where? Two in Room Ten? How did they get inside?* . . . fed up with Mars in short time. Don't know how guys can . . . *All right, Gargan, leave it to me* . . . when you've finished with the green bottle maybe we can . . . dived headlong into the forest and dug himself a hole twenty feet deep."

Click! went the door as relays operated and a dozen heavy bolts slid home. The screen glowed to life, swirled and colored. A face appeared.

"So Gargan was right. What are you two doing there?"

"Sitting and waiting," said Raven. He stretched out his legs, gave a picture of one making himself thoroughly at home.

"I can see that. You've not much choice about it now." The face exposed a toothy and unpleasant smirk. "The guard at the gate swears that nobody has been admitted. Nevertheless, you two are here. There's only one answer to that: you're a pair of hypnos. You took him over and then wiped the marks off his brain." The smirk gave way to a harsh laugh. "Very clever of you. But look where it's got you. See if you can hypnotize a scanner."

"You seem to think it's a crime to be a hypno," said Raven, dexterously kicking the sore spot in a typical pawn-mind.

"It's a crime for a hypno to use his power for illegal

purposes," the other retorted. "And just in case you don't know, it's a crime to break into a private residence."

Conscious that all this was a waste of time, Raven growled, "In my considered opinion, it's also a crime for a thick-headed underling to amuse himself indulging adolescent triumph and let his own boss go hang." His face hardened. "We've come to talk to Thorstern. Better get him before someone paddles some sense into your tight end."

"Why, you loudmouthed marsh-stink!" began the other, going livid. "I could—"

"You could what, Vinson?" inquired a deep, resonant voice that came clearly from the cabinet's loudspeaker. "It is a great mistake to lose one's temper. One should retain control of it at all times. At all times, Vinson. To whom are you speaking?"

Charles gave Raven a gentle nudge. "That sounds like the almighty Thorstern himself."

The face in the screen had turned sidewise and become submissive. "It's a couple of skewboys, sir. They busted in somehow. We've pinned them down in Room Ten."

"Indeed?" The voice was rich, calm, unhurried. "Have they offered any reason for such precipitate action?"

"They say they want to talk to you."

"Dear me! I know no justification for gratifying their desire. On the contrary, it would establish a precedent. I would be expected to hobnob with any and every eccentric who managed to crawl through the walls. Do they think I'm at everybody's beck and call?"

"Don't know, sir."

The invisible speaker changed his mind. "Oh, well, providing this occasion is not used as a pretext to cover future ones, I might as well hear what they have to say. There's a remote chance I might learn something useful. I can deal with them most effectively, *most* effectively if it proves that they are trifling with me."

Servilely, "Yes, sir."

The face slipped off the screen, was replaced by another, large, muscular, square-jowled. Thorstern was well past middle age, had a thick mop of white hair, deep bags under his eyes, but was still handsome in a virile way. His character was engraved upon these broad features, intelligent, ambitious.

His calculating eyes estimated Charles first, taking in all details from feet to head, then moved to the other.

Without slightest evidence of surprise, he said, "Ah, I know you! Only a couple of minutes ago I received a copy of your picture. The name is David Raven."

Chapter 11

Raven gazed back level-eyed. "Now why on earth should you want a picture of *me*?"

"I did not want it," riposted Thorstern, too quick-witted to admit anything even by implication. "It was thrust upon me by our authorities who, on this planet, can lay fair claim to efficiency. Your photograph is being circulated. Apparently our police are most anxious to get hold of you."

"I wonder why?" said Raven, pretending puzzlement.

Harumphing to clear his throat, Thorstern continued, "A person in my position would be gravely embarrassed were he to be found harboring a wanted man. Therefore if you have anything to say you'd better say it quickly, because you haven't got long."

"After which—?"

Thorstern's broad shoulders rose in an expressive shrug. It was done in the manner of a Roman emperor turning thumbs down.

"The police will take you away and my responsibility will cease."

The way in which it was voiced bore irresistible suggestion that there were special, unmentionable reasons why he should then feel free of responsibility. He had the air of one with an entire police force in his pocket.

His mere nod was enough to cause an arrest, his wink sufficient to guarantee that someone would be shot in the back while allegedly attempting to escape. Obviously Thorstern had power and plenty of it.

"You're quite a character," declared Raven, openly admiring him. "Too bad you insist on balling up the works."

"You are impertinent," pronounced Thorstern. "And it is intentional. You hope to disconcert my mind by creating irritation within it. But I am not so childish. Unreasoning emotion is a luxury only fools can afford."

"But you do not deny the accusation."

"I can neither confirm nor deny that which is completely meaningless."

Raven sighed and went on, "If that is your stance, it makes our task so much the harder but no less necessary."

"What task?"

"To persuade you to call off the undeclared war you are waging against Terra."

"Heavens above!" Thorstern widened his eyes in mock astonishment. "Do you really expect me to believe that Terra would send a petty criminal to interview a business man about a purely fanciful war?"

"There is a war and you're running it with the aid of stooges here and on Mars."

"What proof have you?"

"No proof is required," said Raven, flatly.

"Why not?"

"Because you know it to be true even though you don't choose to admit it. Proof would be needed only to convince a third party. There is no third party present. This is wholly between yourself and us two."

"As one whose business and financial interests are large and widespread," informed Thorstern, becoming ponderous, "inevitably I have been the target of all sorts of rumors and insults. I have become hardened to them. They split no atoms with me whatsoever. They represent

114

the price a man must pay for his considerable measure of success. The jealous and the spiteful are always with us, always will be, and I regard them as beneath contempt. But I must admit that this bald and completely unsupported assertion of surreptitious warmongering is by far the most outrageous that has offended my ears to date."

"It is neither fantastic nor unsupported," Raven contradicted. "Unfortunately, it is a grim fact. It doesn't offend you, either. In fact, you take secret pride in it. You are inwardly gratified that someone has proved shrewd enough to recognize you as the big boss. You are tickled to bits because for once your well-publicized dummy Wollencott has failed to grab the limelight."

"Wollencott?" echoed Thorstern, quite unmoved. "I am now beginning to see things a little more clearly. I presume that Wollencott—a melodramatic rabble-rouser if ever there was one—has stamped on somebody's corns. So you've stupidly followed a false trail he has laid and it brought you straight to me."

Charles stirred in his seat and growled at the screen, "I am not in the habit of smelling along false trails."

"No?" Thorstern studied him a second time, saw nothing but an obese individual with plump, amiable face and lacklustre eyes. "So *you* claim the honor of identifying me as the prime motive force behind a non-existent war?"

"If it can be called an honor."

"Then, sir, you are not only a crackpot but a dangerous one!" He made a disparaging gesture. "I have no time for crackpots. It would be best to get you off my hands and let the police deal with you." His face was severe as he finished, coldly, "Like a good citizen, I have the utmost confidence in our police."

Giving him a contemptuous sniff, Charles retorted, "You are referring, of course, to the large number who happen to be in your pay. I know of them. They are feared on this planet and with good reason." His lazy face sharpened suddenly so that for the briefest moment he looked neither fat nor futile. "But we don't fear them!"

"You may find cause to change that opinion." Thorstern switched his attention back to Raven. "I deny all your nonsensical accusations and that is that! If Terra thinks there is need to reassert her authority over Venus let her do so in proper manner. Without a doubt Wollencott is the cause of Terra's trouble. How she's going to cope with him is her problem and not mine."

"We aren't fooled by false fronts or human-shaped red herrings, see? If we snatch Wollencott you will laugh most heartily, replace him with the next stooge on your private list and use the snatching for purposes of propaganda."

"Will I?"

"You won't lift a finger to save Wollencott. On the contrary, you'll assign to him the useful role of Venusian nationalism's first martyr. Terra has something better to do than provide a petty god with one or two saints."

"The said deity being me?" inquired Thorstern, grinning.

"Of course." Raven went on, "Our logical move is to get at the man who pulls the strings of the puppets. That is why we've come direct to you. Our only alternative is to accept that you are not amenable to reason and bring you to heel by more drastic methods."

"That is a threat." Thorstern revealed strong, white teeth. "It comes strangely from one so completely at my mercy. To your other delusions must now be added the weird notion that you are independent of your environment and impervious to circumstances. Stone walls do not a prison make. Hah!"

"Enjoy yourself," Raven advised. "It's later than you think."

"I am now beginning to doubt your inherent criminality," Thorstern continued, ignoring that remark. "I think you are a case for a psychiatrist. You are motivated by a powerful obsession that I, Emmanuel Thorstern, a prosperous Venusian trader, am a kind of Goliath to whom you must play the part of David." He glanced down at a desk not visible in the screen, finished with much acidity, "Yes, I see that your name actually is David. Possibly you are conditioned by it."

"No more so than you are by Thor or Emmanuel."

It produced the first noteworthy reaction in the other's features. Momentarily forsaking his determined composure, Thorstern scowled. Even then he managed to lend the grimace a majestic quality.

He chewed at his bottom lip and rasped, "I have broken men for less than that! I have smashed them!" His clenched fist struck the desk. "I have made them as if they had never been!"

"Well! I see you *do* know the significance of your names."

"I am not uneducated." He lifted a bushy eyebrow. "But I am only a trader—not a fanatic. It is you who are obsessed, not me. I seek power, true, but only in material things. Your insults are dangerous—not to me, but to yourself."

"Your threats are of no consequence. The point is that you may smash certain men but you will never smash Terra. Call off this war while yet there is time."

"Or—?"

"Or Terra will decide that she's had more than enough and will strike in her own way. Like to know how?"

"I am listening."

"She will remove the opposition's key men one by one, starting with you!"

Thorstern wasn't fazed. Neither was he annoyed. Sweeping back his thick mop of white hair, he consulted papers below the level of the screen, spoke judicially.

"My conscience being clear, I have no reason to apprehend summary removal. Furthermore, we are all Terrans in law, subject to the Terran system of jurisdiction which lays down that a citizen is deemed innocent until conclusive evidence of guilt is forthcoming. Such evidence will be impossible to produce, especially in the absence of certain witnesses, including yourselves."

"A counter-threat," Raven commented.

"Construe it as you please. You do not seem to appreciate your own position."

"We know it. We are trapped—you hope!"

"You are in a room with solid walls and devoid of windows. The only door is multiple-locked by remote control and cannot be unlocked except from here. It is an anteroom reserved for interviews with paranormals of unknown power and unknown purposes. We get them here from time to time."

"So it seems."

"I am not so foolish as to rely exclusively on one iron gate which could be passed as somehow you passed it. You can learn a belated lesson from this: whoever fights me does so in time and place of my own choosing."

"Rather elaborate precautions for the home of an honest trader, aren't they?" Raven asked, pointedly.

"I have elaborate interests to protect. The means I have detailed are not all, by a long shot. You have reached only the second line of defense." He bent nearer the screen, added with triumphant emphasis, 'Even in this room from which I am speaking you would find me invulnerable!"

Smiling to himself, Raven said, "It would be nice to put that to the test."

"You will not be given the chance. Get it into your slow thinking minds that ordinary men are not without ability. Some of us—myself especially—know how best to deal with mutants. We think two jumps ahead of them every time."

"You're two behind but you don't know it."

Disregarding that, Thorstern continued, "If you are proud of your teleportatory powers I suggest you try them on the door bolts. Or if you happen to be hypnos, see whether you can fascinate me through a scanner. Or if you are telepaths, try to detect my thoughts. You cannot read my mind, can you? You don't know where I am, in which direction or how far away. I may be within ten yards of you, my thought-stream grounded by a silver-mesh screen. Or I may be speaking to you from the other side of the planet."

"Sounds as if you're scared of someone."

"I fear nobody," said Thorstern, and was speaking truth. He was Thorstern's body without Thorstern's conscience. "But I do recognize the existence of supernormal powers denied to me. Hence I use prudence. On Venus and Mars one can do little else. Our number of mutants is high. It is a factor Terra should take into account before starting something she might not be able to stop."

"Terra has mutants of her own," Raven told him. "More than you suppose. You folk tend to overlook that item, being so bemused by what you've got yourselves. Who lugged the lot of you to new planets in the first place? The Terran space fleet which was and still is manned by Terrans who've spent fifteen to twenty years zooming through the dark and absorbing hard radiations. There have been the same natural results. Many children of space-dogs aren't quite like other people's children."

"I'll take you up on that." Thorstern showed the gratification of one about to make an unanswerable point. "If, as you pretend, there is a war being waged, why doesn't Terra use her own mutants to retaliate in kind?"

"Who said Venus was using mutants for her attacks?" asked Raven.

Thorstern spent one-tenth of a second chiding himself for the obvious blunder, covered up by asking in mock surprise, "Isn't that what is happening?"

"No."

"What then?"

"Something infinitely worse. They're using a new kind of ray to sterilize our womenfolk."

"That's a blatant lie!" Thorstern's voice was loud and ireful, his face flushed.

"Of course it is." Raven displayed no shame. "And you *know* it. You've just said so. *How* do you know it?"

"Nobody would play so lousy a trick." Secretly irked by this second mistake, Thorstern decided that he would make no more. "I have grown tired of this conversation. It is neither entertaining nor informative. I am going to deal with you as I would with any other menacing crazies who break into my home."

"If you can."

"It will be easy. Every skewboy has the same kind of lungs as everyone else. He falls asleep as swiftly and as deeply even though he may be a nocturnal. Despite his powers he is as helpless in his slumbers as any new-born babe. He is no longer what he fancies himself to be, that is, the biological superior of ordinary, talentless people. Asleep, he is no better than a lump of meat. Any village idiot can handle him."

"Meaning you intend to gas us into insensibility?"

"Precisely," agreed Thorstern, pleased with his powers over the powerful. "There are vapor-conduits running into your room for that very purpose. It is part of the defense system. We use our imagination and think ahead of you, see?" Plucking pensively at a bottom lip, he added by way of afterthought, "I like to do things in the simplest way, smoothly, with minimum of trouble."

"But you refuse to do anything about stopping this war?"

"Don't be silly. I really cannot admit that there is a war, much less that I have any part of it. Your mythical conflict fails to interest me. I am treating you as a pair of unsavory characters who have broken into my home. I am going to ensure that the police take you away peacefully, like removing unwanted luggage."

He leaned forward, reaching for something near the edge of the screen.

Already slumped low in his chair, Charles suddenly slid down farther, quietly, undramatically. His plump face was pale, his eyes closing as though for the last time. His legs sprawled at awkward angles.

Raven stood up, removing his attention from the on-looker in the screen. Bending over Charles, he heaved

120

him into sitting position, slid a hand under his vest, gently rubbed him over the heart.

"Quite a diverting little by-play," remarked Thorstern, his lips pursed in sarcasm. He was still reaching toward the screen but with his hand momentarily arrested. "The fat boy plays sick. You massage his chest, looking serious. In a moment or two you will tell me he's having an attack of coronary thrombosis or something like that. He will die unless something is done quickly. I am then supposed to go into a sympathetic panic, withhold the gas, withdraw the bolts and send somebody running to you with a *tambar* bottle."

His back still turned to the other, Raven said nothing. He remained over Charles, holding him in the chair, rubbing near to the heart.

"Well, it won't work!" Thorstern practically spat out the words. "It is too infantile a trick to deceive a halfwit. In fact, I consider it an insult to my intelligence. Moreover, if that fat boy's stroke did happen to be genuine I would be quite content to sit here and watch him die. Who am I to try to thwart the workings of destiny?"

"I am glad you said that." Raven did not bother to turn around. He was splendidly indifferent to what the other intended to do. "People like us frequently are handicapped by ethical considerations. We waste valuable time trying to persuade others not to let us do things that must be done. We tend to postpone the inevitable until it can be held off no longer. It is our characteristic weakness. We are weak where less scrupulous men like you are strong."

"Thank you," said Thorstern.

"So it is much of a relief when prospective victims sweep all our qualms away," added Raven. Sensing that this was the precise instant, the exact moment, he swung round, stared straight at the screen, his eyes silver-flecked and luminous. "Good-by, Emmanuel! Someday we may meet again!"

The other did not reply. He was incapable of it. His

formerly strong and aggressive features were now undergoing a series of violent contortions. The eyes bulged, moved jerkily. The mouth opened and closed, emitting no sounds. A thick layer of sweat broke out on his forehead. He was like one being torn apart.

Still gently chafing the flaccid body in the chair, Raven watched all this without emotion or surprise. Thorstern's tormented features dropped below the level of the screen. A hand appeared, grasping spasmodically. The face came back, contorted in manner harrowing to witness. All this had taken no more than twenty seconds.

Then the eerie phenomenon departed as swiftly as it had arrived. The facial muscles relaxed, the countenance tidied itself though still glistening with perspiration. The deep voice spoke again, cool, calm, collected. Thorstern's voice with an almost indistinguishable timbre that did not belong to Thorstern. Thorstern's mouth and larynx and vocal cords being employed as if he were a ventriloquial dummy. It appeared to be addressing a hidden microphone to the left of the screen.

"Jesmond, my visitors are about to leave. See that they are not obstructed."

The dummy that was—or had been—Thorstern reached forward, touched a stud. The door bolts slid back. It was his last deed in this existence for the whole face changed again, the mouth fell open, the features went through several superswift alterations of amazing flexibility. Then the head vanished from the screen as the body collapsed beneath it. One could almost hear the distant thump.

Charles stirred as Raven shook him with great vigor. Opening his dull eyes, he shivered, felt himself, got slowly to his feet. He teetered a little, breathing heavily.

"We must move fast, David. I thought I had him for keeps, but the cunning devil—"

"I know. I saw the face. A *new* face. Come on!"

Jumping to the door, he jerked it open, hustled Charles through. The cabinet was silent, its screen glowing but

122

blank. He closed the door on it, turned down the passage. There was nobody in sight.

"The cunning devil!" repeated Charles. He panted a bit, breathless with haste and full of grievance.

"Shut up. Save it till later."

Hurriedly they passed the area covered by the still inoperative invisible light beam, out through the door and into the fog that filled the courtyard. A welter of surrounding thoughts poured into their minds, lent urgency to their feet.

"... so this cootch dancer comes on like an educated snake ... Raven is dead, I tell you. He couldn't ... take more than a Hotsy to set fire to that dump ... was reaching for the gas-stud when they got him somehow, I don't know how ... story goes they had a single-seater test-job on Jupiter a couple of years back but I guess that's just another Terran rumor because ... they must be multi-talented mutants no matter who says there's no such animal. In that case ... vein of solid silver over the other side of the Sawtooths, so he's packing and ... can't have got far. Sound the alarm, you dope! No use gaping at a stiff while those skewboys ... well, next thing this Martian floater goes up to walk on the ceiling and the picture falls right out of his pocket and into his wife's lap. She takes just one ... hardly at the gate yet. Get that siren going ... shoot on sight ... ought to have played that ace. Hey, what's all the excitement? ... care what they are or what they can do. They can die like anyone else."

Jesmond, surly as ever, was waiting at the gate. Bad visibility prevented him from recognizing them until they were close. Then his eyes popped wide.

"You? How did you get inside?"

"Is it any business of yours?" Raven gestured at the steel barrier. "Obey orders and open up."

"All right, keep your hair on." Muttering under his breath, Jesmond fumbled with the complicated lock. The evening's disturbances had made him mulish.

"Hurry—we're pressed for time."

"Are you now?" He paused, one hand at the lock, while he glowered at them. "Who's doing this job, you or me?"

"Me!" said Raven promptly. He punched Jesmond on the nose, licked his knuckles. "Sorry, Pal!"

There had been plenty of vim and weight behind the blow. Jesmond went down with a resounding wallop and lay making bubbling noises through his nostrils. His eyes were closed, his mind floating somewhere among the stars.

Turning the lock, Raven flung the gate wide open, said to Charles, "You've done enough. Time you went home."

"Not likely!" Charles gave him a knowing look. "The open gate is a gag, otherwise you wouldn't have smacked down that noisy sleeper. You're going back inside." He commenced retracing his steps into the courtyard, doing it at an agitated waddle. "And so am I."

Then the alarm sounded, an electric siren located high above the black battlements. Beginning with a low and ghastly moan it built up to an ear-splitting screech that ripped through the fog, echoed and re-echoed across surrounding countryside.

Chapter 12

The two hastened through enveloping cloud that pressed cold and damp upon their faces, created pearls of moisture in their hair and trailed streakily behind them in thin, cottonwool wisps. The typical Venusian nighttime odor of crushed marigolds was now very strong. But the fog did nothing to impede their progress; they ploughed straight ahead as if moving in broad daylight.

At the farther end of the courtyard and well beyond the door they had previously entered was a narrow stone archway with a lantern dangling from its center. Of lacquered brass, fanciful in design, it hung in ornate innocence and cast a thin fan of invisible light upon a row of pinhead-sized cells set in the step beneath the arch.

The siren was still screaming banshee-like as Raven sought to trace the leads governing this deceitful setup. Finally he stepped through the arch, Charles following. A moment later the siren ceased its clamor. It died out with a horrid moan. Ensuing hush was broken by angry voices and a host of equally riled thought-forms.

"Might have taken longer than I liked to bust that beam," Raven remarked. "Its lines run all over the place and back through a large switchboard. However, I was lucky."

"In what way?"

"Breaking the beam vibrates a visible telltale—and nobody was watching it at the moment. There seems to be a major panic inside. Everyone shouting orders at everyone else."

Standing close to the wall, he peered around the corner and through the arch toward the gate. A scuffling of many feet could be heard in the gloom. Several forms rushed from the courtyard door toward the main exit. There sounded a jabber of voices, each trying to overshout the others. It was easier to listen to their minds.

"Too late. Gate's open. Here he is, flat out."

"Well, you three were in the room. What were you doing when he got conked? Playing jimbo, eh? Hear that?—any skewboys can bust in or out while these lazy bums play jimbo!"

"Oh, so you came on the run when the alarm sounded? Bah, you were an hour behind the times!"

"Quit arguing. We aren't here to hold an inquest. They can't be more than a few hundred yards away. Let's after them."

"How're we going to do that? Feel our way like blind men? Do you think we've all got radar vision?"

"Shut up! It's the same for them, isn't it?"

"Not on your life. I tell you they're skewboys and multi-talented ones at that! Bet they're sprinting through the haze as if they don't know it exists."

Charles whispered, "If I were like them I'd hate the guts of people like us."

"They do. And I don't blame them—not one little bit." Raven gestured for silence. "Listen!"

"Aw, have it your own way but I'm going after them. They can't escape without making noises. I'm going to shoot at noises and ask questions afterward. Coming along, Sweeny?"

"Yes, sure, I'll come too."

Several pairs of feet crunched gravel beyond the gate and advanced cautiously into outer darkness.

"Suppose they're floaters—how will they make noises then?"

"They'll make them. A floater can't hang in mid-air for ever. What I call a *really* talented fellow is one who can digest a lump of lead."

"Button it, Sweeny. How the devil can we hear them if your dental plates keep up a constant clatter?"

They faded as their minds turned solely to the task of listening for fugitive feet. Those remaining by the gate were still swapping recriminations with the jimbo enthusiasts while trying to revive the stricken Jesmond. Another mess of neural waves was radiating from inside the castle.

"Nothing to show what killed him. Seems like his heart just stopped of its own accord. I tell you it was sheer coincidence. No hypno can function through a scanner, much less cause his subject to die."

"No? Then why did he draw the bolts, order the gate open and make the way clear for those two? He was hypnoed good and proper, I tell you, and through a scanner at that! Those two guys have got something nobody human ought to have."

"You did well there," Charles murmured with approval. "When you scowled into the screen at precisely the right moment it put them clean off the track. They're laying all the blame on you, thinking that somehow you did it with your little peepers."

"I'd hate them to get on the right track."

"Yes, so would I." The plump face puckered as Charles went on. "If only there were some satisfactory way of telling them a few startling truths without thereby giving the facts to the Denebs for free."

"There isn't. There is no way, no way at all."

"I know—but more's the pity." He went quiet, again listened to the other minds.

"You called Plain City yet?"

"Yes, they've a bunch coming along. Couple of telepaths to listen for them mentally, if that'll do any good.

Also half a dozen hypnos, a Hotsy, and a guy with a flock of tree-cats. An assorted bunch of circus roustabouts who can walk tightropes and all that stuff."

"The boss will have fourteen fits when he gets back and hears about all this. Reckon a bug-talker with a hive of hornets might do more—"

"There you are!" Raven nudged his companion. "What we wanted to know. Thorstern's not here but is expected fairly soon. That fellow in the room looked nothing like Thorstern by the time you were using him. His face had relapsed into normal shape. He was lantern-jawed, gaunt and so flexible that he could wave his nose like a hand. A malleable, eh?"

"I realized it the moment I made contact with him." Charles became disgruntled again. "He was so good that I hadn't suspected it up to that moment. It came like a shock—but it was nothing to the shock I gave him!"

"He'll have got over it now. Death is quite a considerable relief to the feelings." He gave a quiet laugh. "Isn't it?"

Ignoring the question as one to which the answer was obvious, Charles continued, "The room was lined with a grounded silver screen to keep his mind tight against probes from outside. His name was Greatorex. He was one of the only three mutants permitted in the place."

"For special reasons, of course."

"Yes. They have been trained to impersonate Thorstern to such perfection that it comes second nature. That's why he talked about being invulnerable even in the room. He was speaking in one breath about two people; the big boss himself *was* invulnerable simply because he wasn't there." He mused with a touch of morbidity, finished, "Those three take turns doing duty for Hizonner as and when required."

"Where are the surviving pair? Did his mind tell you?"

"Somewhere in the city, taking it easy until they are wanted."

"Humph! You can see what it means: if Thorstern is

due back and doesn't know what has taken place, it's likely that he'll come in person. But if somebody has made contact and given him all the lurid details, he may play safe by handing us another malleable, another expert mockup of himself. He'll use one of them to bait a trap knowing we can't refuse to snap at the bait."

"Even so, they won't catch us."

"Neither will we catch him—that's what gripes me." He frowned to himself, suddenly shifted his attention elsewhere. "Listen to this fellow—he's getting ideas!"

It was coming through the wall from somewhere within the black castle. "All right, the gate was open and one of those dopey guards laid out. Does that mean they've taken it on the run? Or does it mean that's the way they want it to look? Maybe they haven't gone at all. Maybe they're still hanging around. If I were a fox I'd wear a hard hat and sit on a horse. I'd live a lot longer. What if they can pick up my thoughts—will it do them any good? They can't stop me thinking. I say we ought to search this dump and the sooner the better."

A thinner, more impatient mind answered, "You're crammed to the ears with ifs, buts and supposings. If I've nothing better to do, I can think up plenty of them myself. For instance, suppose they happen to be supermalleables, what then? You've not only got to find *where* they are but also *who* they are. Heck, one of them might have bloodied his own beak, laid flat on the floor and had a hard time keeping his face fixed while kidding us that he is Jesmond." A brief pause, then, "Come to that, how do *you* know that I am *me*?"

"You won't last long if you're not. They're sending some telepaths from the city and they'll soon find out exactly who you are. I say we should rake this place with a fine-tooth comb. Bet you the boss will tear off a few heads if we don't."

"Oh, have it your own way, Fidgety. I'll order a search. It's trouble for nix, but we'll do it. Tell everyone to carry a gun in his hand and that he'll be excused if found with a strange corpse."

Raven grumbled under his breath, "Some folk lack the ability to leave well alone."

"That comes nicely from you," observed Charles, enjoying a fat smile.

"I asked for it." Raven gazed again into the courtyard, surveyed surrounding walls. "The hunt is on. We've no choice but to try to dodge them until either Thorstern or another spit-image arrives."

The dodging wasn't so difficult. They sat in the thick, all-concealing mist atop a blank, battlemented wall some forty feet high. A tree-cat might have scented them up there. A chirruping supersonic could have got a revealing stream of echoes from them. Even a floater could have found them by obeying his natural instinct to snoop where ordinary pawns could not.

But the hunters were men in the accepted, everyday sense of the term, men without mutational talents. They had their limitations as has every other life-form, great or small—for the great remain within other, different and often inconceivable limits, just as binding, just as restricting albeit in immensely wider sense.

So two of the great sat in the dark upon the wall-top, perched like ruminating owls, while lesser life prowled warily but futilely around the basalt castle, its yards and outbuildings, weapons held ready, trigger-fingers made nervous by the greatest fear of all: fear of the unknown.

To these pawn-minds a mutant was a kind of vaudeville character who had gone too far, developed delusions of grandeur and might at any time unite with ruthless prototypes to make slaves of normal men. A multi-talented mutant would be infinitely worse, a non-human creature disguised in human shape and theoretically capable of anything, anything at all.

The notion of being suddenly confronted by a biological monstrosity which was hypno-telepath-pyrotic-whatever all rolled into one, with no handicaps other than the sole inability to outjump a bullet, was too much for a couple of the searchers.

One sneaked through the archway, pointing a peculiar handlamp on the studs to keep them activated. He sought in vain around the area, eyes wide, back hairs erect, and passed a couple of times right under the feet of the quarry before he gave up and went out.

At the same time another emerged from the courtyard door, detected the sound of secret movement through the arch, stared toward it. Weapons ready, they pussy-footed toward each other and saw a vague form loom up through the fog.

Both barked, "Who's that?" and triggered without waiting for reply.

One was missed by an inch. The other got a slug in his left arm. The sound of shots stirred the edgy castle still further. Somebody in the distance beyond the gate fired vertically at an imaginary floater, plugged a darker patch of fog that was anything but man-shaped. The ether became full of abuse, all of it passionate and most of it coarse.

Leaning forward, Raven looked down past his dangling feet, "If only one-tenth of the ancestral details now being broadcast are true, Thorstern must have raided an orphanage to staff this place."

"I hear something else." Charles glanced upward. "Do you?"

"Yes. Someone's coming. I have a feeling it's the man we want."

The sound was a superswift *whup-whup-whup* as of giant vanes whirling at considerable altitude. The helicopter was coming from the east flying high above the night fog.

A thin orange-colored ray shot from a corner turret of the castle, spiked through overhead cloud, remained gleaming steadily. Noise of vanes grew louder as the oncoming machine gradually lowered toward the beacon. A

131

minute later it was immediately above, at a few hundred feet and making an explosive roar. There was a distinct downdraft from it. Fog coiled and swirled below it, oozing its scents from far-off jungles.

Guided by its own instruments or by radioed instructions from the ground, the copter lowered into the mist, descended through it, landed on the graveled area outside the gate. The orange beam cut off. Several pairs of feet ran through the courtyard and out the gate toward the new arrival.

"Now to join the deputation."

Edging off the stonework, Raven dropped forty feet to the ground. He did not drift down like a levitator. He fell in the same manner with which he had plunged into the forest: a swift and normal plunge followed by last moment deceleration.

Charles followed in exactly the same uncanny way, landing imperturbably and brushing the seat of his pants. Raven pointed through the arch.

"Let's forget that invisible light trap. If somebody does notice the telltale wobbling it will only give him the creeps and add to the fun."

There was a minor uproar of voices and accompanying thought-forms coming from the direction of the shrouded copter. A dozen agitated men all trying to talk at once. Two of the gate guards were lounging outside their post and looking toward the tumult with such intentness that neither took any notice of the vaguely outlined pair who hastened through the gate, passing them within a couple of yards. Whether or not the telltale had operated and been noticed it was impossible to determine. At any rate, the siren did not resume its wild screaming.

The escaping pair went only a little way toward the machine, just far enough for the fog to hide them from the watchers by the gate. At that point they made a half-circle that brought them near to the copter on the side farthest from the castle. None had noticed them, the gloom was so thick, the subject of discussion too all-absorbing.

A man was standing at the top of the copter's landing ladder, listening to the talkers, grim-faced and gimlet-eyed. He looked like the twin brother of the unfortunate Greatorex.

The minds of those addressing him revealed a most curious situation. Not one of them knew with any degree of certainty whether Thorstern himself had died and they were now reporting the fact to one of his dummies, or whether a substitute had suffered and they were telling Thorstern himself—or another substitute.

With masterful cunning the would-be dictator of a world had been frank with them, let them in on his scheme of quadrupling himself, then drilled them to accept any seeming Thorstern as the real Thorstern. So accustomed had they become to their master's in-hiding technique that automatically their minds grouped Thorstern and his three malleables together as one personality many-bodied. It was a tribute to the man; a greater tribute to the others who so ably played his part.

The trick was useful in the extreme. No antagonistic mind-probe could detect a substitution in the screen-protected brain of anyone pretending to be the big boss. He would have to go direct to the mind of Thorstern himself and feel around that—if he could find it.

Neither could any of the leader's rank and file be tempted to take a treacherous crack at him, since they knew the odds were three to one against nailing the right man, and with vengeance surely to follow should they fail. It created within the organizational setup a most discouraging hide-and-seek factor calculated to make any would-be traitor think twice—and then decide discretion to be the better part of valor.

But for once the man atop the ladder was caught napping in spite of all precautions. No silver-mesh screen ensured the privacy of his mind. He was in the open and primarily concerned with getting a clear idea of what had happened in his very hideout and, on the basis of that, decide whether it were safest to stay or depart.

His mind admitted that he was indeed Emmanuel Thorstern and no other, a fact that would have given comfort to the gripers before him had there been a telepath among them. Already he was juggling with the notion of returning to Plain City to give zip to the hunt and sending another impersonator back to the castle to take the full brunt of any second blow that might be made.

"Then this guy glared straight at him as if to say, 'I hope you drop dead!'" continued the frontmost talker. "Whereupon he did just that! I tell you, boss, it isn't natural. It would put a scare into a bunch of skewboys, let alone the likes of us." He spat on the ground. "When a couple of things that aren't human can waltz straight in and—"

"Through the gate, through the alarm system and everything else," chimed in a second. "Just as if they didn't exist. Then they top it by walking out of a triple-locked room."

A third voiced exactly what was in the listening man's mind, "What gives me the willies is the fact that if they can do it once they can do it again and again and again—maybe more besides!"

Thorstern backed half a step. "You've searched the place? Thoroughly?"

"Every inch, boss. Couldn't find hair nor hide of them. We called for some help from the city. They're sending a herd of pussies and a few skewboys. Fight fire with fire."

As if in confirmation there came evidence of the pussies referred to. From far away sounded the faint, irritable yowling of haltered tree-cats.

"They'll do a fat lot of good," opined the first, too pessimistic to care who knew it. "Not unless they happen to meet Raven and the pot-bellied chump on the way. They've had a long start by now. Sweeny and his boys won't get within a mile of them and neither will the city crowd." He brooded a couple of seconds, added, "Nor me either, if I can help it."

Feeling that he had heard enough, Thorstern came to a decision. "In view of all this I'd better go back to the city. I'll stir up the authorities and get some drastic action." He drew himself up. "I am not without influence."

"Yes, boss, sure."

"I'll return here immediately I'm satisfied everything's being done that can be done. Expect me back in a couple of hours' time or three at most."

He said it straight-faced, knowing full well that he had not the slightest intention of returning so long as it might be at his personal peril. Another would double for him on his next appearance.

"If anyone else comes asking for me, tell them I'm away and you don't know where. If a caller proves to be this Raven again, or looks somewhat like him, talks or acts like him, or gives reason to think he's animated by similar ideas, don't argue or give him a chance. Use a gun on him and use it effectively." His hard eye gave them a final authoritative going over. "I will accept full responsibility should anyone make a mistake."

With that he stepped inside the copter, doing it with an air of self-confident deliberation that concealed his inward desire to get away fast. He was shaken though he took every care not to show it.

Someone had not been fooled by the false front put up by Wollencott even though they'd proved suckers for Greatorex. Someone had painstakingly traced all hidden leads and found them running to Thorstern. Someone had power exceeding his own and at least equal ruthlessness. Someone was determined to remove him from his own tortuously constructed scheme of things and—even in this first failure—had proved ability to succeed with appalling ease.

He growled at the pilot. "Get going," and lay back in his seat. His mood was worriedly introspective.

The vanes whirled, the machine did a brief bounce,

rocked slightly and went up. Raven and his companion went up with it by the simple expedient of stepping close and hooking a leg over the landing-wheel braces. Formerly hidden from view of the talkers by the copter's intervening bulk, they became momentarily visible as they soared. A group of startled faces got a good look at them for two or three seconds before they disappeared into overhead cloud. Reaction was angry and confused.

"Quick, give me that gun! Quick, I say! You got ten thumbs?"

"Let go, you fool! What's the use of firing blindly? You can't see them now."

"Easy, Meaghan, you might hit the boss."

"Or the pilot. D'you want a couple tons of metal dropped on your crust?"

"Got to do something. Darn those skewboys! If I had my way I'd slaughter them all on principle. It'd make life easier for most of us."

"Phone the city again. They'll shoot them off the undercarriage as the copter comes down."

"This is where a couple of well-armed floaters would be useful. Why not—?"

"Stick around, Dillworth. The pilot may smell a rat and descend." The speaker perked his ears, caught the steadily rising *whup-whup-whup*. "No, he's carrying on. Stick around all the same."

"Where are you going?"

"Inside. I'll contact the boss on the radio and tell him what's underneath."

"Good idea. A shower of slugs through the floor will blow them off their perch."

The copter came out of the cloud into bright starlight plus the shine from a mock moon called Terra. They had emerged from the haze at two thousand feet. In parts it thickened to ten thousand while in others—especially the higher shelves of the rain forests—there was none. Daytimes it rose in a complete strata to forty thousand leaving the ground dull but clear.

136

To one side the Sawtooths spiked against a sable background powdered with stars. Nearby, percolating through the mist, was the glow of Plain City with an orange beam pointing vertically from its westward rim. Far to the south was another almost indiscernible glow coming from Big Mines.

Heading directly for the Plain City beacon, the pilot was content to skim a mere hundred feet above the fog. There was no point in gaining greater altitude for so short a run. He sat hunched over the controls with Thorstern grim and silent at his side, and kept his attention on the orange beam. Subconsciously he sensed that the machine was less lively than it had been an hour ago. Kind of sluggish. But he wasn't worried about it. Night-times the atmosphere's oxygen content varied from hour to hour and tended to make his motors seem temperamental.

He was already over the city when the radio beeped and he put out a hand to switch it on. At the same time the door opened and Raven stepped inside.

"Good evening," he said to Thorstern pleasantly.

With his hand still hovering over the switch, the pilot threw an incredulous glance through the windshield to confirm that he really was airborne and flying high, then growled, "How the blue blazes—!"

"Stowaway reporting, sir." Raven grinned at him. "And there is another outside uncomfortably riding the rods. A much bulkier one." He returned his attention to Thorstern, followed that person's intent gaze to a side pocket. "I wouldn't, if I were you," he advised. It was said in ordinary tones yet sounded threatening.

Deciding that the radio might as well be answered, the pilot flipped his switch and snapped, "Corry here."

A voice drummed from the tiny loudspeaker. "Tell Mr. Thorstern to grab a gun and send a dozen slugs between his feet. Those two guys are squatting on the undercarriage."

"He knows," said the pilot.

137

"He knows?"

"That's what I said."

"Good grief!" The voice turned in an aside to someone else. "The boss already knows." Then it came back. "What's he doing about it?"

"Nothing," the pilot reported.

"Nothing? How's that?"

"Don't ask me. I'm only the pilot."

"You don't mean—" The other's rising tones suddenly cut off. Came a sharp click as the distant transmitter closed down.

"He's jumped to conclusions," observed Raven. "He thinks you and Mr. Corry are tied up in sacks and that he's been talking to *me*."

"And who may you be?" inquired Mr. Corry, his tone suggesting that only hobos came aboard in mid-air.

Thorstern spoke for the first time. "Keep out of this— there's nothing you can do."

His bothered brain provided an interesting example of how inconsequential thoughts sometimes come upper-most in times of crisis. He was in a jam. Judging by what had occurred at the castle, it was a very tight one. There was every reason to believe he was in danger of his life and before long might follow the hapless Greatorex into oblivion. Added to which was the quasi-guilty realization that he had asked for trouble and could not justifiably complain about getting it aplenty.

But all he thought of at that moment was, "An antigrav cab has a load-limit of five hundred pounds. A copter can haul more than a ton. If I'd used an antigrav I wouldn't be in this fix. It couldn't have lifted with two inside and two clinging outside. After this, no more copters for me— not unless I have an escort."

"You have an escort—my friend and myself," Raven pointed out. He shoved the door open. "Come on. We're stepping out."

Thorstern stood up slowly. "I'd break my neck."

"You'll be all right. We'll have hold of you."

"What's to stop you letting go?"

"Not a thing."

The pilot chipped in. "If you two are floaters let me tell you it's against the law to leave an air machine while it's flying over an inhabited area."

Taking no notice of this, Raven continued with Thorstern, "You have several alternatives. Firstly, you can make a snatch at that side pocket and see what happens. Or jump out on your own and see how high you bounce. Or crash the copter and be scraped out of the junkpile. But if you prefer you can come with us and get down in one piece."

Thorstern's mental reaction to that was, "He can hypnotize me into doing anything he wishes, anything at all, even to dying against my will, by remote influence, through a scanner. It would be better to do things of my own accord. I can bide my time. It's his hour now—mine later. Other circumstances provide other opportunities."

"That's using hoss-sense," Raven approved. "Stay with us until we blunder. You can then tear out our hearts."

"I know you're a telepath and can treat my mind like an open book." Thorstern moved toward the door. "And more besides. There is nothing I can do about it—yet."

He braced himself as Raven backed out ahead of him, grasped an arm, and Charles reached up to take the other. Just as those able to levitate almost from birth have minds conditioned by their own peculiar ability, so are others conditioned by their limitations.

Thorstern had brains and his full share of animal courage but nevertheless his whole nature rebelled against an unhampered leap into space. With a parachute or an antigrav belt he would not have hesitated for a moment. With no more than other, hostile hands grasping him it wasn't so good.

So he closed his eyes and held his breath as they left the machine. He felt sick in the pit of his stomach when they plummeted down. Thick atmosphere heavy with vapor enshrouded him and streamed upward, making his pants belly out and his hair stand on end. The air stream whistled past his ears.

He was conjuring fearful visions of a rocky wall or tilted roof rocketing from underneath whiteness to smash his legs or break his body when a powerful pull on both arms slowed him down. Still he kept his eyes shut and strove to control his insides. A gable end rose from the mist, brushed his feet, slid upward. He landed in a street.

High above the pilot was gabbling into his transmitter. "Couple of fellows grabbed him at two thousand four hundred feet. I took it for granted they were floaters but they went down like stones. Eh? No, he didn't resist or give me any orders. Near as I can tell they must have hit in Sector Nine, somewhere around Reece Avenue." A pause, followed by, "Not if I know him. There was something mighty queer about the whole business. He went without wanting to—but he went!"

Raven said, "Your pilot Corry is on the police band and screaming for help."

"I don't think it will be of much use." Thorstern looked around, trying to identify his surroundings in the dim light and poor visibility. "But no matter."

"Becoming fatalistic?"

"I accept conditions temporarily beyond my power to change. At my time of life I have learned to wait. No game goes wholly in one's favor all the time." Pulling out a handkerchief he wiped beads of condensation from his lavish mop of hair. "It is the last move that counts."

The statement was devoid of misplaced confidence or braggadocio. It was the voice of experience, the considered opinion of one whose complicated plans frequently had suffered obstructions, delays, setbacks, all of which had been overcome next week, next month or the following year. He could display infinite patience when the need arose, still keeping the main purpose in sight and pushing toward it the instant the way became clear.

He was admitting that this unlucky night he was beaten and might well be finished for keeps, but warning them that so long as he lived there was always tomorrow, another day. It was a form of defiance, a revealing of teeth when cornered. There wasn't much else he could do—just then.

Chapter 13

Mavis opened the door and let them in without being summoned by knock or ring. Expressing neither pleasure nor surprise, she had the matter-of-fact air of one who has kept in constant touch with events and knew what was happening at any given moment.

In the manner of a mother mildly reproving a small and wayward child, she said to Charles, "You are going to regret this. I can feel it coming." With that, she returned to her kitchen.

"Now we've got still another type of mutant," grumbled Charles, unabashed. He flopped into a chair, making its well-worn seat bulge down between the legs. "A prognosticator."

Staring toward the kitchen in open approval, Thorstern remarked, "It's a pleasure to hear somebody talking sense."

"Everyone talks sense according to his or her particular lights. Each man his own oracle." Raven pushed a pneumaseat toward him. "Sit down. You don't have to freeze up stiff just because you're in bad company."

The other sat. Already he was striving to drive away a series of thoughts that insisted on coming into his mind. He was most anxious not to nurse them because they could be seen whenever either of these two saw fit to peer inside his skull and, for all he knew, they were peering without cease.

He could not be certain of constant eavesdropping. A telepath can feel or sense or detect another mind groping within his own. A non-telepath cannot. Thorstern was unordinary rather than extraordinary and that was a handicap of which he was acutely conscious in his present predicament; at other and safer times he would have dismissed the handicap with a lordly wave. So he tried to swat the thoughts as one would swipe at half a dozen annoying flies, but they hung around and kept on buzzing.

"This pair of multi-mutants can protect their thoughts. Probably the woman can also. But I can't hide mine and doubt whether they can shield them from others. Already the patrols will be scouring the streets, some concentrating on this neighborhood. They'll include whatever telepaths can be dug up at this late hour. So unless this room has built-in screens to give privacy there's a fair chance that some passing mind-probe will recognize my thought-stream and trace its source. He will then summon the troops and—"

He managed to shoo it away for a few seconds, but again it returned to completion. "Wish I knew whether a spray of thoughts is as individually characteristic as a voice. Maybe they all seem alike. If so, I'll be out of luck unless I can choose the right moment to radiate an unmistakable giveaway. If this pair happen to pick it up too, they may do something drastic. I'll have to take a chance on that."

Giving Raven a surly eye, he said, "I have jumped out in mid-air. I have sat down when told. I have obeyed orders. What next?"

"A talk."

"It's two in the morning. You could have talked tomorrow and at a reasonable hour." He pursed sour lips. "Was there any real need for all this preliminary melodrama?"

"Unfortunately, yes! You've made it hard to gain contact. Moreover, you've chased me around as if I were the dog that snitched the Sunday roast."

"Me?" Thorstern lifted an incredulous eyebrow.

"You and the organization over which you preside."

"Meaning my extensive trading interests? Nonsense! We have something better to do than chivvy people. Seems to me you're animated by a persecution complex."

"Look, we've been through all this before. The turn loses its novelty the second time round. Didn't you get a record of our conversation with your very accomplished impersonator?"

Much as he would have liked to deny all knowledge of any malleables doubling for him, Thorstern was too wise to let his mouth utter something simultaneously contradicted by his mind. He could not hope to deceive with mere words. But he could be evasive, play for time, fight a delaying action.

So he said, truthfully, "I've not had the details of what you told Greatorex. All I do know is that he is dead and that you had a hand in it. I don't like it." His voice gained a touch of toughness. "Eventually you won't like it, either!"

Charles emitted a short laugh and interjected, "That's a nice, vivid, satisfying picture of people hanging by their necks. Your imagination operates in full colors. I like the way you make their tongues stick out, black and swollen. A few of the details are inaccurate. The knots are in the wrong place—and I don't possess two left feet."

"Do I have to endure criticism in addition to mental prying?" Thorstern asked Raven.

"He couldn't resist it. Sadistic pleasures ask for adverse comment." He paced to and fro, the prisoner's gaze following. "Under the delusion that Greatorex was really you, we asked him to stop cutting off Terra's toes. He fed us a phoney line, doing it as to the manner born. We gave him fair warning that toe-cutting is a practice the victim has every right to resent. He insisted on playing the tune as before. Superb as his act proved to be, he was hamstrung by his own limitations."

"Why?" asked Thorstern, watching beetle-browed.

"Not being you, it was not within his power to make a major decision on your behalf. Knowing you, he wouldn't dare. He could do no more than play to the best of his ability the part in which he had been so well drilled. By virtue of his peculiar position he was without the initiative that could have saved him." He made a that-is-that gesture. "And so he is dead."

"For which you are now sorry?"

"Sorry?" Raven faced him, eyes bright with silvery motes shining in the irises. "Certainly not! We couldn't care less!"

It sent a most unpleasant sensation down Thorstern's spine. When there was a highly desirable end in view he could be decidedly cold-blooded himself, but never did he display it with such unashamed callousness. An unctuous washing of hands with much solemn deploring was his technique for brushing off a cadaver with decent dignity. If Greatorex—less burdened with guilt than himself—could be dismissed so airily, like a piece of trash . . .

"Seems there are others who enjoy sadistic pleasures," he stabbed, reasonably enough.

"You misunderstand. We are not happy about the matter but neither do we grieve. Call it splendid indifference."

"Practically the same thing." This was an opportune moment to appeal to a telepathic patrol if one happened to be nearby. "I don't know how you did it, but I call it murder!"

Mavis came in with a percolater and cups. She poured for three, set out a plate of cookies, retired without a word.

"You wish to talk about murder?" Raven asked. "That's a subject you're qualified to discuss."

That was an obtuse crack at himself, Thorstern felt. An undeserved one. Whatever else he might be, he was not a bloodthirsty monster. True, he was running what

145

whining Terrans saw fit to call an undeclared war but in reality was a liberation movement. True also that a few lives had been taken despite instructions that blows be struck to exact minimum loss of life and maximum loss of economic power.

A few killings had been inevitable. He had approved only those absolutely necessary to forward his designs. Not one more, not one of any sort. And even those he had dutifully deplored. He was by far the most humane conqueror in history, bidding fair to achieve the biggest and most spectacular results at the least cost to all concerned.

"Would you care to explain that remark? If you are accusing me of wholesale slaughter I'd like you to state one instance, one specific case."

"There are only individual cases in the past. The greater atrocities are located in the future, if you consider them essential—and if you live that long."

"Ye gods, another prognosticator!" commented Charles, this time completely without humor. Indeed, he made it smack of grim foreboding.

Raven continued with Thorstern, "Only you know how true that is, how far you are prepared to go, how great a cost you are willing to pay to boss a world of your own. But it is written in the depths of your mind. It stands out in letters of fire: *no price is too high*."

Thorstern could find nothing to say. There wasn't an effective answer. He knew what he wanted. He wanted it cheaply, with as little trouble as possible. But if tough opposition should jack the price sky-high in terms of cash or lives it would still be paid, with regrets, but paid.

At the present moment he was helpless in the hands of this bellyaching pair. They could end his stubborn ambitions, but they would have to finish him like Greatorex. He had no doubt they could do it. That they were willing to do it was something that remained to be seen. *He* would have no qualms.

Stealthily, in the hope that none would notice, his attention turned toward the door. But he could not suppress concomitant thoughts no matter how hard he tried. If a patrol had overheard that talk about murder they would not necessarily bust in at once. They might first go for help of a formidable kind. There was a chance, any minute, of a rowdy diversion during which he might break free.

Raven was still talking although the other only half listened. "If your Venusian nationalist movement really were no more than a means of gaining self-government we could find it in us to sympathize despite the violence of its methods. But it isn't what it pretends to be. Your brain reveals that it's your personal instrument of self-glorification. It is designed solely to gain you the power you crave. You poor little crawling, creeping grub!"

"Eh?" Thorstern's attention snapped back.

"I said you're a poor little crawling, creeping grub, hiding from the light, squirming around in the dark and pathetically afraid of a thousand things including anonymity."

"I fear no—"

"So you yearn for petty predominance over a colony of similar grubs during a mere heart-beat in the span of time. After which you will be gone, for ever and ever. Dust into dust. An empty name in a useless book, mouthed by myopic historians and cursed by weary school children. In distant time some naughty moppet may be punished by having to write a tiresome essay about you. The rise and fall of Emperor Emmanuel." Raven's sniff was loud and contemptuous. "I suppose you call that immortality?"

It was too much. Thorstern's thick hide was thin in one spot. He enjoyed insults because they were acknowledgment of his strength and ability. He appreciated enmity because it gratified his ego to know he was feared. Jealousy he viewed as an oblique form of worship. Hatred served only to magnify him. The one thing he could not endure was to be regarded as a no-account, a piker, a comparative seeker of butts on the sidewalk. He could not tolerate being thought small.

His features livid, he came to his feet, thrust a hand in a pocket, extracted three photographs and flung them on the table. His tones were savage.

"You've some good cards and they tickle you pink. But I've seen them. Now take a look at a few of mine. Not all of them, for you'll never see the rest!"

Picking up the top one. Raven studied it imperturbably. A blown-up photograph of himself, rather old, not very good but still good enough to serve for purposes of identification.

"It's being exhibited on the spectroscreen every hour," said Thorstern, with vicious pleasure. "Reproductions are being issued to patrols as fast as they can be turned out. By midday tomorrow everyone will know your face— and the reward will push the search." He was full of ireful triumph as he stared at the other. "The tougher you get with me the tougher I'll make it for you. You pranced easily into this world in spite of all preparations to grab you on arrival. See if you can get out of it." He switched to Charles. "And the same applies to you, Fatman."

"It doesn't. I have no intention of departing." Charles settled himself lower in his chair. "I'm quite comfortable here. Venus suits me as much—or as little—as any other ball of dirt. Besides, my work is here. How can I do it if I don't stay with it?"

"What work?"

"That," said Charles, "is something you wouldn't understand."

"He walks dogs and is ashamed to admit it," Raven chipped in. Tossing the photograph onto the table, he picked up the second, glanced at it. His features went taut. Flourishing it in front of the other, he demanded, "What did you do to him?"

"Me? Nothing."

"You did your dirty work by proxy."

"I gave no specific instructions," denied Thorstern,

taken aback by Raven's reaction. "All I told them was to pick up Steen and make him tell what had occurred." He assumed an expression of fastidious revulsion as he glanced at the offending picture. Running in a typical path, his mind dutifully deplored the sight. "So they did it."

"And enjoyed the doing by the looks of it." Raven was annoyed and showed it openly. "They made a gory mess of him. Now Steen is dead through no fault of his own. I don't mind that anymore than he minds it."

"Don't you?" Thorstern was surprised by a comment so contradictory of visible reaction.

"No. His end doesn't matter a hoot. It would have come sometime even though he lived to be a hundred. No man's end matters." With a jerk of disgust he flipped the photograph aside. "What I do dislike most intensely is the fact that he was slow to die. He took a long time over it. That is bad. That is unforgivable." The eyes shone with sudden fires. "It will be remembered when your turn comes!"

Again Thorstern felt a cold shiver. He was not afraid, he told himself. It wasn't within him to admit fear. But he conceded himself a certain degree of apprehension. He had played a card hoping it would serve as a dire warning. Perhaps it had been a mistake.

"They exceeded my orders. I administered a most serious reproof."

"He reproved them," said Raven to Charles. "How nice!"

"They pleaded that he was stubborn and made them go farther than they'd intended." Thorstern decided it might pay to enlarge on this subject while yet it was hot. No rescue party had responded to his earlier talk about murder. Maybe somebody would pick up his dissertation on Steen. Any form of hollering would do so long as it brought results.

He went on. "They used a telepath to try to pick his mind, from a safe distance so Steen couldn't make a dummy of him. It was no use. He could catch only what

149

Steen was thinking and he insisted on thinking about other things. So they had to persuade Steen to mull over what had made him pull a fast one on us. He didn't want to. He tried not to. He tried very hard." Thorstern spread hands to emphasize personal helplessness and lack of blame. "By the time he became co-operative they had overdone the persuading."

"Meaning—?"

"His mind turned, same as Haller's did. He babbled a lot of crazy stuff and passed out for keeps."

"And what was the crazy stuff?"

"He said that you were an entirely new, redoubtable and previously unsuspected type of mutant. You've a detachable ego. He said you had swapped bodies with him against his will."

"By heavens!" interjected Charles, popping his eyes in mock astonishment. "Now we've got bio-mechanics, prognosticators, ego-masters and whatever. There's going to be no end to this."

"It was unadulterated blah," continued Thorstern, peevishly. "I checked with several of our leading authorities on paranormal aptitudes. They declared it ludicrous—but they knew why Steen told it."

"What was their diagnosis?"

"That he'd been out-hypnoed by one of his own type far more powerful than himself. They've no case on record of such absolute dominance but theoretically it is possible."

His gaze shifted sidewise, for the first time noticed his cup of coffee now half cold. Licking dry lips, he picked it up, drank it in three or four gulps.

"For a short time you made Steen believe he was *you*. And you made him send Haller off balance, at which point his delusion ran out. Now, ordinary as I am, I can do some mindreading of my own. You're thinking that if I don't play it your way you will put the same sort of bee on me."

"Will I?"

"Either that or dispose of me outright as you did with

Greatorex. Whichever course you take will be futile. If you fix me up like Steen it will wear off. Hypnosis always wears off within twenty-four hours at most. Whatever I'm compelled to do during that time I can undo later."

"True," admitted Raven, gravely.

"While if you finish me completely you will have a mere body on your hands. A body can't call off a war. You've told me six times that the dead don't care. Take a bite out of your own philosophy and think how little I'll care about Terra's troubles. Bah, I'll be less concerned than is Greatorex!" A notion struck him and he demanded, "How did you finish Greatorex? Even a super-super-hypno cannot persuade a man to lay flat and expire. What did you *do* to him?"

"The same as we'll be compelled to do to you once we're convinced that there is no alternative." Raven stared significantly at the other. "Get it into your mulish head that we have few compunctions in dealing with an obstacle. We differ from you only in that we make it mercifully swift. We don't let the subject linger. *That* is the real crime: to prolong deliberately the act of dying!" He studied his listener, finished, "Greatorex went so fast he hardly had time to fight it. Steen was denied that fundamental privilege."

"I told you—"

Raven brushed the words aside. "You are not going to make the planet Venus your personal property and, sometime in the future, join with the Martians to hold Terra to ransom in her hour of trial. If humanity ever gets into a tight corner it's going to be humanity that'll fight its way out, not just Terrans. All of us! So you will cease hostile action against Terra and persuade the Martians to follow suit. Alternatively, you will be removed from the scene forever, after which we shall deal similarly with your successors, whoever they may be. We shall destroy them one by one until your entire movement collapses from sheer lack of leadership." He pointed to the tiny radium chronometer in the ring on Thorstern's middle finger. "You've five minutes to make up your mind."

"I've more than that, much more. In fact, I've got just as long as I like." He poked the third photograph across the table. "Take a look at that."

Not bothering to pick it up, Raven bent over and examined it. His expression did not change in the slightest.

"Who is it?" inquired Charles, too lethargic to get up and see for himself or exercise any other visual sense.

"Leina," informed Raven.

Thorstern laughed. It was a grating sound. He was enjoying his own foresight to the full. In particular, he was pleased with his success in keeping his mind away from the subject of Leina until this moment. Not once had a thought of her drifted through his brain. And again a pawn had out-guessed a mutant.

Nothing delighted him more than to be a jump ahead of a paranormal. It was his characteristic weakness which would have greatly interested any ecologist studying the effect of an environment containing superior life-forms.

"Your woman," he mouthed with unconcealed scorn. "We know her habits, movements, aptitudes. We know, for instance, that she's another superior breed of hypno, like yourself. Steen said so. He wasn't lying, not in his condition. Maybe that's the attraction between you and this heavyweight tart. I can't imagine any other unless you're fond of elephants and—"

"Leave her physical proportions out of this. She was not constructed to suit your taste. Get to the point."

"The point is," said Thorstern, unable to resist showing relish, "that the moment I die or go nuts or obviously out of character"—he tapped the picture with a heavy forefinger—"she pays!"

"That's a laugh," said Raven.

"I hope you'll enjoy it when you find her dead."

"I won't weep," Raven assured, carelessly. It was not at all sardonic. He made it true, dreadfully true.

Even Thorstern thought it horrible. He looked uncertainly at Charles, seeking confirmation of his own feelings in that person's revulsion, found him mooning boredly at the ceiling. His attention came back to Raven, his features incredulous.

"She can die slowly."

"Do you think so?"

"I am positive of it. Unless she happens to have a weak heart she can take ten times longer than did Steen. How would you like that?"

"I think it disgusting."

"Eh?"

"The mastermind, the mighty conqueror, hides behind a woman's skirts."

Back came the old fury at belittlement, but Thorstern managed to beat it down and say, "Listen who's talking—somebody willing to let a woman pay for his sins."

"She won't mind," smiled Raven, offering him a completely unexpected angle.

"You're mad!" declared Thorstern, beginning to believe it.

"Greatorex doesn't mind. Neither does Haller. And Steen is coldly indifferent. So why should Leina care? Why, even you—"

"Shut up, you murderous maniac!" Thorstern was on his feet again, both fists clenched until the knuckles showed white. His voice was loud with a mixture of strain, near-relief and triumph. "You've left it too long. You were so cocky you wanted to chew the fat all night. And we've been overheard, see?" He made an ecstatic gesture toward the front door. "Hear those feet? Twenty of them? Fifty! A hundred! The whole city is roused!"

"Too bad," said Raven, watching him blank-faced.

"Take me and see what it buys you," invited Thorstern, full of nerve. "In a few seconds the rush will come after which you'll get what you've earned." Trying to keep a wary eye on Raven and at the same time watch the front, he added with emphasis, "Unless I am in complete possession of myself and order them to hold their hands."

153

"It appears that we're in a bad fix," commented Charles, blearing in fat reproof, gazing at the door.

Thorstern was now standing with compressed lips while his mind ran its untrammeled course without regard for who could read his thoughts. *They dare not try anything* now. *The cost would be too great. They will postpone designs to a moment that will never come. They will be dealt with according to Terran law. The case will be sewn up good and tight, beyond Heraty's power to unstitch. Or I could arrange an accident. That might be quicker and more effective. Yes, one way or another—*

Like Charles, his full attention was on the door beyond which he had heard—or could have sworn he had heard—the cautious scuffling of many feet. A few of the patrol, he decided, might be made jittery by the presence of such formidable characters as Raven and the other. They'd be dangerously touchy. When they broke in he would have to move fast and roar orders faster lest he fall foul of someone too trigger-happy to look where he was throwing it.

He stiffened, noting out the corner of an eye that neither of the others had moved. Hah, they were resigned to a situation from which there was no escape. Teleportatively manipulated, the lock began to turn slowly and apparently of its own accord.

Chapter 14

The door commenced to move, drifting inward inch by inch as if wafted by a gentle breeze or inobtrusively edged by the ultra-cautious hand of someone lurking in the outer dark. A yellowish coil of night fog slithered through the gradually widening gap and brought odors of resin, rotting leaves, warm bark and wet fungi.

No sound came through the opening other than the dull thumping of fuel pumps over at the spaceport and faint strains of music from four or five streets away where restless nocturnals were trying to live the fuller life. There was utter silence within the room, not even the whispering of a drawn breath. This and the door's tedious motion created an immense tension that was as much as Thorstern's overstretched nerves could stand.

His eyes were straining at the gap, his ears shocked by the total lack of anticipated uproar, his mind trying to operate along ten channels at once. Who was there, waiting outside? Did they have weapons ready? Fingers taut, triggers already partway back? If he made a mad jump for that opening would he leap into a deadly volley and go down for ever and ever and ever?

Or had they a telepath to warn them of his intentions

so that they would hold their fire? But, of course, a
telepath could not thus warn them because he was still
hesitating, had not reached a decision. A telepath could
read his thoughts and yet be completely unable to forecast
a split-second conclusion. There were no prognosticators
in any positive sense.

The moments crawled like eons while he watched the
door which now had ceased its motion halfway round its
arc and remained invitingly ajar. The dark gap to the street
tantalized him.

Why the devil were they waiting? Were they fearful of
the risk to himself if they charged blindly through? Perhaps they had a plan that required him to take certain
synchronized action. In heaven's name, why were they
waiting?

More fog rolled in. Noticing it for the first time, he
was smitten with a plausible solution—gas! Yes, that was
it, that was the idea! Send gas in with the fog. Anyone
familiar with the defenses of the castle, and especially of
Room Ten, would have thought of it right away. So they
wanted him to stay firmly put until he collapsed along
with his captors. Then they would enter in safety, revive
him, give him the other pair to pull to pieces.

It was possible that Raven and the fat one knew what
was coming. It had sparked brightly within his own mind
and therefore they must have seen it—unless they had
been too busy probing the think-boxes beyond the door.
Can a telepath deal with more than one brain at a time?
Can he probe several simultaneously? Thorstern was not
certain. He lacked data on the point. Anyway, these two
would get the same result from outer minds—gas! And
what could they do about it? Nothing! The mightiest of
mutants is as much an animal as any pawn in that he *has*
to breathe.

His nostrils tried to detect the insidious approach of
the invisible weapon though he knew almost certainly that
it would be odorless. There should be other signs. A slow-
ing of the pulse. Slightly more labored breathing. A sud-

den miasma in the mind. Eagerly he kept watch on himself, alert for symptoms, and waited a mere half-minute that he sensed as half an hour. Then he broke. It was too much. He could endure no more, no more, no more.

With an agonized bellow of, "Don't shoot! Don't shoot!" he sprang into the gap in the doorway. "It's me! It's Thor—" His voice died away.

Staring with stupefaction into the shrouded night, he posed there a short time while his brain broadcast its reactions.

"Nobody here. Nobody, not a soul. They fooled me. They made me hear things, imagine things. They treated me like a rat in a laboratory, stimulated to see which way it turns in its fight for life. Then they released the lock and opened the door. Hypnos and teleports at one and the same time. That's multitalented, no matter what the experts may say. The hell-devils!" His neural impulses suddenly boosted to maximum amplitude. "Run for it, you idiot, run!"

And then the unexpected happened, the sort of thing that upsets the best laid plans of mice and men. Thorstern's tremendous psychic strain had brought it on, invited it.

With one hand braced on the doorpost, the empty street before him, inwardly bolstered by the certitude that armed search-parties must be somewhere in the locality, he lifted a foot for the first swift step in a wild dash for freedom. He never made it.

His body poised for the effort, he stood unmoving while a thoroughly bewildered expression came into his hard face. Slowly he put down the uplifted foot, slowly sank to his knees like one prostrating himself before an unseeable god. His agitated thought-stream had now gone into a violent swirl that flung out odd words and phrases.

"No . . . oh, *don't!* . . . I can't, I tell you . . . let me alone . . . *Steen* . . . It wasn't my fault . . . oh, let me—"

He toppled forward, writhed around in soundless pain. Already Raven was bending over him, features tight and serious. Charles had come hurriedly out of his chair, manifestly taken by surprise. Mavis appeared in the kitchen doorway, her eyes condemning but her lips saying nothing.

Raven grasped the stricken man's right hand and at once the bodily contortions ceased. Retaining his grip, he twisted his own arm and bent the elbow several times as one does when trying to cling to a wire loaded with excruciating voltage. He seemed to be battling against something, struggling with something. Thorstern opened his mouth, gasped like a landed fish.

"No, no, go away . . . leave me . . . I—"

Lumbering around to the other side, Charles helped lift the heavy body, take it across the room and settle it in a chair. Mavis closed the door but did not bother to reset the lock. Frowning to herself, she returned to the kitchen.

In a little while Thorstern gulped once or twice, opened shocked eyes, heaved himself upright in the chair. There were weird thrills running through his nerves and a highly unpleasant sensation like effervescence in his blood stream. His limbs lacked strength and his insides seemed turned to water. Much as he hated to admit it even to himself he was more shaken than ever he'd been in his life. His face was colorless, like wax. Curiously enough, his mind retained no memory of the words he had uttered in his throes, no knowledge of what had really taken place.

Glowering at Raven, he said in trembling tones, "You squeezed my heart."

"I did not."

"You almost killed me."

"Not guilty."

"Then it was *you*." He turned his head to glare at Charles.

"Me, neither. The truth is that we saved you—*if* you can call it salvation." Charles smiled at a secret thought. "But for us you would now be one of the late lamented."

"Do you expect me to believe that? One of you two did it."

"How?" inquired Raven, examining him both outwardly and inwardly.

"One of you is a teleport. He unlocked and opened that door without stirring an inch. He squeezed my heart the same way. *That's* what you did to Greatorex!"

"A teleport moves objects by exterior influence," Raven contradicted. "He can't get inside people and rearrange their plumbing."

"I was nearly gone," insisted Thorstern, rocked by his nearness to death. "I could feel my heart being compressed, my body going down. It was as if I were being dragged by main force out of my own body. Somebody did it!"

"Not necessarily. A million die every day without anyone's assistance."

"I can't die like that." He made it childishly complaining.

"Why not?"

"I'm fifty-eight and there's nothing wrong with me." Gingerly he felt himself, gauged the thumping inside his chest. "Nothing wrong."

"So it seems," said Raven, pointedly.

"If I am fated to go naturally, of a heart attack, it is too much of a coincidence for me to drop at this very moment."

He'd made a good point there, he decided. Pinned it on them effectively. Though it would do no good whatever, he was anxious to saddle them with the blame for no other reason than because they were so insistent about refusing it. He could not understand that. Why should they deny bringing him down flat in the doorway when they could boast about it with far more intimidating effect?

But deep, deep down inside him—thrust into an obscure corner where he wouldn't have to look at it—lurked the dreadful idea that perhaps they were right. Perhaps his time was more limited by destiny than he had assumed.

No man is immortal. Maybe he had only a little time to go and the sands were trickling out fast.

Dragging it right into the light and compelling him to survey it, Raven said, "If you were so fated it would most likely come at a moment of considerable nervous strain. So where is the coincidence? Anyway, you did not run and you did not die. Next week you may expire. Or tomorrow. Or before dawn. No man knoweth the day or the hour." He pointed at the other's midget chronometer. "Meanwhile, the five minutes have become fifteen."

"I give up." Finding a large handkerchief, Thorstern wiped his beaded forehead. His breathing was erratic and he remained sheet-white. "I give up."

It was true. More penetrating minds could see the truth inside him, a genuine verity born of half a dozen hastily thought up reasons, some contradictory but all satisfying.

"Can't run in top gear forever. Ease down and live longer. Got to look after myself. Why build for somebody's benefit after I've gone? Wollencott is twelve years younger than me, thinks he'll be the big boss when I'm down the hole. Why should I work and scheme and sweat for his sake? A ham actor. A malleable I raised from the gutter and made into a man. Just a trap-shooting mutant. *Floreat Venusia*—under a stinking mutant! Even Terra does better. Heraty and most of the Council are normals— Gilchist assured me of that."

Raven made a mental note of that last bit: Gilchist, a World Councilor. The traitor in the camp and undoubtedly the character who had betrayed him to the underground movement on Terra. The man whose name Kayder and the others did not know because they didn't want to know it.

"Or if it's not one mutant it'll be another," morbidly continued Thorstern's mind. "One of them will bide his time, take over my empire like taking milk from a kitten. I was safe enough while all attention was focused on Wollencott but now they've gone back of him and found me. The mutants have powers. Someday they will organize themselves against the common run of men. I wouldn't care to be here then!"

His eyes lifted, discovered the others watching. "I've told you I give up. What more do you want?"

"Nothing." Raven nodded toward the wall phone. "Like me to call an antigrav to take you home?"

"No. I'll walk. Besides, I don't trust you."

Arising shakily, he felt his chest again. Within him was suspicion of their ready acceptance of surrender and their casual release. Judging them by himself, he felt sure that another and different trap was waiting somewhere for him to walk into. Had they timed something to happen at the other end of this road, well away from the house? Perhaps another heart-squeeze, to the finish?

"*We* trust *you* because of what is visible in your mind," Raven told him. "It's your hard luck that you lack the ability to see into ours. If you could you would know beyond all shadow of doubt that we play square. You won't be touched by us—unless you renege."

Mooching to the door, Thorstern opened it, looked them over for the last time. His face retained its pallor and had aged a little, but he had recovered a measure of his dignity.

"I have promised to put a stop to all hostile action against Terra," he said. "I shall keep my promise to the letter—that *and no more!*"

Stepping into the dark, he gave his parting shot a touch of absurdity by carefully closing the door behind him. It would have been more fitting had he thrust it wide or slammed it enough to shake the house. But fifty years ago a tall and bitter woman had boxed his ears for slamming doors and, all unknown to him, the ears still tingled.

Following the walls he hurried along the road at the best pace he could muster. Visibility extended to three yards and that made him like a half-blind man.

Now and again he stopped to listen through the mist, then hastened onward. At this unearthly hour there would be few people about other than fidgety nocturnals or

161

roaming patrols. He had covered an unestimable distance before he detected noises to his left.

Cupping hands, he hailed, "Are you there?"

Feet speeded up. The patrol loomed out of the yellow haze, six of them, heavily armed. "What's the matter?"

"I can tell you where to find David Raven!"

Back in the room Charles stopped his careful listening. "He has tried desperately to remember—but he can't. He is muzzy-minded. Doesn't know which way to send them. He'll soon give up and go home."

Crossing heavy legs, he nursed his stomach. "When he flopped in the doorway I thought for a moment that you were taking him for your very own. Then I picked up your mental yelp of surprise."

"And I thought it was you snatching his ego." Raven frowned to himself. "It caught me napping. Good job I reached him so quickly or he'd have been gone."

"Yes, a heart attack." The moon eyes grew bright. "One more stunt like that and the news will be out."

"Somebody was irrationally precipitate," said Raven, looking serious. "Somebody had a one-track mind and couldn't wait to be educated. That's wrong, very wrong. It mustn't happen again!"

"He held out a long time and gave up slowly, which makes an invitation almost too strong to resist," reminded Charles with the air of one explaining everything. "So the would-be emperor of Venus was mighty lucky. If he had gone it would have been relatively quick. Oh, well, he's a tough character with more than his share of fortitude. Nothing less could have scared him into reasonable pacifism. Maybe it was all for the best. His mind holds no notion of what really occurred and that is the main thing."

"Perhaps you're right. If he had expired we'd have had more of his fooling around, lots more. Wollencott would have to be dealt with and probably the other pair of impersonators likewise. Either of the latter would be sweetly placed to occupy the seat of the mighty and deceive everyone but telepaths. Added to which there may be a hidden list of sharp-witted non-mutant individuals nominated by Thorstern as his successors, one or two of whom might be located on Mars. This surrender has saved us a lot of grief. Without it we'd have had to follow through to the bitter end."

"A surrender with mental reservations," Charles commented. "He couldn't help stewing them while fumbling his way along the road."

"Yes, I heard him."

"He's a sticker if nothing else. Firstly, he reserves the right to feed his promise to the ducks if at any future time he can discover a way to make himself absolutely mutant-proof. He estimates the chance of that as about a million to one against but he insists on covering that remote chance. Secondly, he reserves the right to slap you clean into the next galaxy but can't imagine a satisfactory method just yet."

"That's not all," contributed Raven. "I'm guessing here on the strength of what we know of his character: he'll get into direct touch with the World Council, criticize Wollencott, heartily damn the underground movement, deplore their misdeeds, sympathize with Terra and offer to put a stop to the whole business for a worthwhile consideration. He'll try to sell his surrender to Terra and make a good profit on it."

"He might, at that!"

"Let him. It's no business of ours. The main purpose has been achieved and that's all that counts." He mused a while, went on, "Thorstern won't like destroying his organization. He will call off the hounds but hate to break up the pack. Only thing that would soothe his soul would be to form a bigger and better pack, openly and legally. There's one way he could do that, and that's with the knowledge and approval of the most influential of his recent opponents, including Heraty and several of the World Council."

"For what purpose? They know nothing of the Denebs and therefore—"

"I told Thorstern that humanity will fight its way out of its own fixes. He may remember it. He is ignorant of the Denebs, as you've just remarked, but may decide— and convince others—that the hour of trial is here already. Pawns versus mutants! Being what he is, Thorstern automatically thinks of human beings as solely of his own kind, while mutants are not quite human, or quasi-human."

"Ah!" Charles narrowed his eyes. "Plenty of intolerance exists today. It wouldn't need much boosting."

Raven shrugged. "Who knows it better than we? Look what he gains if he can co-operate with Martian and Terran prototypes in arranging a synchronized three-world extermination of paranormals. It would give him back his private army, this time composed only of his own pawnkind, gratify his ego, satisfy his hatred of mutants and provide him with the excuse and the means of removing the chief source of peril to himself. I can't see how he can avoid thinking of it sooner or later. He's got brains and courage and is thoroughly stubborn."

"It wouldn't be easy. The mutant minority is a very small one yet plenty large enough to make extermination a major problem."

"Numerical ratios aren't the whole of it," Raven declared, propping himself against a corner of the table. "I can see two obstacles, both big."

"Such as which?"

"One: they can wipe out only the *known* paranormals. How many more remain unknown? How many are beyond identification by ordinary minds and intend to remain that way?"

"It makes the job impossible to complete. Thorstern may not start it at all if he realizes he can't finish it."

"Maybe he will," agreed Raven, with some doubt. "Obstacle number two is the natural consequence of civilizations coexistent on three planets. Suppose Thorstern tries to persuade them to arrange simultaneous pogroms designed to rid humanity of its too-clever boys. Each planet immediately suspects a trap. If it slaughters its own mutants while the others do not—"

"Mutual distrust." Charles nodded in understanding. "No planet will be eager to take a risk that might place it at a grave disadvantage compared with the others." He thought again, continued, "It could be a big risk, too. What if *two* worlds wiped out their own talent and the third did not? Boy, how soon could it gain mastery over the others! In such an event I could give a shrewd guess at which would be the third world and who would be bossing it."

"Three planets will all see the same picture. Terrans and Martians are neither more nor less dopey than Venusians. So whichever way Thorstern turns he'll have a tough proposition on his hands. The trouble is he's the sort who likes tough propositions. He views them as a challenge to his abilities. I don't think we've heard the last of him yet."

"Neither do I. And, David, we're top of his list for a summary removal." A chuckle sounded low in his belly. "*If* he can do it."

"I'm going back to Terra. Thanks for the hospitality." Crossing the room, Raven put his head through the kitchen doorway, said to Mavis, "Goodby, Delicious!"

"And good riddance, Nuisance!" She gave him a false scowl that fooled him not at all.

He pulled an atrocious face at her, went outside, waved a careless hand at Charles. "You have been a pal. See you in the morgue."

"Someday," promised Charles as if looking forward to this treat. He watched the other fade into the fog, closed the door, waddled back to his chair.

With her mind but not her voice, Mavis told him emphatically, "You are going to regret all this."

"I know it, Honey."

Chapter 15

A rare assortment of craft lay scattered across the numerous dispersal points of the spaceport. Antigravs, copters large and small, several ancient autogyros owned by unshaven prospectors, two dapper World Council courier boats, an auxiliary-engined balloon belonging to a party of virus-tracking scientists, a scarred and battered Martian tramp bearing the name of *Phodeimos*, two passenger ships, one awaiting mail and the other under repair and, finally, a rusty contraption, half gyro, half motor-cycle, abandoned by some crazy gadgeteer.

Sodium lamps shed a cold, unholy light over this mechanical menagerie. Night mist was still hanging around but had thinned considerably as the huge but invisible sun started to poke its rim over the horizon. In less than an hour the fog would soar and leave the ground clear.

The whole place was heavily but inefficiently guarded, with small groups of men lounging near the fuel tanks and repair shops. Others mooched singly around the perimeter or between the silent ships. Not one was mentally alert. Bored by a long night devoid of incident and within half an hour of being relieved by the daytime shift, each was solely interested in seeing thirty minutes whisk past so that he could pack up and beat it for breakfast and bed.

Raven appreciated this common state of mind; it created psychological conditions in his favor. Timing is a factor important to success in anything and the clock is a greater autocrat than most folk realize. Attempting something difficult, one could be rebuffed when the clock's hands were in one position and scrape through when in another.

He had reached to within a hundred yards of the perimeter and was exercising caution. Undoubtedly these guards had been warned to look out for him. Thorstern's surrender would not have caused that warning to be withdrawn.

Most of these armed watchers were ordinary, untalented men ignorant of power-wranglers on this world or any other. A few of the others might be followers of Thorstern in fact—or Wollencott in fancy—and these would have additional, unofficial orders what to do should Raven show up. There was no way of telling which was which because one and all were thinking only of the end of their spell of duty and the petty relaxations to follow.

This fellow coming near had a vivid imagination filled with a large plate of bacon and eggs. He was also a roamer and a floater, which made him a most suitable victim.

Watching him for some time, Raven found this guard was one of the few on an irregular beat, free to wander at will among the grounded machines. A couple of times the guard had registered a moment of strain, left the surface and soared over a vessel that he could not be bothered to walk around. The other guards, all apparently earthbound, had observed these occasional floatings with bland indifference. About ten percent of them had special aptitudes of their own, each much superior to all others in his own view.

Drawn by what he felt as a mere impulse and had no cause to suspect as anything more, the guard ambled boredly round the corner of the little tool shed behind which Raven was waiting. On a similar impulse derived from the same source, he held out his chin at a convenient angle. He was most cooperative and Raven genuinely regretted the poorness of his reward. He smacked the chin, caught the body with its bacon and eggs still whirling, lowered it to ground.

Wearing the other's badged cap and official slicker he came from behind the house and traipsed into the field. The victim had less height. The slicker came barely to Raven's knees but it would not be noticed. The nearest guards were two hundred yards away. Trouble would most likely come from a telepath. If one made a distant pass at him and got a complete blank he'd know immediately that this was more than a mere floater—then the band would start to play with a vengeance!

Bending his arm to hold the gun in its crook exactly as the other had carried it, he came to the passenger ship waiting for mail. It was the *Star Wraith*, one of the latest models, fully fueled and ready to blow. There was no one on board. He tensed and soared over it, landing lightly on the other side.

For all the mess of stuff lying around his choice of an escape vehicle was limited. The gyros, copters and antigravs, were strictly localized contraptions. There was nothing capable of leaving the planet other than the *Star Wraith* and the pair of courier boats. Either of the latter would do providing they were fueled and serviced. Thank goodness that on this moonless world there was no danger of grabbing a short range Moon-boat by mistake.

The nearer courier boat had full tanks and was all set, but he passed it by for a look at its fellow. That, too, lacked nothing but its pilot. Both vessels were without personnel and neither was locked. He preferred the second solely because a quarter-mile clearance lay behind its tail whereas the other was nicely positioned to make ashes of a time-worn autogyro that someone might love more than his mother. He chose the second.

Just then a mind behind the little tool house returned

from its involuntary vacation, forgot former visions of breakfast, tried to co-ordinate itself. Raven detected it at once. He had been expecting it, waiting for it. The blow had been enough to gain him a couple of minutes and that was all he required, he hoped.

"What did I run into?" it mumbled confusedly. A few seconds, then, "I got slugged!" A slightly longer pause followed by a shrill and agitated, "My cap! My gun! Some mangy pup of a tree-cat has—"

With a deceitfully casual air Raven rose as if to float over the selected ship, instead hit the lock twenty feet up and got inside. Closing the circular door, he snapped its fasteners and sealed it, made his way to the pilot's seat.

"Somebody bopped me!" continued the mind. "Jeepers, he must have been ready!" It faded out for a moment, came back with increased strength as he bellowed both mentally and vocally, "Look out, you dreamers! There's a guy up to something! He pinched my—"

Amid the resulting medley of thought-forms that promptly switched from the subject of off-duty to on-duty four stronger ones emerged from nothingness, felt blindly around ship after ship. They reached the courier boat, touched Raven's mental shield, tried in vain to spike through it, recoiled.

"Who are you?"

He did not reply. The ship went *dum-dum-dum* as its pumps and injectors commenced operation.

"Answer! Who are you?"

They were mentalities of quite a different caliber from the host of others milling around. They were sharp, precise, directable, and knew an armor-plated mind the moment they encountered it.

"Another tele. Won't talk. Got his shield up. He's in that courier KM44. Better surround it."

"Surround it? Not likely! If he lets go a blast from those big propulsors he'll incinerate the tail-side of the circle!"

"I doubt it. He daren't risk a jump before the fog lifts."

"If it's that fellow Raven there are going to be some awful ructions because we're supposed to—"

"I tell you we don't know who it is. Might be just some space-crazy kid squatting there and egging himself on to let her blow." As a pious afterthought, "If he does, I hope he breaks his neck!"

"Bet you it's Raven."

The radio dinged inside the pilot-cabin and the cause of all the excitement flipped the switch. A hoarse voice emanating from the control tower burst forth with outraged authority.

"You in KM44—open the lock!"

He did not respond to that, either. Things were still *dum-dumming* halfway back to the tail. Various meters quivered and a red line on an ivory strip had crept to a point marked: READY.

"You in KM44. I warn you—"

Smiling, he glanced in the rear view periscope, saw a line of armed men fanned out a couple of hundred yards behind his pipes. His forefinger scratched a button, depressed it for a fraction of a second. Something went *whop*! And the vessel gave a slight kick and a neat ball of superheated vapor bulleted backward. The advancing foe raced madly from the center of the target.

The enraged speaker in the control tower was now reciting a harrowing list of pains and penalties selected from regulations one to twenty, sub-sections A to Z, and had become so engrossed in this data on what the human frame could be made to suffer that he was blind to everything outside. He was the only person Raven had ever heard who could mention the most trying items in italics.

The stud went down a second time. A terrific blast of orange-white flame spouted from the rear end. The resulting roar deafened everyone for a mile around but inside the ship it sounded as nothing more than a high moan.

Yammering steadily on, the radio continued with sadistic gusto, "... but where the said *crime* incorporates *illegal* use of police and customs exemptions the *penalty* on conviction shall be not less than *four times* that prescribed in sub-section D7 without prejudice to any *further* increases given hereunder in sub-sections—"

Switching the radio to reverse the flow of language, Raven snapped back, "Look, chum, nobody can *live* that *long*!"

Cutting both transmitter and receiver, he slid the off-lever forward and shot away on a column of fire.

A million miles out he set the auto-pilot, examined his rear view screens for evidence of pursuit. There were no signs of any. The likelihood of being chased from Venus was small because futile. Ships had yet to be built capable of catching up with the kind he was using.

It was remotely possible but not probable that some vessel already in the void might be ordered to try to intercept him. But the broad gulf between Earth and Venus was not crammed with boats at this particular stage of interplanetary development.

The forward screens and detectors showed nothing noteworthy ahead except one pinpoint of infra-red radiation too far away to identify. Probably the *Fantôme* homeward bound. She should be somewhere around that region right now.

Content to let the auto-pilot do the routine work, he sat awhile in the tiny control cabin and surveyed the awesome spread of the cosmos. His air was that of one who has seen it a thousand times and hopes to see it ten thousand more. He could never grow weary of its tremendous splendor.

Nevertheless he left the sparkling view, lay in the tiny bunk and closed his eyes—but not to sleep. He shut them the better to open his mind and listen as he had never done when listening to the secret thoughts of ordinary men. The vessel's steady purring did not distract him in the slightest, neither did the rare *psst*! and momentary flare of colliding particles of cosmic dust. For the time being his receptivity of the audioband had ceased to exist while his mind stretched higher listening powers to the utmost.

They could just be heard, the sounds he was seeking, if one overcame one's fleshly muffling by straining hard enough and concentrating sufficiently. Eerie mental voices vibrating through the endless dark. Many of these mysterious impulses lacked amplitude, had flattened waveforms and had become greatly attenuated by travel across illimitable distances. Others were stronger because relatively nearer, but still far, far away.

"Black ship making for Zaxsis. We are letting it run without hindrance."

"They are about to leave for Baldur 9, a red dwarf with four planets, all sterile. They consider this one a dead loss and aren't likely to come back."

"Spurned the planet but grabbed the largest satellite because it is rich in heliotrope crystals."

"Came down with a squadron of forty and searched the place from pole to pole. Seemed in a great hurry."

". . . off Hero, giant blue-white in sector twelve of Andromeda. One hundred eighty black ships traveling fast in three fan formations of sixty apiece. A real Deneb expedition!"

"This Deneb made an emergency landing with two tubes busted. He waggled his palps until we understood and helped him do repairs. We acted plausibly stupid, of course. He was grateful in a superior way. Gave the kids several strings of rainbow beads and went away without suspecting."

"Black ship of cruiser type was heading straight for Tharre. We muddled its pilots' minds and turned it back."

"Think he got the notion intuitively but had no way of proving it right. He was dangerously close to the truth and didn't know it. But he liked the idea well enough to make it the basis of a new religion. It might have created an explosive situation if the Denebs had picked up some of that theology. So we destroyed it at the very start by translating him to his next stage and mourning with his kind."

"Enormous black battleship holding eight thousand Denebs has taken possession of a lesser moon. Said they'd send a picket-boat to swap trade with us once in a while but they're not enthusiastic. They have seen us—and all they've seen is a gang of backward aborigines."

"... long string of a dozen in hot pursuit. Funny how they can't resist chasing the uncatchable."

"Well, I'm all right but she is old and gray and wants out. The years go by the same for us as for those over whom we watch. So if some other couple—"

"...clustered all over this asteroid giving them the hearty come-on and the Denebs fell for it as usual. They came whooping up and blasted the rock to dust and went away happy. We never did like that rock; it had a very eccentric—"

"The convoy steamed straight past making for the Horse's Head, sector seven, but dropped this half wrecked lifeboat containing one ancient and bleary Deneb. He says he'll stick around and prospect for crystals while the others go on looking for what is right under his elastic nose."

"Armada of eight hundred ships setting out from Scoria to avenge that pair that disappeared. They have shielded the pilots' brains with platinum casques and have new type force projectors installed on every ship. Somebody means business!"

"Made up their minds to play safe and char the world all over merely because the wave-lattice creatures inhabiting it are shiny, only semi-visible and suspiciously un-Deneblike. We couldn't allow that! So we tickled the load in their armory. It made a mess!"

Ham radio had nothing on this for it was neither radio nor amateur: it was long-range *beamed* telepathy and decidedly professional.

The babble continued through the whole trip. A black ship here, another there, a hundred hell-bent for somewhere else. Denebs were doing this, Denebs were doing that, landing on some worlds, departing from others, ignoring a good many more, sometimes craftily attracted toward one, sometimes dexterously turned away from another, all the time helped or thwarted by this widespread host of faraway entities according to the unknown rules of an unknown game.

By and large the Denebs seemed to discard most worlds either at first sight or after a brief stay, yet still they kept on searching, poking, probing through an enormous area, methodically or non-methodically combing the cosmos for what they could not find. If one thing could be positively determined about them it was that they were incurable fidgets.

Raven spent all his time either listening to this talk from the great deeps of infinity or gazing through the fore observation port at the unending concourse of stars. Now and again his eyes held an abstract quality and into his face came an expression suggestive of a curious hunger. All thoughts of Thorstern, Wollencott, Carson, Heraty and the rest had been put aside; their ambitions and rivalries were of submicroscopic insignificance when compared with mightier events elsewhere.

"The Denebs picked a hundred thousand minds before they decided the years aren't long enough to permit a search through five hundred millions. So they have gone. They've departed as ignorant as when they arrived."

". . . sat around for three full circumsolars. They clucked with patronizing amusement over our rocketships, even borrowed a couple to play with and handed them back with thanks. But when you crashed that cruiser they'd sent in pursuit of you, they became really hot and took off after you like—"

"There is a distinct trend toward Bootes for some reason best known to themselves. Better be ready for them coming that way!"

"Laethe, Morcin, Elstar, Gnosst, Weltenstile, Vä, Périè, and Klain. Between two and ten thousand Denebs on each, all seeking rare minerals. They treat the local life-forms as tame but useless animals, throw them uneatable tit-bits. All the same, they've been extremely jumpy since—"

"Nine ships coming down, acting like they're full of their usual suspicion."

It went on and on and on, unhearable to all but minds naturally equipped for the purpose. No pawn-mind could detect them. No Deneb mind, either. Atmosphere blanketed the telepathic beams, and the warps around giant suns bent them a little, had to be estimated and taken into consideration. But in free space, transmitting to suitable receivers correctly attuned, almost all of them got through.

They told of lonely suns and scattered planets and gypsy asteroids as familiarly as mere man could mention the commonplace features of his home town. They identified locales, gave precise sector references and named a thousand names—but not once did any of them mention Terra, Venus, Mars or any of the family of King Sol.

There was no need to refer to any of those worlds for their time had not yet come.

A couple of six-seater police boats jumped off the Moon and tried to follow the stolen courier on its way in. They were out of luck. It plunged at Terra as if it had fifty light-years yet to run, shot sidewise when far ahead of the pursuit, vanished over the planet's eastward rim. By the time the others curved round to that hemisphere the boat had landed and become lost in more scenery than twelve pairs of eyes could scrutinize.

It reposed on a rocky moor where another take-off would damage nobody's property. Raven stood by its cooling tail and studied the sky awhile but the police boats did not appear above the horizon. Probably they were zooming disconsolately three or four hundred miles to the east or west.

Crossing thick heather, he reached a dirt road, went to the farmhouse he'd noted when coming down. He used its phone to call an antigrav which arrived in short time from the nearest village. Within an hour he was at the headquarters of Terran Intelligence.

As long-faced and lugubrious as ever, Carson signed to a seat, put hands together as if about to pray, and spoke with his mind.

"You're a prime headache. You've given me more work to do in a week than usually I get in a month."

"How about the work you gave *me*?"

"That wasn't so tough by the looks of it. You walked out of here and you've walked back with your tie straight and your nose blown. In between times you've annoyed important people and scared the wits out of others. You have thumbed your beak at every existing law and now I've got to cover up your misdeeds, somehow, heaven alone knows how."

"I haven't busted every law," Raven denied. "There are some intact. I have yet to distill ten gallons of *tambar* out in the hills. What I'd like to know is this: *are* you covering me up? The Moon patrols took after me on my way in despite my using a courier boat."

"A stolen one." Carson nodded aggrievedly at a thick bunch of papers on his desk. "You create crime faster than I can whitewash it. I am trying to whitewash that courier right now. But don't worry. The worry is all mine. Some folk seem to think it's the sort of thing I'm paid for. So I've got to find a way to turn this bare-faced pinch into an officially permitted borrowing." He rubbed his chin, looked rueful. "And don't you dare tell me you smashed it to bits on landing. Where have you stashed it?"

Raven told him, adding, "I'd have brought it straight into the spaceport but for those cops trying to sit on my neck. Their chase made it look as if I was wanted. Lately I've been wanted quite enough to do me for a time."

"I'll have a pilot pick it up and bring it in." Carson poked the papers away from him. "Woe, woe, all I get is woe."

"Running from Venus to here takes quite a while even

in a superfast courier boat," Raven pointed out. "So I've lost touch with local affairs. What's happened to provide the woe?"

Carson said, "Last week we killed two characters caught in the act of trying to destroy an important bridge. Both proved to be Mars-born. Next day a power station went sky-high, plunged ten towns into darkness and stopped industry over a hundred square miles. On the Saturday we found an ingenious contraption planted at the foot of a dam and snatched it away in the nick of time. If it had exploded the result would have amounted to a major disaster."

"Then haven't they—?"

"On the other hand," Carson went on, ignoring him, "Scientists now report that the Baxter blowup almost certainly was a genuine accident. They say the fuel proves to be highly unstable in certain exceptional and unforeseen conditions. They claim to have found a cure already."

"That's something worth knowing."

Carson made a gesture of impatience. "It's once in a blue moon I get an authoritative report like that and until I do I'm compelled to regard every accident as something possibly and probably deliberate. We have been handicapped all along the line by inability to distinguish human error from sabotage. Why, we can't even get rid of suspects. We are still holding eight of them taken from that underground dump. Mars or Venus-born skewboys, every one of them. If I had my way I'd deport them and prohibit their re-entry, but it can't be done. Legally they are Terrans, see?"

"Yes, that's the trouble." Raven leaned forward over the desk. "Do you mean to tell me that this war is still continuing?"

"No. I won't go so far as to say that. It certainly was continuing up to the end of last week but maybe it is now ended." He surveyed the other speculatively. "Day before yesterday Heraty came along to tell me our worries are now finished. Since then there have been no reports of

177

further incidents. I don't quite know what you've done or how you have done it, but it has been effective *if* what Heraty says is true."

"You have heard nothing about a man named Thorstern?"

"I have." He shifted uneasily in his chair but kept command of his thoughts. "For a long time we've had Intelligence operatives hanging around Wollencott, said to be the leader of Venusian insurgents. Eventually two of them sent in reports saying that this Thorstern was the real driving force behind the movement but they weren't able to dig up convincing evidence in support. It seems this Thorstern goes around tastefully attired in several layers of legality and nobody can prove a darned thing unless he strips."

"That all?"

"No." Carson admitted it with reluctance, not wanting to keep on the subject. "Heraty said that Thorstern is dickering with him."

"Is that so? Did he say what about? Did he offer any details?"

"He remarked that he doubted Thorstern's good faith or, for that matter, that he really is what he claims to be, namely, the man who can call a halt to Venusian intransigence. Thorstern offered to prove it."

"How?"

"By removing Wollencott—just like that!" Carson snapped his fingers. He was silent awhile, then sighed and went on, "That was the day before yesterday. This morning we received a message from Venus giving the news that Wollencott had just fallen out of an antigrav and bounced too hard for his health."

"Umph!" Raven could visualize the wallop, almost hear the crunch of bones. "Nice way to dismiss a faithful servant, isn't it?"

"Better not say that openly—its libelous."

"I can traduce one or two more. World Councilor

Gilchist, for example. He is what might fairly be called a louse."

"What makes you say that?" Carson's expression had become alert.

"He is your suspected fly in the ointment. Thorstern himself said so without knowing he was betraying a traitor." He thought a bit, added, "Don't know what a newcomer like Gilchist resembles, but I sniffed around the Council's minds during that interview and I didn't smell a rat. How was that?"

"He wasn't there." Carson scribbled a short note on a slip of paper. "Four members were absent because of sickness or urgent business. Gilchist was one of them. He turned up a few minutes after you left."

"His urgent business was to put a hurried finger on me," Raven informed. "What are you going to do about him?"

"Nothing. There is nothing I can do merely on your say-so. I'll pass this information to Heraty and the rest is up to him and the World Council. It's one thing to state a fact; another to prove it."

"I guess you're right. Anyway, it's of no consequence if they don't take any action concerning him or even if they award him a gold medal for being sly. Basically, few things of this earth are of real consequence." He stood up, moved to the door, paused with a hand on the panel. "But there is one item with fair claim to a little weight insofar as anything is weighty. Thorstern is a normal individual. So is Heraty. You and I are not."

"What of it?" asked Carson, uneasily.

"There are men whose nature won't let a defeat go unavenged. There are men hard enough to sit in an antigrav and watch a loyal supporter dive to destruction. There are men who can become very frightened if properly stimulated. That is the great curse of this world—fear!" He stared hard at the other, pupils wide, irises shining. "Know what makes men sorely afraid?"

"Death," ventured Carson in sepulchral tones.

"*Other* men," Raven contradicted. "Remember that—especially when Heraty tells you only a little and carefully omits to give you the rest!"

The other did not inquire what he meant. He had been long accustomed to the defensive techniques of normal, non-talented people. They interviewed him in person when they had nothing to conceal, wrote him or phoned him from a safe distance when they had something to hide. More often than not they did have something to hide.

He sat silent as Raven went out, watched the door close. He was a mutant and hadn't failed to recognize Raven's subtle warning.

Heraty, he thought, was fond of doing business by phone.

A tawdry little office up four flights of worn and dirty stairs was the haunt of Samuel Glaustraub, a rudimentary hypno barely able to fascinate a sparrow. Somewhere back in his ancestry there had been one mutant whose talent had skipped a few generations and reappeared greatly weakened. From other forebears he had inherited a legalistic mind and wagging tongue, which features he valued far above the tricks of any skewboy.

Entering this office, Raven propped himself against its short, ink-stained counter and said, "Morning, Sam."

Glaustraub looked up, dark eyes querulous behind horn-rimmed glasses. "Should I know you?"

"Not at all."

"Oh, I thought maybe I should." Putting aside some documents he'd been consulting, he left his desk, weighed up the caller cagily. Deep inside, his mind was complaining to itself, "Where's he get the Sam? Does he think I'm his valet?"

"What, in clothes like those?" Bending over the counter, Raven eyed the other's baggy pants.

"A telepath, eh?" said Mr. Glaustraub, showing big yellow teeth. He smoothed the pants self-consciously.

"Well, I don't care. Fortunately I have a clear conscience."

"I envy you. Few people can say as much."

The other frowned, sensing implied skepticism. He said, "What can I do for you?"

"You have a client named Arthur Kayder?"

"Yes, his case is due to be heard tomorrow." He shook a sorrowful head. "I shall defend him to the best of my ability but I'm afraid it will be in vain."

"Why?"

"He is charged with public utterance of homicidal threats and, since the plaintiff has not entered suit because of absence, the charge has been made by the public prosecutor. That makes it very tough. The evidence against him is recorded vocally and pictorially, will be produced in court and cannot be denied." He gave Raven an apologetic examination. "You're a friend of his, I presume?"

"His best enemy so far as I know."

"Ha-ha!" Glaustraub gave a forced laugh, making his belly quiver. "You are joking, of course?"

"Wrong first time, Sammy. I'm the boy he yearns to strip down to a skeleton."

"Eh?" His jaw dropped, he hurried to his desk, scrabbled nervously through a mess of papers, then asked, "Your name David Raven?"

"Correct."

It upset the other. He took off his glasses, tapped them worriedly, put them on and went around looking for them.

"They are on your nose," Raven informed.

"Are they?" The confirmatory squint was violent and gave him a villainous appearance. "So they are. How silly of me." He sat down, stood up, sat down again. "Well, well, Mr. Raven! The hostile witness!"

"Who said I'm a witness against him?"

"Well, I assume so. Seeing you have returned in time to appear on behalf of the prosecution I—"

"Supposing I don't appear—what does the prosecution do then?"

"Proceeds just the same. The recorded evidence will be deemed sufficient to secure conviction."

"Yes, but that's only because my supporting testimony can be taken for granted. What if I say I knew Kayder was only kidding?"

"Mr. Raven, you mean—?" Glaustraub's hands started trembling with excitement. "You really think that?"

"Like heck I do! He meant every word of it. Kayder would enjoy nothing more than to lie on purple silk eating grapes while listening to me dying the death of a thousand cuts."

"Then why...why—?" The lawyer gaped around, hopelessly confused.

"I'd rather kill a man outright than let him waste years in clink. Anyway, I don't think Kayder ought to suffer long incarceration merely for shooting off his fat trap." Leaning across the woodwork, he nudged Glaustraub who promptly jumped a foot. "Do you?"

"Who, me? Of course not! Decidedly not!" He asked uncomfortably, "Are you willing to appear as witness for the defense?"

"Not if there's an easier way out."

"You could swear an affidavit," the attorney suggested, filled with a curious mixture of doubt, suspicion and hope.

"That'll do me, Samuel. Where do I swear it?"

Glaustraub grabbed a hat, slammed it on back to front, pawed the desk for his glasses, found them on his nose, and took his caller down two flights at a sedate gallop. He ushered him into another office occupied by four men, all overweight. With their aid he concocted a document which Raven read carefully and signed.

"There you are, Sam, old boy."

"This is generous of you, Mr. Raven." His hands loved the affidavit, his eyes gleamed, his mind pictured the coming masterstroke when Glaustraub for the defense arose amid breathless silence and in calm, confident, well-modulated tones proceeded to snitch the prosecution's britches. Here was a rare opportunity for drama. For once

Glaustraub was supremely happy. "Exceedingly generous, if I may say so. My client will appreciate it."

"That is the idea," said Raven, darkly.

"I'm sure you can depend—" Glaustraub's voice broke off and he swapped expressions as he became smitten by the horrid thought that the coming drama might have a price on it. A stiff one. "I beg your pardon?"

Raven explained, "I *want* your client to appreciate it. I want him to think of me as Santa Claus, see?" He prodded a forefinger and again the other jumped. "When a bunch of bums comes after one's scalp there's nothing like a little gratitude for creating discord in the ranks."

"Really?" Glaustraub felt that a lot of cogent points were evading him this morning. He fumbled around the region of his ears.

"They're in your pocket this time," said Raven, and went away.

Chapter 16

The house looked pleasingly quiet and peaceful as Raven approached. Leina was within; he knew that as certainly as she knew he was coming. Your woman, Thorstern had called her, making it sound reprehensible. Yet their association, though unconventional, was utterly devoid of immorality. Other places and other people have other standards of decency and make them very high.

Pausing by the gate, he examined the fresh crater in the field outside. The hole was big enough to swallow an antigrav cab. Apart from this queer feature the house and its surroundings were exactly as he had left them. His attention shifted to the sky, watched the far-off white trail of a Marsbound freighter going toward the stars, the many, many stars.

Reaching the front door, he turned its lock teleportatively, in the same way that Charles had opened the castle gate. It swung wide. Leina was waiting in the lounge, big hands folded in generous lap, her eyes showing gladness.

"I'm a bit late."

He did not offer any warmer greeting. Neither did he kiss her. The warmth was mutually sensed beyond need of futile physical expression. He had never kissed her, never wanted to, never had been expected to.

"I stopped to take the bite off Kayder. Before I went away it was worth putting him someplace safe but now it's no longer necessary. Things have changed."

"Things never change," she observed.

"The little things have changed. I'm not referring to the big ones."

"The big ones are all-important."

"You're right, Brighteyes, but I don't agree with what you imply, namely, that the little things are unimportant." Under her steady gaze he found it needful to justify himself. "We don't want them to fall foul of the Denebs— but neither do we want them to destroy themselves."

"The latter would be the lesser of two evils—regrettable but not disastrous. The Denebs would learn nothing."

"They'll never be any wiser as it is."

"That may be," she conceded. "But you have sown a few seeds of forbidden knowledge. Sooner or later you will be forced to uproot them."

"Womanly intuition, eh?" He grinned like a mischievous boy. "Mavis feels the same way about it."

"With good reason."

"When the time arrives the seeds can be obliterated, every single one of them. *You* know that, don't you?"

"Of course. You'll be ready and I'll be ready. Where you go I shall go." Her brilliant optics were unblinking, unafraid. "Yet I still think your interference wasn't called for and was extremely risky."

"Risks have to be taken sometimes. The war is ended. In theory, humanity is now able to concentrate on getting farther out."

"Why do you say, 'In theory'?"

His face sobered. "There is a slight chance that they may let the opportunity go by in favor of having another and different conflict."

"I see." Moving to the window, she stood with her

back toward him while she looked over the landscape. "David, in such an event will you again insist on taking part?"

"No, definitely not. Such a war would be aimed against our own kind and those thought to be of our kind. So I won't be given the chance to chip in. I'll be smacked down without warning." He went across to her, slid a comforting arm around her waist. "They may deal with you at the same time and in the same way. Do you mind?"

"Not in the least so long as everything remains covered."

"It might not happen, anyway." His gaze turned to the window, found the view beyond. Abruptly he changed the subject. "When are you buying the ducks?"

"Ducks?"

He indicated the crater. "For that pond you're making over there." Without waiting for a reply, he insisted, "What happened?"

"I returned from town last Friday afternoon, made to open the door, sensed something inside the lock."

"What was it?"

"A tiny sphere like a blue bead with a white spot on it. I could see it with my mind. It was so positioned that a key inserted in the lock would press on the white spot. So I teleported it out, laid it over there and made a pebble drop on the white spot. The house shook."

"Some mini-engineer undertook a risky job," he commented, evenly. "Not to mention the teleport who placed it in the lock." Once more his strange callousness revealed itself as he ended, "If the trick had worked as planned, nobody would have been more surprised than you, eh?"

"One person may have been," she corrected. "You!"

The night was exceptionally clear, the stars bright and beckoning. To the naked eye the crater walls stood out clear and sharp on the terminator of the three-quarter Moon. From horizon to horizon the vault of space resembled an enormous curtain of black velvet lavishly powdered with sequins, some sparkling steadily, some intermittently, of all colors, white, blue-white, pale yellow, pink and delicate green.

Lying in a tilt-back chair under the roof's glass dome, Raven studied this scene of incomparable majesty, closed his eyes and listened, opened them to look again. Beside him in a similar chair Leina did the same. These were their own personal, intimate nights: in chairs beneath the dome, looking and listening. There were no bedrooms in this house, no beds. They did not need them. Just the chairs and the dome.

Daytimes they also looked and listened but did it with less concentration and more spasmodically, with their attention more on this world than the countless ones outside. Together they had looked and listened by day and by night for years. The task would have been unbearably monotonous but for the fact there were two of them at it. The presence of one broke the solitude of the other. Moreover, the things they "saw" and "heard" had the merit of infinite variety.

On Terra and far, far beyond Terra things always were happening, always, always. And never did incidents come twice the same. This was the task of the eternal watcher, a responsible job and highly essential. Each was like a sentinel in a midnight tower, protecting a sleeping city by watching the forest beyond the walls for any inward creeping foes. Many shared this job, holding themselves ready to sound the alarm should the need arise, Charles and Mavis on Venus, Horst and Karin on Mars, thousands more—aye, tens of thousands—all posted in pairs.

His mind turning to this last couple, he eyed a pink light hanging low in the sky and called, "Horst! Horst!"

It came after a while, slightly dulled by Terra's atmospheric blanket, "Yes, David?"

"Know what your insurgents are doing?"

"Mostly arguing with each other, David. They have split into several groups. One wants to continue against Terra. Another resents what it calls the treachery of Venus and wants to strike at her. Yet another is anti-mutant. The largest group is disgusted with everything and about to break up."

"So they're going through a period of chronic indecision?"

"That's about it."

"Thanks, Horst. Love to Karin."

He redirected his mind. "Charles! Charles!"

This time it came quicker and with a little more strength. "Yes, David?"

"Any news?"

"Thorstern left for Terra yesterday."

"Know the reason?"

"No, but I can make a guess. It's for something deemed advantageous to himself."

"That's a foregone conclusion. Well, I'll watch for him when he gets here. Let you know what I discover."

"Do that. You've heard about Wollencott?"

"I have. Nasty business."

"Clumsy," endorsed Charles. "Wollencott might have landed in some soft place and suffered injuries that meant slow dying. As it happened he didn't, but that was sheer luck." His mental beam cut off a moment, came back. "Here, the organization appears to be reluctantly falling to bits but its potential will remain and it can be rebuilt anytime. I can't help wondering."

"And I know why."

"Why?"

"Mavis keeps reminding you that you've blundered."

"True," admitted Charles, dolefully. "And I know how you've guessed it."

"How?"

"Leina keeps telling you the same."

"Correct," said Raven. "We've agreed not to agree."

"Same here. You would think I was a juvenile delinquent by the way she looks at me sometimes. The main issue will be protected no matter what happens, so why do women get the heebies?"

"Because, my boy, they look at these worlds from a feminine viewpoint and it's a maternal one. You and I have been throwing the baby too high. It makes them nervous to watch us."

"I suppose you're right." Charles' thought-form became sardonic. "But how do *you* know all this? How many babies—?"

"I use my imagination," interrupted Raven. "'By, Charles."

All that came back was a telepathic grunt. He glanced at Leina. She was reposing in her chair, eyes closed, face to the stars. For a little while he studied her fondly and was not looking at the fleshly features visible to ordinary men. The face was no more than a borrowed mask behind which he could see the real Leina. Most times he failed to notice that she had a face—somebody else's face—and saw only what shone forth from the great orbs.

She was quite unconscious of his scrutiny. Her mind was tuned elsewhere and absorbing the never ending chatter of the heavens. Soon he followed her example, listened to messages dimmed by distance and atmosphere but still discernible.

"Scouting warily around Bluefire, a condensing giant. Twenty black ships of destroyer type."

". . . repeatedly, but complete lack of common ground makes it impossible to communicate with these Flutter-ers. Can't even make them sense that we're trying to speak to them, much less warn them. If the Denebs arrive and become hostile toward them we'll have to take appropriate action and—"

"Calling from Thais. I got in right away without arousing suspicion. Struck it lucky in finding a suitable one on his way out. He had superswift co-ordination and said, 'Yes, by all means.'"

"The Benders have remarkable visual powers despite that they are low in the scale. See us clearly, call us the Shining Ones and insist on worshiping us. It is very embarrassing."

189

"We swept past Jilderdeen unnoticed and saw that the Denebs are building an immense crystal-growing plant in its temperate zone. The implication is that they're there for keeps."

". . . poor savages have chosen us for their annual sacrifice to the Twin Suns. Just sheer bad luck that they should pick us two out of all the tribe. It won't be long now! Somebody else had better be ready to take over after we're gone."

That last message bit into his being. Poor savages. All watched worlds were so possessed, including this one, because all children can be poor savages by a genuinely adult standard. He stirred, sat up, felt restless. The stars blazed down but the world around him was deep and dark, bitterly dark.

Over the following three weeks he kept close tab on world news distributed by the radio and spectroscreen networks. It was boringly uneventful but he stuck to the task in the dogged manner of one who waits for something that must not be missed although it may never come.

No mention of erstwhile anti-Terran activities came over the air. This was not remarkable for there had been no hint of any sort even when they were at their height.

Neither was anything said about development of spaceships or prospects of plunging father into unknown deeps. Bureaucratic love of secrecy again was responsible. The autocratic type of mind insists that news of public interest must not be divulged in the public interest.

Patiently he checked not only the news but also the unending flow of twaddle put over in the guise of entertainment, selecting likely items for close personal examination and seeing them through in all their wearisome completeness. From his peculiar viewpoint, he was like an elderly man compelled to endure hours of face-pulling and rattle-shaking designed to amuse a bunch of mewling babies.

At the end of the third week the fully colored three-dimensional spectroscreen commenced a new thriller serial of four parts. Just another of a regular series of emotion-tickles, it featured a telepathic hero who had looked long and ardently into the non-mutant heroine's mind and found it pure and sweet and clean. The villain was depicted as a low-browed, lower-minded insectivocal with a lopsided sneer and a penchant for the sinister fondling of poisonous centipedes.

It was trash of a kind intended to occupy minds that otherwise might find time to think. Nevertheless, Raven followed the whole performance with the avidity of an incurable addict. When the end came, the villain had been foiled, virtue had triumphed amid soft lights and falling rose petals, and a symbolic boot had crushed a symbolic centipede, he sighed like one satiated—then went to see Kayder.

The man who answered his ring was a pawn resembling a broken-down pugilist. He had a smashed nose, ragged ears, wore a gray sweater.

"Kayder in?"

"Don't know," he lied. "I'll see." His small sunken eyes carefully measured the caller. "Who'll I say?"

"David Raven."

It meant nothing to him. He shambled down the passage, his mind reciting the name as though it would slip away if he didn't go into a clinch with it. Presently he returned.

"Says he'll see you."

Legs bowed and arms swinging so that his fists were level with his knees, he conducted the other to the rear of the house, announced in a hoarse voice, "Mr. Raven," and lumbered away.

It was the same room as before, same ornaments, same desk, but the the boxes had gone. Kayder stood up as he entered, tried to decide whether or not to offer his hand, finally contented himself with indicating a chair.

Raven sat, stretched legs out front, smiled at him. "So Sammy did it. He had his little hour."

"The case was dismissed on payment of costs. It set me back a hundred credits but was cheap at the price." Kayder's heavy features quirked as he added, "The old buffoon on the bench saw fit to warn me that even evidence like yours wouldn't save me if I abused the public communication channels a second time."

"Perhaps Sammy annoyed him by overdoing the drama," Raven ventured. "Anyway, all's well that ends well."

"It is." Leaning forward, Kayder eyed him expectantly. "And now you've come to collect?"

"An astute assumption rather crudely expressed," opined Raven. "Let's say I've come to put the squeeze on you."

Pulling open a drawer, Kayder looked resigned. "How much?"

"How much what?"

"Money."

"Money?" Raven echoed it incredulously. He eyed the ceiling, his expression pained. "He talks about money!"

Kayder slammed the drawer shut. "Look, I want to know something: why did you get me in bad one minute and lug me out of it the next?"

"They were different minutes."

"Were they? In what way?"

"In the first there was a conflict and you were a menace safer out of the road. In the second the trouble had ceased or was about to cease and the need to pin you down had vanished."

"So you know the war has been called off?"

"Yes. Have you had orders to that effect?"

"I have," said Kayder, with some sourness. "And I don't like it." He made a gesture indicative of impotence. "I am being candid with you. There's no other choice with you reading my mind whenever you feel like it. I don't care for this sudden collapse but there's nothing I can do about it. The entire movement is going rapidly to pot."

"Which is all to the good. You were fighting for self-

192

government—if the secret dictatorship of one man can be called self-government."

"Wollencott was a natural born leader but he hadn't the guts to be a dictator."

"He didn't need the guts," said Raven. "The intestinal items were supplied by Thorstern."

Kayder raised a surprised eyebrow. "Why drag Thorstern into this?"

"You know of him?"

"Every Venusian knows of him. He's one of the planet's seven biggest men."

"He's the biggest," Raven corrected. "In fact, he's so big he thinks Venus ought to be his personal property. He owned Wollencott body and soul until he gave him his freedom recently."

"Gave him his freedom? You mean—?" His mind stimulated into furious thought, Kayder sat erect and let his fingers drum on his desk. From time to time he frowned to himself.

After a while, he growled, "It could be. I have never met Thorstern in person. He is generally thought of as a hard and ambitious character. If Wollencott was picking up steam from someone else, Thorstern is the likeliest source." He frowned again. "I never suspected him. He kept himself well concealed.

"He did."

"Thorstern, ye gods!" Kayder stared at the other. "Then why did he get rid of Wollencott?"

"Thorstern was persuaded to give up his systematic bleeding of Terra and confine himself to more legitimate activities. So Wollencott, a former asset, immediately became an embarrassing liability. Thorstern has a way of ridding himself of unwanted liabilities."

"I hate to believe all this," Kayder showed resentment. "But I've got to. It all adds up."

"Your mind says more," Raven pointed out. "It says the anti-Terran organization has divided into splinter groups and you fear that some may try to curry favor with the authorities by ratting on the others. You think there are now too many people who know too much."

"I'll take my chances along with the rest," said Kayder, grimly. "Ratting's a game that can be played both ways. I have less on my conscience than some."

"Is a hypno named Steen on your conscience?"

"Steen?" He rocked back. "I never got him. He sneaked aboard the *Star Wraith* couple of days after you left on the *Fantôme*." He gave his listener a significant glance. "I had more than enough to think about just then, remember?"

Raven nodded without sympathy. "I remember."

"So I heard no more about him."

"He died—very slowly."

"So did Haller!" Kayder shot back with sudden vim.

"Wrong on two counts. Haller went more or less of his own volition. Above all, he went quickly."

"What's the difference? One's as dead as the other."

"The difference is not in their ultimate condition," said Raven, seriously and with emphasis, "but in the speed of their transition to it. Once upon a time you evinced a nasty desire to reduce me to my framework. Had you done it with praiseworthy swiftness I could have passed it off with a light laugh." He gave a light laugh by way of illustration. "But if you had made the process unjustifiably prolonged I would have resented it."

Popping his eyes, Kayder exclaimed, "That's about the craziest piece of talk I've ever heard!"

Raven said, "It's a crazy trinity of worlds we're in."

"I know that, but—"

"Besides," he continued, ignoring the interruption, "you've not yet heard the half of it. I didn't come round merely to pay a social call and indulge an hour's idle gossip."

"You've told me that already. You want something and it isn't money."

"I did you a favor. Now I want you to do one for me."

194

"Here it comes!" Kayder regarded him with undisguised suspicion. "What's the favor?"

"I want you to kill Thorstern should the necessity arise."

"Aha, you do? Look, you saved me something though I don't know what. The maximum was seven years in clink but I might have got away with six months. Let's say you've saved me six months upward—do you think that is worth a murder?"

"You have overlooked my qualifying words: should the necessity arise. If it does arise it won't be murder—it'll be summary execution."

"Who's going to say when the time has come?" asked Kayder, looking shrewd.

"You."

"In that case I'll never reach a decision."

"I don't recall you being so finicky a few weeks ago."

"I've had enough. I'm going to carry on with my trading business and behave myself providing other folks leave me alone. Moreover, although the authorities insist that I'm a Terran, I still think of myself as a Venusian and I'm not going to slaughter a fellow Venusian merely to show my gratitude to a Terran." Hooking thumbs in vest pockets, he took on a stubborn expression. "I'd be glad to do you a favor but you ask too much."

"I'm asking very little if you only knew it."

"Too much!" Kayder repeated. "And I'll tell you something else: when it comes to killing somebody you are fully capable yourself. Why don't you do your own dirty work?"

"A fair question. There are two excellent reasons."

"Yes?"

"For one, I've already drawn too much attention to myself and am anxious not to attract more. For another, if the need to remove Thorstern should arise there's every likelihood that the first sign of it will be my own departure from this vale of tears."

"You mean—?"

"I'll be dead."

Kayder said, "You know what is in my mind: I'm indebted to you just so much that when you're dead I won't be especially happy. But it's no use pretending I'll be sorry, either."

"You'll be sorry!" Raven contradicted.

"Care to tell me why?"

"Because it may mean that you're next."

"Next? Next for what?"

"For wiping out of this world."

Standing up, Kayder spread hands on his desk and spoke harshly. "You're getting at something. Who is going to wipe me out? Why should he want to? Seeing that you and I have been on opposite sides, why should I now be on the same list as you?"

Waving him down and waiting for him to compose himself, Raven informed, "From the viewpoint of the masses we share one thing in common—neither of us is normal."

"What of it?"

"Ordinary people are leery of paranormals. It can't be said that they love them."

"I'm not love-starved. I'm used to their attitude." He gave a careless shrug. "They recognize those better endowed by nature and are envious of them."

"It is also an instinctive wariness approaching fear. It is a natural and ineradicable part of their defense-mechanism. Some most remarkable things can be done with mass-fears if you can arouse them to sufficient intensity, control them, direct them."

Stewing it moodily, Kayder offered his conclusions, "I can't read another man's mind but that doesn't mean I'm dopey. I can see where you're going. You think Thorstern may try to regain power of a different but equally satisfactory kind by stirring up an anti-mutant crusade?"

"He might. He used the aptitudes of mutants—such as yourself—to further his schemes. Now, the way he may look at it, the same or similar aptitudes thwarted him, denied him victory, even menaced his life. Being

196

normal himself, he'll realize that he might gain ascendancy over his fellows if all of them were normal likewise."

"All this is sheer speculation," Kayder objected, but showing uneasiness.

"Just that and no more," Raven agreed. "Nothing may happen. Thorstern's drive may go in quite innocuous directions. If so, there will be no need to take action against him."

"He'd be playing a mighty dangerous game if he tried it. Mutants may be few in number but once united by a common peril from hordes of—"

"You're thinking along my original lines," Raven chipped in. "I have switched off them since. I've gone on to another track."

"How d'you mean?"

"Thorstern is fifty-eight. These days plenty of people live to a hundred and retain their faculties into the late nineties. So barring accidents or assassination he has a good while to go."

"What difference does that make?"

"He can afford to be patient and take a longer way round to achieve the same result by less arduous means."

Kayder blinked and suggested, "Make it a bit clearer."

"Way back in the past," Raven informed, "some wiseacre remarked that the most effective technique is not to fight a thing but to set its own parts fighting one another."

It registered like a shock.

"Change your way of thinking," Raven invited. "Go from the general to the particular. There is no such creature as a standardized mutant. The word is a collective noun covering a biped menagerie." He watched the other for effect as he continued, "And, being what you are, I'll bet you consider insectivocals to be the cream of the crop."

"An equivalent notion is nursed by telepaths," observed Kayder, pointedly.

"That's a jab at me, but no matter. Each variety of

197

mutant thinks himself superior to the others. Each is as suspicious and jealous as any mere pawn."

"Well?"

"Such a state of mind can be exploited. Type can be set against type. Remember one thing, my bug-ridden friend: superior powers aren't necessarily accompanied by superior brains."

"I know that much."

"There are telepaths of such acute receptivity that they can probe your mind way out to the horizon yet are so inherently dim-witted that they've trouble with any thought more abstruse than c-a-t spells 'cat.' Mutants are humans with all the faults and follies of humans. Brother Thorstern, being an instinctively good psychologist, won't overlook that useful fact!"

By now Kayder's mind had readjusted. He could see the dire possibilities, was compelled to acknowledge their existence. The picture was anything but a happy one.

"If he tries this out, how do you think he'll start?"

"Systematically," said Raven. "First of all he will gain the secret support of Heraty, the World Council and influential pawns on three planets. His next step will be to collect and correlate all data on mutants that can be assembled from every available source, analyze it, reach a positive decision as to which two types exercise the most destructive powers and therefore are the most dangerous. He will choose one of those types to play the part of ye goode and faythfulle knight, the other for the role of baby-eating dragon."

"And then?"

"Let's say he decides the most effective play is to persuade pyrotics to exterminate insectivocals. Forthwith all the propaganda services of three worlds start mentioning insectivocals in a most casual way but invariably in an unflattering context. This continues, building up subconscious prejudice against them, showing them in an increasingly unfavorable light until eventually most humans—by which I mean pawns and other-type mutants alike—think of insectivocals as prize stinkers with no competition."

"Hell in a mist!" rasped Kayder.

"That much having been done, along come insidious suggestions that insectivocals hate pyrotics because of the latter's bug-killing powers. From time to time the public is given gentle hints that it's a good thing we have pyrotics around to take care of us."

"Like heck it is!" Kayder said, purpling.

"At the proper moment—and don't forget that precise timing is all-important—a well-publicized official speech is made in defense of insectivocals, appealing for unity and tolerance and authoritatively denying an absurd rumor that educated bugs plan to take over the three planets with the aid of treacherous insectivocals. That does a lot of good. It makes the public—again including other-type mutants—jump to the conclusion that there's no smoke without fire."

"They won't swallow all that guff," protested Kayder, inwardly knowing that they might.

"The public will swallow anything, anything at all no matter how crazy, provided it appears to bear the seal of official approval, is sufficiently long sustained, never contradicted, and plays upon their fears," retorted Raven. "Imagine they're now thoroughly aroused—what comes after?"

"You tell me."

"Something to trigger the situation thus deliberately created." He sought for an example, concocted one on the spur of the moment. "A specially placed skeleton is 'found' on its face in the Sawtooths and is given a hundred times more publicity than it deserves. An inspired rumor flies around that an innocent pyrotic has been stripped down by a murderous insectivocal. Further emotion-arousing fairy tales follow immediately after. A picked rabble-rouser sets a mob on the run when by most remarkable coincidence the police are busy elsewhere. The news of *that* whizzes around and loses nothing in the telling."

Bending forward he stared straight at Kayder. His eyes were cold, cold.

"Before you know it, you and every other identifiable insectivocal will be racing for dear life with a howling pack of ordinary people after you, other-type mutants in the lead and pyrotics panting to get at you first!"

"While Thorstern sits back and smiles?" suggested Kayder, showing big teeth.

"You've got the idea, chum. With the aid of scared humanity he roots out the last findable insectivocal and makes the type extinct. Then follows a carefully calculated period of peace and tranquility before the propaganda services start their new build-up on the next victims, mini-engineers for example."

"He'll never do it," declared Kayder.

"Maybe not—and maybe! Did you see that last serial on the spectroscreen?"

"No, I didn't. I can find better ways of wasting time."

"You missed something worth noting. It featured mutants."

"That's nothing. They've run mutant characters before."

"Yes, of course. So this serial may be without significance. Or it may represent the beginning of an insidious campaign planned to end when nobody lives who has an extraordinary aptitude." He waited a bit, added, "The hero was a telepath and the extremely obnoxious villain was an insectivocal."

"He'll never do it!" repeated Kayder in louder tones. A pulse was beating in his forehead. "I'll kill him first!"

"That's all I ask. I came to you because you owe me a favor. Also because recently you were the boss of a collection of talents and probably can call upon them again. You've death-dealing power and the gumption to use it. Leave Thorstern alone to live in peace but watch to find which way he's going. If you can see that for the second time he intends to create human disunity—"

"He won't live long enough," Kayder promised with savage determination. "And I'll be doing you no favor. I'll be protecting myself. I'll have no scruples if and when the time comes. A man is entitled to defend himself." He eyed Raven calculatingly. "Just as a guess I'd say *you* will need protecting long before me. What action are you going to take?"

Raven stood up and said, "None."

"None?" Kayder's heavy brows arched in surprise. "Why not?"

"Perhaps, unlike you, I'm unable to take suitable action regarding myself." He opened the door. "Or perhaps I enjoy the prospect of becoming a martyr."

"If that's a wisecrack, I don't get it. If it isn't, then I *know* you're crazy!" Kayder wore a worried frown as he watched the other leave.

Chapter 17

Back in the house Raven sprawled in a pneumaseat and said to Leina, "There's going to be more interference if events make it desirable. But not by our kind. Human schemes will be countered by humans. Are-you happy about it?"

"I'd have liked it better if that had been arranged in the first place," she gave back a little tartly.

"They're entitled to their tiny fragment of destiny, aren't they?" He threw her a quizzical glance.

She breathed a sigh of resignation. "The trouble with males is that they never grow up. They remain hopeless romantics." Her great eyes looked right into him. "You know perfectly well that these puny bipeds are entitled to nothing but preservation from destruction at the hands of the Denebs."

"Have it your own way," said Raven, giving up the argument. There was no point in pursuing it with her—she was too entirely right.

"And furthermore," she went on, "I have been listening while you were busy with less weighty affairs. Twelve black ships have been reported in the region of Vega."

He stiffened. "Vega! That's the nearest they've come to date."

"They may come nearer. They may arrive here in the end. Or they may shoot off in some other direction and not be seen in this cosmic sector for ten thousand years." She did not add more but he knew what she was leaving unsaid, "This is a bad time to take foolish risks."

"An error in tactics doesn't matter where there is ability to conceal it and recover," he pointed out. "I think I'll go catch up on the news."

Upstairs he reclined and opened his mind and sought to extract from the ethereal babble that portion emanating from the region of Vega. It was not easy. Too many talking at once.

"The tripedal hoppers of Raemis fled into the damp marshlands and are fearfully declining all contact with the Denebs. The latter seem to think the world unsuitable for any purpose. They are making ready to depart."

". . . twisted the pilots' minds and turned the entire convoy toward Zebulam, a near-nova in sector fifty-one of the Chasm. They are still bulleting along under the delusion that they're on correct course."

"I asked him for it. He'd discarded it so suddenly and violently that he was too confused to give permission. By the time he'd collected his wits it was too late, the opportunity had passed. So now I've got to wait for another. Meanwhile—"

"These Weltenstiles got the fright of their lives when a cruiser came out of the dark and fastened tractor-beams upon them. It didn't take the Denebs one-thousandth of a time-unit to realize that the ship they'd caught was a crude contraption manned by comparative savages. They let it go unharmed."

". . . twelve in fan formation still heading toward Vega, blue-white in sector one-ninety-one, edge of the Long Spray."

He sat up and gazed at the night sky. The Long Spray gleamed across the zenith like a gauzy veil. Terrans called it the Milky Way. Between here and one significant pinpoint in the dark were a thousand worlds to divert the attention of oncoming ships. But they might persist on course, ignoring other attractions. When left alone to go their own sweet ways the Denebs were unpredictable.

The end foreseen by Leina arrived after another three weeks. During that time neither radio nor spectroscreen networks made mention of recent interplanetary animosities, while their other offerings revealed no sinister trend in any direction. Mutants had again been featured in various items of entertainment but the everlasting roles of hero, heroine and villain had been distributed with fine impartiality.

Elsewhere twelve long black ships of space had nosed a quarter turn to starboard and now were approaching the eight unoccupied planets of a minor binary system. Temporarily, at least, the drive toward Vega was arrested.

The morning sun shone down, bright and warm. The sky was a clear blue bowl marred only by a streak of low cloud on the eastward horizon and a great curving vaportrail rising into the stratosphere. Once more the *Fantôme* was Venus-bound.

A four-seater copter gave first indication that errors must be paid for, that the past has an unpleasant way of catching up with the present. It droned out of the west, landed near the crater already beginning to produce a crop of colorful weeds. One man got out.

Leina admitted him to the house. A young, well-built type with frank, eager features, he was a very junior operative of Terran Intelligence, a sub-telepath able to probe minds but without a shield for his own. From the viewpoint of those who had sent him this made him an excellent choice for his special mission. Essentially he was open and disarming, the sort to establish confidence.

"My name is Grant," he introduced himself. Conditioned by his own status, he spoke vocally, knowing that mental communication placed him under a handicap when dealing with a true telepath. "I have come to tell you that Major Lomax of Terran Intelligence would like to see you as soon as may be convenient."

"Is it urgent?" Raven asked.

"I think so, sir. He instructed me to bring you and this lady in the copter if you were ready to leave at once."

"Oh, so he wants *both* of us?"

"Yes, he asked for you and the lady."

"Do you know what it is about?"

"I'm afraid not, sir." Grant's expression was candid and his unprotected mind confirmed his words.

Raven gave Leina an inquiring glance. "Might as well get it over now. What do you say?"

"I am ready." Her voice was low, her eyes brilliant as she studied the visitor.

His face flushing, Grant fidgeted and prayed for some means of closing his mind which insisted on thinking, "She is looking into me, right inside of me, right at where I'm hiding inside of myself. I wish she couldn't do that. Or I wish I could look at her in the same way. She is big and cumbersome—but very beautiful."

Leina smiled but tactfully made no remark, said instead, "I'll get my coat and handbag, David. Then we can go."

When she reappeared they went to the waiting machine which rose smoothly under whirling vanes and drifted westward. Nobody said anything more during the hour's flight. Grant kept strictly to business, handled the controls, maintained his thoughts in polite and disciplined channels.

Leina studied the bright landscape turning below, giving it the undivided attention of one who is seeing it for the first time—or the last. Raven closed his eyes and attuned himself to calls far above the normal telepathic band.

"David! David!"

"Yes, Charles?"

"They are taking us away."

"We, too, Charles."

The copter lost altitude, floated down toward a stark and lonely building standing upon a windswept moor. A squat, heavily built edifice, it resembled an abandoned power station or perhaps a onetime explosives dump.

Touching earth, the machine jounced a couple of times, settled itself. Grant got out, self-consciously helped Leina down. With the others following he went to the armor plate front door, pressed a button set in thick concrete at its side. A tiny trap in the armor plate opened like an iris diaphragm, revealed a scanner peering at them.

Apparently satisfied the trap closed over the eye. From behind the door came a faint, smooth whirr of machinery as huge bolts were drawn aside.

"Like a fortress, this place," remarked Grant, innocently conversational.

The door swung ajar. The summoned pair stepped through and left the other to return to his copter.

Turning on the threshold, Raven said to Grant, "It reminds me of a crematorium."

Then the armor plate cut him off from view and the bolts slid back into place. Grant stood a moment staring at the door, the concrete, the great windowless walls. He shivered.

"It does at that! What a lousy thought!"

Moodily he took the copter up, noticing that somehow the sun had lost much of its warmth.

Behind the door stretched a long passage down which a distant voice came reverberating. "Please continue straight ahead. You will find me in the room at the end. I regret not being there to meet you but know you will forgive me."

It was real enough, that voice, suave, courteous, but curiously impersonal and devoid of warmth. And when they found the speaker his looks matched his tones.

Seated in a chair behind a long, low desk, Major Lomax proved to be a lean individual in his early thirties. He had light blue eyes that gazed fixedly and rarely blinked. His fair hair was cropped to a short bristle. The most note-worthy feature was his extreme pallor; his face was white, almost waxy and had a permanent tautness on one side.

Motioning to a double pneumaseat, the only other resting place in the room, Lomax said, "Kindly sit there. I thank you for coming so promptly." The blue eyes went from Raven to Leina and back again. "I apologize for not escorting you from the door. I am rather handicapped. It is difficult for me to stand, much less walk."

"I am very sorry," said Leina with womanly sympathy.

There was no easy way of detecting the reaction. A swift probe showed that Lomax was a top-grade telepath with an exceptionally efficient shield. His mind was closed as securely as could be done by any human being. Despite that they might have driven through this defense with a simultaneous and irresistible thrust. By mutual consent they refrained from trying. The other must have sensed their first tentative pass at him, but no sign of it showed on his pale, strained countenance.

Positioning a thin wad of typewritten papers in front of him, Lomax continued in the same cool, unemotional voice as before.

"I don't know whether you now suspect the purpose of this interview, neither can I tell what action on your part may be precipitated by it, but before we begin I want you to know that my function is prescribed here." He tapped the papers. "It has been worked out for me in complete detail and all I must do is follow it through as written."

"You make it sound ominous," offered Raven. "Oh, well, carry on."

There was no visible reaction to that either. The sheet-white face remained as fixed and expressionless as that of a mummy. It suggested that its owner could and would play to perfection the part of an intellectual automaton.

Picking up the top sheet, Lomax read from it, "First, I have to give you a personal message from Mr. Carson, head of Terran Intelligence, to the effect that when informed of this interview he strongly disapproved, opposed it by all legitimate means at his command, but was overruled. He wishes me to convey his sincere regards and assure you that no matter what may take place within this building he will always hold both of you in the greatest esteem."

"Dear me!" said Raven. "This is getting worse."

Lomax let it go by with complete impassivity. "This interview will be conducted only on a vocal basis. There is a reason, for it is being recorded for the benefit of those who arranged it."

Putting the top sheet aside, he took the next one and continued in the same robotlike way. "It is essential that you know I have been chosen for my present task because of a rare combination of qualifications. I am a member of Terran Intelligence and a telepath well able to cover his own mind. Last but by no means least, I am very much of a physical wreck."

Glancing up, he met Leina's great optics and for the first time displayed a faint shadow of expression in the form of vague and swiftly suppressed uneasiness. Like Grant and many others, he was disturbed when looked into so deeply.

He hurried on. "I shall not bore you with full details. In brief, I was involved in a crash and badly injured. Everyone did their best for me but my remaining days are not many, the waiting time is increasingly painful and I shall be glad to go."

The blue eyes lifted, stared straight at them with bold and unmistakable defiance. "I want you to keep that in mind because it is most important: I am in the abnormal mental state of a man who will be glad to die. Therefore I cannot be intimidated by the threat of death."

"Neither can we," assured Raven, amiably bland.

It disconcerted Lomax a little. He had expected nothing less than a heated and indignant demand as to who was threatening his life. Concealing his surprise, he returned his attention to the papers.

"Further, although I do not fear my own dissolution, I shall be compelled to react should my existence be endangered. I have undergone a special course of mental conditioning which has created a purely reactive circuit within my mind. It is not part of my normal thinking processes, cannot be detected or controlled by any other mind-probe. This circuit automatically keys-in the instant I am in peril of losing either my life or control of my free personality. It will force me to do something *unthinkingly*, instinctively, the result of which will be the immediate destruction of all three of us."

Raven frowned and commented, "Somewhere back of all this is a badly frightened man."

Ignoring that, Lomax went determinedly on. "What I shall do is not known to me nor will be until the very moment I do it. Therefore you have nothing to gain by combining to beat down my mental shield and search my mind for what is not consciously there. You have nothing to gain by trying to hypnotize me or seize control of me by any other supernormal means. On the contrary, you have everything to lose—your lives!"

The pair on the pneumaseat glanced at each other, did their best to look outwitted and aghast. Lomax had a precisely defined part to play—but so had they.

It was a curious situation without parallel in human annals, for each side was in mental hiding from the other, each was holding a trump card in the form of power over life and death, each *knew* that victory for itself was certain. And each in his own way was right!

Looking at Lomax who refused to meet her eyes, Leina complained with some exasperation, "We came here in good faith thinking perhaps our help was needed. We find ourselves being treated like uncommon criminals guilty of heaven alone knows what. No charge has been made against us and we are denied the proper processes of the law. Just what are we supposed to have done to deserve all this?"

"Exceptional methods must be applied to exceptional

cases," remarked Lomax, quite unmoved. "It is not so much what you have done as what you may do eventually."

"Can't you be more explicit?"

"Please be patient. I am coming to it right now." He resumed his sheets. "This is a condensation of facts sufficient to enable you to understand the reason for this meeting. Certain matters brought to the attention of the World Council—"

"By a schemer named Thorstern?" suggested Raven, picturing Emmanuel's scowl when this came over the recording system.

"...caused them to order a thorough inquiry into the nature of your activities, especially during your recent operations on behalf of Terran Intelligence," continued Lomax, stubbornly. "Which inquiry was later extended to this lady with whom you—reside."

"You make it sound nasty," reproved Leina.

"Data was drawn from a large number of sources considered reliable and the resulting report, which was complete and exhaustive, made President Heraty decide to appoint a special commission to study it and issue a recommendation."

"Somebody must think we're important." Raven slid a glance at Leina who responded with an I-told-you-so look.

"Composed of two World Council members and ten scientists, this commission held that on the basis of the evidence before them you had displayed supernormal powers of eight distinct classifications, six known and two previously unknown. Or, alternatively, that in addition to the telepathic power which you have never tried to conceal you also possess hypnotic power of such redoubtable strength that you have succeeded in compelling witnesses to attribute other aptitudes you don't really have. Either the witnesses are dependable or they have been deluded by you. Either way the result is the same: the evidence suggests that you are a multi-talented mutant." He did a

210

double-take at the paper, murmured with a touch of annoyance, "That's obviously wrong," and changed it to, "You are *both* multi-talented mutants."

"Is that an offense?" inquired Raven, not bothering to contradict.

"I have no personal views regarding this matter." Lomax leaned forward, held his middle a moment while his face went even whiter. Then he recovered, said, "Kindly permit me to continue. If the evidence had favored no more than that, the World Council would have been compelled to accept that multi-talented mutants do exist in spite of so-called natural laws. But the data is equally in support of an alternative theory toward which some members of the commission lean while others reject it as fantastic."

The listening pair stirred on the pneumaseat, showed curiosity and mild interest. No more than that. No apprehension. No fear of being rooted out like surreptitious scuttlers in the dark. At every moment they were living the part they wished to play, as determined as Lomax to see it through to the bitter end.

"You are entitled to know the cogent items," Lomax carried on. He discarded another sheet. "A careful reexamination of your antecedents shows that both of you might well be persons considerably out of the ordinary by our standards of today. It was by substantially the same method that Mr. Carson traced you in the first place and reached the same conclusion."

He paused while his features quirked to a jolt of agony inside him, then said more slowly, "But the ancestry of David Raven should at best have produced no more than a superb telepath, a mind-probe of unusual penetrating power and extremely acute receptivity. It is conceivable—and contrary to no known laws—that his mental strength might be sufficient to make him impervious to hypnotism, thus causing him to be the first hypno-proof telepath on record. But that is all. That is the limit of his hereditable aptitudes." He gave the rest of it extra emphasis as he went on, "He could *not* exercise hypnotic or quasi-hypnotic powers of his own, even as a multi-talented mutant, because there is not one hypno among his forebears."

"That may be—" began Leina.

Lomax chirped in, "The same remarks apply to you. They apply also to your two confreres on Venus, which pair are now having the same kind of interview in similar precautionary conditions."

"With a similar threat hanging over them?" Raven asked.

Lomax took no notice. Perfectly disciplined, he was answering no questions other than those pertinent to the stage reached in his task.

"Item number two: we discovered that David Raven either had died or shown all symptoms of death and then been resuscitated. The doctor who performed this feat can no longer be called upon for evidence, having died himself three years ago. The incident is not remarkable when considered by itself, as an isolated occurrence. Such things *do* happen though rarely. It becomes noteworthy only when examined in conjunction with other facts."

The blue eyes shot a glance at Leina before he continued, "Such as the fact that this lady once went swimming, was caught in a powerful undercurrent, apparently drowned, but revived by artificial respiration. *Plus* the facts that your two prototypes on Venus have had equally hairsbreadth escapes."

"You've had one yourself," Raven riposted. "You told us so at the beginning. You're lucky to be alive—if it is luck!"

Strongly tempted to admit the escape but deny the pleasure of living in his present condition, Lomax hesitated, nursed his middle, then plowed grimly on.

"Item number three has indirect significance. You have been told by Mr. Carson of certain Terran spaceship experiments so there is no harm in adding more. He did not give you the whole of it. To cut it short, our last exploring vessel went farther into the void than you may suspect. Upon its return the pilot reported that he had been chased by unidentifiable objects of unknown origin. All that his instruments could tell him was that these objects were metallic and radiated heat. There were four of them moving in line abreast at distance too great to permit examination with the naked eye. But they changed course when he changed and undoubtedly were in pursuit. They had greater maneuverability and far more speed."

"Nevertheless he escaped?" put in Raven with a skeptical smile.

"The escape is fully as much a mystery as the pursuit," Lomax retorted. "The pilot says the four were overtaking rapidly when a few strange sparkles and gleamings appeared in front of them, whereupon they swung into reverse course and went away. He is convinced that these four were artificial fabrications and his belief is officially endorsed."

"And what does this mean to us?"

Taking a deep breath, Lomax declared with impressive solemnity, "There is other life in the cosmos and not so far from us either. Its forms, powers, techniques and ways of thought remain matters of pure speculation. It may be humanoid enough to pose as veritable humans, gaining plausibility by using the identities of real humans who have died."

He whisked a sheet aside, continued with the next. "Or it might be a parasitic by nature, able to seize and animate the bodies of other creatures, masquerading thereafter in guise mighty close to perfection. We have no data to go upon in these respects, but we can think, imagine, and conceive the infinite possibilities."

"Frightened men have bad dreams," observed Raven.

"I think it's all terribly silly," Leina put in. "Are you seriously suggesting that we may be zombies motivated by intelligent parasites from somewhere else?"

"Lady, I am suggesting nothing. I am merely reading

papers prepared by my superiors whose conclusions and motives I am not disposed to question. That is my job."

"Where does it get us?"

"To this point: the commission has informed President Heraty that all four of you—the couple on Venus as well as yourselves—are of identically the same type. Secondly, they are quite unable to define the origin of that type with reasonable certainty. In defiance of the rule that only the dominant talent is inherited, you *may* be multi-talented mutants of natural human birth, in which case the so-called laws of genetics will have to be modified. On the other hand, you *may* be a non-human form of life, disguised in our shape and form, living among us unsuspected until lately."

"For what purpose?"

It did not faze him in the least. Passing a hand over his bristly hair, he looked physically and mentally weary as he answered, "The purposes of other life-forms are obscure. We know nothing about them—yet. We can, however, make a justifiable assumption."

"And what is that?"

"If its intentions were friendly another life-form would make contact openly, without attempting concealment."

"Meaning that surreptitious contact is proof of hostile designs."

"Exactly!"

Leina said with some morbidity, "I can think of nothing more absurd than to suggest that human beings are not human beings."

"For the second time, lady," said Lomax, displaying frigid politeness, "I am not making suggestions. I am no more than a deputy appointed to inform you of the conclusions of experts. They say that you two are multi-talented mutants or non-human life-forms and more probably the latter."

"I think they're impertinent," opined Leina, becoming femininely inconsequential.

Lomax let it pass. "If it should be the case that some

other form of life has dumped scouts upon our three worlds, unknown to us, the logical conclusion is that their ultimate purpose is antagonistic. It's the criminal who climbs in through the back window. The honest man knocks at the front door."

"You have a point there," admitted Raven, undisturbed.

"Therefore if a life-form powerful enough and intelligent enough to conquer space ahead of ourselves has planted a secret advance party among us, well, it means that humanity soon has to face its greatest crisis ever!" He waved a hand to indicate the fortresslike surroundings. "Hence this extraordinary procedure. Alien invaders stand outside our laws, are not entitled to claim the protection of them."

"I see." Rubbing his chin, Raven regarded the other thoughtfully. "What are we supposed to do about all this wild speculation?"

"The onus now rests on you of proving beyond all manner of doubt that you are natural-born humans and not another life-form. The proof must be watertight. The evidence must be incontrovertible."

Chapter 18

Raven growled in pretended anger, "Darn it, can you prove you're not something out of Sirius?"

"I won't argue with you or permit you to disturb my emotions." Lomax jabbed an indicative thumb at the last sheet of paper. "All I'm concerned with is what it says here. It says you will produce undeniable proof that you are human beings, by which is meant the kind of superior life native to Terra."

"Otherwise—?"

"Terra will assume the worst and take steps to protect herself by every means available. For a start she will wipe out all three of us here in this room, simultaneously deal with those on Venus and make ready to repel any later attack launched upon us from outside."

"H'm! All three of us, you say. Tough on you, isn't it?"

"I told you why I was chosen," Lomax reminded. "I am quite ready to go should it prove necessary, especially since I've been assured that the method to be employed will be superswift and painless."

"That is a great comfort," put in Leina, enigmatically.

He eyed them in turn. "I shall go with you solely to

deprive you of the last possible way out, your only avenue of escape. There will be no opportunity for one of you to ensure survival by confiscating my person. No other life-form—if such you should happen to be—is going to walk out of this trap in the guise of a man named Lomax. We survive together or die together according to whether or not you produce the evidence my superiors require."

He was slightly pleased about that. For the first time his resented physical condition had given him power of an invincible kind. In given circumstances such as existed here and now, the ability to contemplate one's own death with absolute calmness could be a veritably appalling form of strength.

If one were devoid of fear while one's opponents were filled with it, the conflict could end in only one way: with the defeat of the cravens. In common with those behind him he was taking it for granted that any form of life, human or nonhuman, would value its own survival too highly to share his own abnormal nonchalance about destruction.

In that respect neither he nor those who had planned this situation could have been more mistaken. The difficult thing was for prospective victims to conceal the fact. Their essential tactic was not to reveal it outwardly and to give the recording apparatus a series of reactions manifestly natural from the human point of view.

So in suitably disturbed tones, Raven remarked, "Many an innocent has been slaughtered by the chronic suspicions and uncontrolled fears of others. This world has never lacked its full quota of witch hunters." He fidgeted as if on edge and asked, "How long do we have to talk ourselves out of this fix? Is there a time limit?"

"Not by the clock. Either you dig up the proof or you don't." Lomax registered tired indifference as to which way it went. "If you can't, the knowledge that you can't will drive you to desperation sooner or later. You will then have to try a hazardous way out. When that happens I will—" He let his voice trail off.

"You'll react?

"Effectively!" Resting elbows on the desk, he propped his chin, took on the air of one prepared to wait for the inevitable. "I am very patient and you're free to take full advantage of it. But I advise you not to play for time by trying to sit here for a week."

"That sounds like another threat."

"It is a friendly warning," Lomax corrected. "Although they have given far less cause for suspicion the pair on Venus are classified with you and are receiving precisely the same treatment. All four of you are birds of a feather, will be released or executed together."

"So a coupling exists between here and there?" inquired Raven.

"Correct. Emergency action here causes a signal to be beamed which precipitates the same action there. The same holds good in reverse. That is why we've kept the two pairs apart. The more time one pair wastes, the greater the chance of the issue being settled for them by the other couple."

"Well, it's a neat arrangement," Raven conceded.

"You have *two* chances of bidding this world good-by for ever: at my hands should you cause me to react, or at the hands of your allies on Venus." Lomax revealed the shadow of a smile as he added, "You are in the most unhappy position of the man who remarked that he could cope with his enemies but only God could save him from his friends."

Emitting a deep sigh, Raven lay back and closed his eyes as if concentrating on the problem in hand. That Lomax might try to listen to his thoughts did not worry him in the least. He had complete confidence in the inviolability of his own mental shield and in the inability of any Earth-type telepath to tune so high in the neural band.

"Charles! Charles!"

The response took a long time coming because the other's mind was absorbed in his predicament and had to be drawn away.

"Yes, David?"

"How far have you got?"

"We're now being told how four Denebs took after a Terran but were turned away." A mental chuckle, followed by, "I just can't imagine what turned them."

"You are lagging behind us a few minutes. We're near the end here. Who's dealing with you?"

"A very old man. Quick witted but on his last legs."

"We've got a young one," Raven informed. "Rather a sad case. So much so that it wouldn't be thought extraordinary if he had a serious attack and collapsed under the strain of this interview. We could make it look good and sound good on the recorder system. Deplorable but natural. I think we can successfully cover up by taking advantage of his condition."

"What do you propose?"

"We'll feed the microphones a little real life drama. We'll use it to establish a plausible semblance of innocence. Then he'll have his attack, we'll react naturally and he'll also react to that because he can't help it. The result will get you out of your jam because we here will have jumped the gun and thus denied you the chance to say a word in your own defense."

"How long will it be?"

"In a few minutes' time."

Opening his eyes and sitting up like one who has discovered a bright and hopeful solution, Raven said excitedly, "Look, if my life is known in detail it will be obvious that my body could have been confiscated only at the time of my death and resuscitation."

"No comment," said Lomax. "Others will decide that point."

"They'll agree." He asserted it with confidence. "Now if we accept this far-fetched notion that some other life-form could take over the material body of another creature, how could it also confiscate something so immaterial as that creature's memories?"

"Don't ask me—I'm not an expert." Lomax made a brief note on a pad. "But carry on."

"If I can relate a wealth of childhood memories from the age of three upward," continued Raven, with excellent imitation of triumph, "and have most of them confirmed by persons still living, where do I stand then?"

"I don't know," said Lomax. "The suggestion is now being considered elsewhere. A signal will tell me whether or not you may extend the theme."

"What if I show that during my youth I self-consciously suppressed my powers, knowing that I was a freak? What if I show that the alleged coincidence of four similar freaks in a bunch is attributable to no more than that like clings to like?"

"It may suffice or it may not," Lomax evaded. "We shall hear pretty soon." His face suddenly squirmed from some inner torment and beads of perspiration popped out on his forehead. He pulled himself together, displaying an iron will. "If you've anything more to offer now's the time."

Looking around the room Raven *saw* the scanner lens, the recorder leads buried deep in the wall, the tiny pin in the floor near Lomax's right foot, the connections running from it to a machine in the cellars. Without any difficulty whatever he could examine the machine and estimate the efficiency of the lethal ray it was designed to produce.

He and Leina had become aware of all these features at the very first. It would have been easy to detach various leads by remote operation, teleportatively, without moving from the pneumaseat. It would have been easy to jam the pin or break the power supply to the concealed executioner below. Despite Lomax's belief to the contrary, the way out lay wide open and had been from the start—unfortunately a successful break would have been a complete giveaway.

The present situation showed too much had been revealed. At whatever cost suspicions must be lulled in manner carefully calculated to create false conclusions and, at the same time, the sources of forbidden information must be removed, plausibly and for ever. The shadowy figure at the other end of the recorder system must be fed soothing data on which they could compute and get the wrong answer every time.

Concealment was the paramount issue. No fragment of truth must lurk in any biped mind lest someday it be extracted by others. Humans lived in protective ignorance and should continue to do so at whatever cost. A little knowledge could be a highly dangerous thing. They must be denied it for ever and ever and ever.

As for the freedom beckoning beyond the armorplate door, it was only a poor, restricted, third-rate kind of liberty. The freedom of a child to play in the street. The freedom of a babe to wet its triangle and shake its rattle, the freedom of a caterpillar to crawl to mock safety around the underside of a leaf.

Casually his hand touched Leina's, making them of one accord. There were scanners to watch what was about to occur, they would require care. Then there was only the blind, idiot recording system, the little pin, the lethal projector.

"There are and always have been unknown mutants in addition to known ones," he said, making it pleadingly persuasive. "It is a fact that makes ancestral data inadequate and misleading. For example, if my maternal grandfather, being an unmitigated scoundrel, took great care to conceal his hypnotic powers which he preserved solely for illegal purposes, it stands to sense that—"

He broke off while Lomax had another spasm of internal agony that bent him forward. Before Lomax could recover, Leina obligingly contributed a startled yelp of, "Oh, David, look!" and right on top of it shouted, *"What's the matter, Lomax?"*

At the same moment both minds thrust with irresistible strength through the other's mental shield. Lomax had no time to inquire what the devil they were talking about, no time to deny that anything was the matter, not even a

221

split-second to recover and wipe the brief pain from his face. He heard Leina's exclamation and Raven's following question, both uttered in tones of shocked surprise, then came the fierce stab at his brain. He faltered farther forward. The reactive circuit sprang into instantaneous operation. Automatically his foot rammed down on the hidden pin.

For a fragmentary moment his mind shrieked aloud, "I've done it! Heavens above, I've—!"

Then the cry cut off.

There followed a period of soul-searing chaos and absolute bewilderment. Lomax did not know, could not tell whether it was long or short, a matter of seconds or eons. He did not not know whether it was now light or dark, cold or warm, whether he was standing up or lying down, moving or still.

What had occurred when he pressed that pin? Had some new and awful device been tested on himself and the other two guinea pigs? Had it hurled him into the past, the future, or some other dimension? Or worse still, oh, infinitely, worse, had it added a mutilated mind to his mutilated body?

Then it struck him that he could no longer sense the throbbing agony that had made his life a personal hell these last two years. Sheer surprise and an overwhelming flood of relief stopped his mind's mad whirling. He began to coordinate slowly, uncertainly, like a little child.

It now seemed that he was floating either up or down amid a mighty host of brilliant bubbles, large and small. All around him they drifted lazily along shining in superbly glowing colors while among them pale wisps of smoke wreathed and curled. He was, he thought, like a tiny, rudderless boat on a wide, iridescent and bubbly river.

The pain had gone, unbelievably gone, and now there was only this sleep, dreamy swaying along the mainstream of blues and greens, crimson and gold, starry sparklings of purest white, fitful gleams of silver, momentary flashings of little rainbows, on, on into the infinitude of peace. He was slumbersome and content to slumber for ever and ever, for as long as time goes on.

But then his mind stirred as a sense became active and prodded it into reluctant attention. It now seemed that with the palely coiling wreaths of smoke amid the bubbles came an immense multitude of voices that somehow were not really voices but could be heard or sensed or understood and all speaking one tongue.

Some talked in quick, staccato phrases from places tremendously afar. Others were nearer and more leisurely. It was strange that while each had a sort of mental audibility he could also tell—somehow, he did not know how—the precise direction from which each one came and the exact distance of its source relative to the others. A few were near him, very near, voicing mysterious things among the curls of smoke, the spheres and the colors.

"Stay with him!"

"He may have no reason to be vengeful but stay with him—we want no more dangerous impulses like Steen's."

"Said he was ready for this so he should be quicker to adapt."

"It's never easy no matter how ready one may be."

"He must learn that no man can be an enemy."

"The flower cannot hate its own seeds nor the bird its eggs."

More senses sprang into operation even while he wondered whether this was the delirium of mental mutilation. In a confused, out-of-focus way he became conscious that the entities he had known as Raven and Leina were still present, sharing his dream environment. They were holding him without actually touching him, drifting with him through the mists and the bubbles. They were not the same yet he knew who they were beyond all doubt. It was as if he could now see what was to be seen if one looked right into them.

All at once this hazy sense of perception that was not sight cleared itself, adjusted, swung into full and complete

223

functioning. The myriad bubbles fled away as if blown by a mighty breath and took up new positions at enormous distances. They were suns and planets, glowing and spinning within the great spaces of eternal dark.

His new vision was non-stereoscopic, devoid of perspective, but had in lieu an automatic and extremely accurate estimation of relative distances. He *knew* merely by looking which bubbles were near, which far, and exactly how much farther.

Still with the other two in attendance, he heard one cry, "Charles! Charles!" and a reply eerily vibrating from far away, "Coming, David!" The names used were not those names but he thought of them as those names because he could not grasp the new ones—though somehow he knew to whom they referred. This phenomenon did not arouse his curiosity or stimulate his mind to speculation, for he was concentrating on the vision of the bubble-filled cosmos and overcome by its incomparable wonder.

The surfaces of many spheres could be "seen" in splendid detail. On a lot of them strange creatures lived and swarmed, hoppers, creepers, crawlers, flutterers, flame-things, wave-form entities, beings of infinite variety and most of them low in the scale of life.

But one widespread form was high. It had a long, thin, sinuous body covered in dark gray hide, a well developed and efficient brain, many dexterous limbs and e.s.p. organs. It enjoyed telepathic power confined to its own special band. Its individuals could compute as individuals or combine mentally to compute as a mass-mind.

These things roamed far and wide in slender, pencil-shaped, jet black space vessels, exploring other worlds, patrolling the gulfs and chasms between, mapping, charting, reporting to numerous bases and always ceaselessly searching, searching.

The Denebs!

In their own esteem these were the lords of creation. Absorbing data being fed to him from he knew not where,

Lomax understood a lot about the Denebs. They stood right at the top of the life-scale of bubble-bound creatures, had great tolerance of all other life-forms considered lower than themselves. To these they did no harm, regarding them as satisfactory targets for patronizing superiority. But the Denebs had one great shortcoming—they could not abide the notion of sharing the cosmos with a life-form equal to themselves—or higher.

And there was one still higher!

So for countless centuries the Denebs had been feverishly seeking the home world or worlds whence came unbearable competition. They would destroy rivalry at its source—if the source could be found. Their black ships prowled and poked and probed and searched amid the endless multitude of bubbles, disturbing but not destroying the hoppers, creepers, crawlers and sometimes nosing around the colonies of little white grublike bipeds established on many widely separated spheres.

Lomax felt a peculiarly intense interest in this last type of creature. Poor little grubs, squirming and wriggling around, building or trying to build or hoping ultimately to build rudimentary, ramshackle rocketships that never would touch more than a fringe of creation. Mournful grubs, sorrowing ones, ecstatic ones, ambitious ones, even petty dictator-grubs.

In all probability there were individuals among them slightly better endowed, talented above the grub-norm. These would think themselves superior merely because they could exercise a minute, fragmentary portion of powers entirely normal but said to be supernormal. Some could, perhaps, read other grub-minds to the pitiful limit of a bubble's horizon. Some could, perhaps, fascinate another grub, creating fear of themselves by compelling obedience.

Doubtless every colony of them had developed a grub-culture, a grub-philosophy, a grub-theology. Being unable to conceive anything infinitely higher, some might go so far as to think of themselves as made in the image of a mighty super-grub.

Now and again one more daring than the rest might have sneaked from the hiding place of its own grub-conditioning and peered furtively into the dark and seen a great, bright-eyed moth like a nocturnal butterfly beating gloriously through the endless night. And it would cower down, sorely afraid, totally unable to recognize—itself!

An enormous surge of life filled Lomax's being as the data filed itself and became estimated. The grubs! The nestlings! Alive with tremendous power, he saw Raven and Leina, Charles and Mavis as he had never seen anyone before. They were with him still, helping him, watching him, urging him to adapt to the environment.

The little two-legged grubs, he was crying. Ours! Our nestlings waiting their natural metamorphosis! If the Denebs—long unable to recognize them for what they are—should now learn the truth from one discerning mind in one colony they will systematically destroy the lot. If one grub learns too much, all may be slaughtered from one end of the heavens to the other.

"Never!" assured the one he had known as Raven. "It will never be known to any of them. There are two watchers in every nest, each living inside a grub-body taken with permission of its former owner exactly as I took the body of David Raven with his permission. They are guardians. They enter in pairs. It needs one to watch, but two to break earthbound solitude."

"The place we left, *you* left?"

"Two more already have gone in."

They began to leave him, moving silently into the immense deeps that were their natural playfields. The Denebs were highest of the bubble-bound, but *these*, the higher ones, were bound to nothing once their childhood's grub-existence had ended. They went like wide-eyed, supersensitive, multi-talented creatures of the great spaces.

Those pale, weak two-legged things, wondered Lomax, what had they called themselves? Oh, yes, Homo

Sapiens. Some among them were precocious and hence regarded themselves as Homo Superior. It was pitiful in a way. It was pathetic.

As instinctively as a baby moves feet it is not consciously aware of possessing, or a kitten similarly puts forth claws, so did he spread huge, shining, fan-shaped fields of force and swoop in the wake of his fellows.

He was alive as he'd never been alive before. And filled with a fierce exultation.

For he knew what he had become and what the little white grubs had yet to be.

Homo In Excelsis!

By the year 2000, 2 out of 3 Americans could be illiterate.

It's true.

Today, 75 million adults...about one American in three, can't read adequately. And by the year 2000, U.S. News & World Report envisions an America with a literacy rate of only 30%.

Before that America comes to be, you can stop it...by joining the fight against illiteracy today.

Call the Coalition for Literacy at toll-free **1-800-228-8813** and volunteer.

**Volunteer
Against Illiteracy.
The only degree you need
is a degree of caring.**

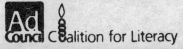

Ad Council · Coalition for Literacy

LV-2